"Just let me hold you."

Nothing else he could have said just then would have blunted the edge of panic so effectively. Whether he wanted to hold her for himself or for her, she didn't know. But either way, the motion of Mike's hand kept Katie where she was. With slow, easy strokes he traced a path from her neck to her thigh, the movement seeming as soothing to him as it was to her.

She knew exactly what he was doing. He knew as well as she did that once they moved from each other's arms, nothing would be quite the same. But as long as they stayed where they were, they could postpone the moment they would have to face what they'd done. More than willing to avoid the moment for as long as possible, she curled into the protection of his arms, and let herself think only of how she'd always wanted to be exactly where she was....

* * * *

**Christine Flynn is
"...one of the genre's master storytellers."**
Romantic Times magazine

Dear Reader,

Autumn inspires visions of the great outdoors, but Special Edition lures you back inside with six vibrant romances!

Many of the top-selling mainstream authors today launched their careers writing series romance. Some special authors have achieved remarkable success in the mainstream with both hardcovers and paperbacks, yet continue to support the genre and the readers they love. *New York Times* bestselling author Nora Roberts is just such an author, and this month we're delighted to bring you *The Winning Hand,* the eighth book in her popular series THE MACGREGORS.

In *Father-to-Be* by Laurie Paige, October's tender THAT'S MY BABY! title, an impulsive night of passion changes a rugged rancher's life forever. And if you enjoy sweeping medical dramas, we prescribe *From House Calls to Husband* by Christine Flynn, part of PRESCRIPTION: MARRIAGE. This riveting new series by three Silhouette authors highlights nurses who vow never to marry a doctor. Look for the second installment of the series next month.

Silhouette's new five-book cross-line continuity series, FOLLOW THAT BABY, introduces the Wentworth oil tycoon family and their search for a missing heir. The series begins in Special Edition this month with *The Rancher and the Amnesiac Bride* by Joan Elliott Pickart, then crosses into Romance (11/98), Desire (12/98), Yours Truly (1/99) and concludes in Intimate Moments (2/99).

Also, check out *Partners in Marriage* by Allison Hayes, in which a vulnerable schoolteacher invades a Lakota man's house—and his heart! Finally, October's WOMAN TO WATCH is talented newcomer Jean Brashear, who unfolds a provocative tale of revenge—and romance—in *The Bodyguard's Bride.*

I hope you enjoy all of the stories this month!

Sincerely,

Karen Taylor Richman
Senior Editor

Please address questions and book requests to:
Silhouette Reader Service
U.S.: 3010 Walden Ave., P.O. Box 1325, Buffalo, NY 14269
Canadian: P.O. Box 609, Fort Erie, Ont. L2A 5X3

CHRISTINE FLYNN

FROM HOUSE CALLS TO HUSBAND

Published by Silhouette Books
America's Publisher of Contemporary Romance

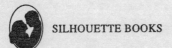

For our daughter, Dawn Flynn, R.N.,
with tons of love and thanks for all the information,
encouragement and advice

SILHOUETTE BOOKS

ISBN 0-373-24203-4

FROM HOUSE CALLS TO HUSBAND

Copyright © 1998 by Christine Flynn

Books by Christine Flynn

CHRISTINE FLYNN

admits to being interested in just about everything, which is why she considers herself fortunate to have turned her interest in writing into a career. She feels that a writer gets to explore it all and, to her, exploring relationships—especially the intense, bittersweet or even lighthearted relationships between men and women—is fascinating.

The Pledge

Graduation day

We, the undersigned, having barely survived four years of nursing school and preparing to go forth and find a job, do hereby vow to meet at Granetti's at least once a week, not do anything drastic to our hair without consulting each other first and never, ever—no matter how rich, how cute, how funny, how smart—marry a doctor.

Katie Sheppard, R.N.

Dana Rowan, R.N.

Lee Murphy, R.N.

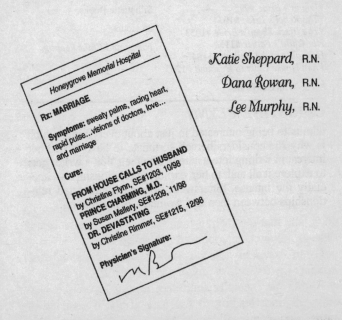

Honeygrove Memorial Hospital

Rx: MARRIAGE

Symptoms: sweaty palms, racing heart, rapid pulse...visions of doctors, love... and marriage

Cure:

FROM HOUSE CALLS TO HUSBAND
by Christine Flynn, SE#1203, 10/98
PRINCE CHARMING, M.D.
by Susan Mallery, SE#1209, 11/98
DR. DEVASTATING
by Christine Rimmer, SE#1215, 12/98

Physician's Signature:

Chapter One

It was only two weeks into January and Katie Sheppard had already broken four of her five New Year's resolutions. She'd yet to clean a single closet. She hadn't registered for the yoga class that was supposed to reduce stress and expand her mind. And last night, while blubbering her way through her favorite movie, she'd blown her diet with an entire pint of Häagen-Dazs. Now, instead of cutting back on the hours she volunteered at a free women's clinic—resolution number four—she'd actually agreed to help expand its program. If the day didn't end soon, she had the feeling number five would also bite the dust. In a way, she supposed it already had.

When asked to take on more than I can comfortably handle, I will learn to say no, and mean it.

Right, she mentally muttered, pulling open the heavy stairwell door leading to her unit. If she'd sounded any more convincing talking to the clinic's director, whom she'd bumped into in the hospital's cafeteria, she would have wound up running the whole bloody program.

Her female friends were more generous, but her friend Mike was right—her backbone was made of mush.

"Dr. Brennan was looking for you a few minutes ago, Katie. Did you see him?"

Speak of the devil.

Deciding she'd have to finish beating herself up later, Katie did an about-face as she passed the telemetry unit's nurses' station with its long white counters and banks of cardiac monitors. A hot pink stethoscope hung around her neck, the bell and earpieces dangling against the top of her light blue scrubs. Wincing as she loosened a strand of frustratingly curly, wheat-colored hair caught under the neon-colored tubing, she sidestepped an orderly and headed for the middle-age model of efficiency seated behind the high counter.

Alice Ives, the unit's secretary and everyone's self-appointed mom, had barely glanced up when she'd spoken. The woman's attention was riveted to the photos one of the other cardiac nurses had brought in of her family's Christmas vacation in Hawaii. Katie had taken her turn drooling over them between patient assessments, morning rounds and a staff meeting.

"Did he say what he wanted?"

"Only that it could wait. He's doing a procedure in 307 if you want to catch him. By the way," she added, still flipping through photos, "he didn't seem too happy about whatever it was."

Confusion settled in Katie's dark brown eyes. If Mike said it could wait, then what he wanted probably had nothing to do with a case. Where his patients were concerned, he invariably wanted answers five minutes ago.

"I won't interrupt him," Katie said, wondering if something had gone wrong with his research study—the one he'd roped her into helping him with. "But if he finishes in the next few minutes, I'll be down with the new admit."

Reaching over the counter, she slid her clipboard from where she'd left it before she'd gone on the break she wished she hadn't taken, and paused long enough to see which picture had Alice so transfixed.

It was the one of a palm tree silhouetted against an orange and magenta sky. A lovers' sunset, she thought, feeling a little wistful herself. "Living vicariously is the pits, isn't it?"

The older woman sighed like a preteen with a crush on a rock star. "I'd kill to go to those islands," she admitted, touching the image of the palm tree. "With two kids in college and another starting next year, the only sand Larry and I will see for the next ten years will be on the beach at Lincoln City. And it won't stop raining there until July."

"The Oregon coast certainly isn't known for sun," Katie agreed, thinking of the beach an hour and a half drive through the mountains from Honeygrove. "But we do have all that gorgeous, rugged shoreline."

Alice peered over the top of the purple-rimmed half glasses that matched her grape-colored pantsuit. "You sound like you're describing a man. That's what you should be checking out, too, you know? Men. Not scenery. You're never going to get the family you want if you don't start looking a little harder."

A tolerant smile curved Katie's mouth. "How did we get from discussing your desire to go to Hawaii to my lack of a man?"

"It's that association thing. You know, the one where someone says something that reminds you of something else? But as long as we are talking about it, is there anything new and exciting you've been keeping from me?"

"I don't have time for 'new and exciting,'" Katie muttered, thinking she'd have even less time for herself now, thanks to her starchless spine.

Alice made a disapproving sound. "Time is all you will have if you don't get out there and circulate, girl. Maybe *you* should go somewhere exotic," she suggested, her confidential tone barely audible over the muffled clatter of lunch trays being collected and a page coming over the loudspeaker. Behind her, a technician continuously scanned the monitors, green lines spiking over gray screens. "You're thirty years old. Single. And your only dependent is a cat. If I were in your position," she confided, punching at a blinking light on the console as the phone continued to ring, "I'd be gone in the time it took me to pack a book and a bathing suit.

"Three-G, Alice speaking," she answered, arching her penciled eyebrow at Katie in subtle challenge.

"Hey, Katie." The tech at the monitors kept her focus on one of the screens. "The patient in 316 has had ten beats of V tach. You want to check it out?"

Alice's outspoken observations sounded suspiciously like those Katie heard more and more lately from her own mother. But thoughts of turning into an old maid vanished along with images of muscular males and mai tais. The telemetry unit of Honeygrove Memorial Hospital handled heart patients who weren't sick enough for the Cardiac Intensive Care Unit, but too sick for the medical floors. Three-sixteen was Eva Horton, a spry seventy-four-year-old who'd suffered a heart attack while out for her morning walk. Her indomitable spirit had survived open-heart surgery and enough drugs to drop an elephant. If her heart stayed in the arrhythmia of ventricular tachycardia, however, she wouldn't survive much longer.

Maneuvering around a tall, stainless steel meal cart, Katie aimed for the break between a stuffed laundry cart and a gurney coming down the crowded hall. When she had assessed Eva twenty minutes ago, the woman had been totally stable, her vitals good, her potassium level fine.

Rounding the corner into the room, still working to pinpoint what was going wrong, she deliberately slowed her stride. The young aide preparing to give Eva her bath walked out of the bathroom as Katie ran a practiced eye over the face of the thin, silver-haired woman propped up in the bed.

"How are you doing?" Katie asked, picking up the woman's wrinkled hand. Professional as she was, she had a definite soft spot for this widow who'd confided that she simply didn't have time to have a bad heart. She had grandchildren to spoil, a foursome in bridge she couldn't let down and a shower to grout. At the moment, however, the once-energetic woman's skin was pale and clammy, perspiration misted her upper lip, and the edges of her mouth had a distinct blue outline.

"I feel funny." Eva swallowed, pressing her hand to her chest when Katie released it. "A bit short of breath."

She had been off oxygen since yesterday. Reaching for it even as the woman spoke, Katie turned on the airflow, but she didn't get the cannula in place. In the time it took to blink, the woman's eyes rolled back behind her gold-rimmed bifocals, and her head sagged forward like a rag doll's.

The thin clear oxygen line swung against the wall of outlets and ports like the pendulum of a clock as Katie snatched up the phone by the bed.

The nurses' aide, a statuesque brunette barely over

twenty and new on the floor that week, stood clutching the washbasin she'd just filled. Her already pale skin suddenly looked as ashen as the patient's.

"Get her flat," Katie ordered, wondering what the girl was waiting for. With the phone cradled against her shoulder, Katie lowered the side rails. "And get a backboard under her." Her mind racing, she whipped the patient's glasses off and started ripping off the gown. "Code Blue. Three-G. Room 316," she said into the phone, and threw the pillow in the general direction of a chair.

The phone still rocked in its cradle when she grabbed the backboard the aide pulled from the foot of the bed and shoved it under the unconscious woman. From beyond the room, a bell-like chime sounded an instant before an amazingly tranquil voice came over the intercom. "Code blue. Three-G. Room 316. Code blue. Three-G. Room 316."

The code was repeated a third time, but Katie scarcely heard it. At that very second elsewhere in the hospital, she knew that nurses, technicians and doctors were bolting for the stairways. Any person available answered a code, no one taking the chance that others would take care of it. Within the minute, there could be twenty people in the room, each prepared to handle a part of what one person couldn't effectively do alone.

Except for the aide. She hadn't moved.

Katie tipped back her patient's head to get a straight airway. "Don't just stand there," she insisted, her own heart pounding. "Get a mask. You breathe. I'll compress. Come on!"

The young aide shook her hands as if ridding them of water, her eyes flashing fear and panic. "I've never done this for real before. Only in class."

"Then pretend it isn't for real if it helps! Just do it!"

Had a patient's life not hung in the balance, the empathy Katie could rarely suppress would have tempered her response. It was the aide's first code and she was freaking. Having slid into a dead faint the first time she'd witnessed surgery, Katie could hardly be critical. But she had no time to feel frustrated, and even less time to waste. The patient had no pulse.

"Where's that cart?" she called, a little frantic herself as she crossed her hands on the older woman's ominously still chest and began rapid compressions. "I need help here."

"You got it."

It vaguely occurred to Katie that Mike must have finished whatever he'd been working on. Six feet two inches of what her irascible buddy Dana called a black-haired, blue-eyed studmuffin barreled through the wide doorway with an open white lab coat over his dress shirt, slacks and tie. With one sweeping glance, he noted the brunette fumbling with a breathing mask, assessed the situation on the bed and slipped into action.

"I've got her, Katie. You breathe."

The deep timbre of Mike's voice had been described as everything from the low rumble of distant thunder to the slow burn of good brandy. Half of the female staff claimed his voice alone was enough to accelerate a woman's heart rate. Katie was more interested in his hands. The instant they slipped under hers to take over the compressions, reassurance registered through the adrenaline rush that got everyone through a code. She'd trust Mike with her own life. He'd already saved it a couple of times. He'd saved her rear anyway. But she'd only been a kid at the time.

"I'm on three, four..."

"Five," Mike said, taking over the count while Katie breathed air into the woman's lungs.

The code cart rolled through the door with two nurses, a tech and an electrical cord trailing behind it. As sometimes happened, someone had simply grabbed the cart and ran without unplugging the defibrillator first. The code cart was actually a big red toolbox on wheels, and Cindy, a redheaded RN with a million freckles, hit the charge switch on the defibrillator anchored to the top. A second later, the paddles were ready and she frantically tore away the plastic lock on the cart's base to open the drawers and trays of meds and supplies.

In those same seconds, a respiratory therapist began bagging the patient, relieving Katie of having to breathe for her, and Mike snatched the paddles. He had them a fraction of an inch from the patient's chest when Katie called for gel pads.

Mike froze, the tension in his body almost palpable as a package came sailing across the bed. Katie snatched it up, ripped it open and slapped on two hand-size orange conduction pads, one on the right ribs, the other near the bright red scar bisecting the chest. She knew Mike wouldn't like the delay, but the pads conducted the electricity better, and without them, the paddles left burns that hurt like the devil.

He had the paddles in place even as she pulled back.

"Clear."

His brisk command was followed by a heavy, hollow thwump as two hundred joules of electricity bucked the body on the bed. Eva landed as she'd been, and lay as limp as before.

From across the room, Katie heard something solid hit a wall and slide to the floor.

"Somebody check the bathroom," she called, quickly adding the three leads from the defibrillator monitor to the other leads already on the patient's chest so they could see what was going on. "I think the aide's in there."

Next to Katie, a nurse in blue scrubs like her own was hanging an IV, connecting it to the catheter in the patient's needle-bruised arm. Behind the redhead tossing out supplies from the code cart, someone in green scrubs was recording the beehive of activity on a clipboard. The doorway was jammed with personnel leaving because there were enough people working the code and others arriving to see if they were needed.

Katie had the third lead in place. Atop the cart, the monitor jumped to life, the white lines spiking over a black screen indicating a shuddering heart. "She's still in V tach."

"Go to three hundred," Mike called.

Another sharp, "Clear," and the patient's body bucked once more.

The frenetic pattern of the deadly arrhythmia still looked like tremors on a seismograph.

"Three sixty."

Mike applied the paddles again.

"That did it. She's in sinus," Cindy announced, watching the heartbeat on the cart's monitor.

Sinus rhythm was good. It was normal. It was exactly what they wanted.

Mike's glance met Katie's in a split second of mutually acknowledged relief even as Eva moaned and her eyes fluttered open. The respiratory therapist eased the bag from her mouth. Confusion, then panic, washed over the woman's suddenly flushed face.

Wanting to ease her fear, Katie murmured, "It's okay, Eva. We're right here."

"What's going on?" The tremor in Eva's voice was mirrored in her hand as she reached to clutch the sheet

Katie pulled up to cover her exposed chest. "Why are all these people here? Wasn't I sitting up?" Without her glasses, identities were hard for the woman to establish. She blinked past the dozen people surrounding her bed to focus on the darkly attractive man towering over her. "Dr. Brennan? Where did you come from? Why are you here?"

Katie's hand rested on Eva's shoulder. Feeling the woman tremble, she automatically gave Eva a comforting squeeze, and glanced at Mike as he handed her a blood pressure cuff. The faint smile carving lines into his lean cheeks was intended to reassure his patient, but his blue eyes remained intent while he explained to Eva that her heart had jumped out of rhythm, and that they'd had to use electricity to get it back in sync again.

Fear and anxiety were a patient's inevitable responses to such an episode. So were tears. They gathered in the corners of the older woman's eyes, then slipped down her cheeks as the gravity of her situation sunk in. Katie, her thoughts divided between the various needs of her patient while she strapped on the cuff and took the woman's blood pressure, glanced toward the box of tissues on the far side of the bed.

Mike was already ahead of her. Handing the shaken woman a tissue, he told his patient to try breathing deeply, then pushed his hands into the pockets of his slacks. With his focus on the monitor, he explained that she would be moved to CICU as soon as they could get her there.

"Just until we're sure you're stable," he assured.

Over the tearing sound of Velcro releasing its grip, Katie removed the cuff and passed on the reading. "I'll go with you and make sure you're settled."

"That would be a good idea," Mike replied, seeing how tightly his patient was holding her hand.

"Is this going to happen again?"

It wasn't often that the patient's surgeon was around when a patient crashed. But since he had been—and since it was Mike—Katie knew she wouldn't be left to interpret explanations or decode words that often left patients more frightened than they already were. Even as the activity continued around her with Katie administering the drugs Mike ordered and the respiratory therapist adjusting the oxygen cannula around her head and under her nose, Eva responded to the considerate way Mike answered her questions. Or maybe, Katie mused, thinking of the comments others had made, what the patient responded to was simply the deep, soothing timbre of his voice. It held authority, assurance, certainty. Strength. As Katie watched the agitated beats slow on the monitor, she wondered if maybe his voice couldn't calm a heart, as well as excite one.

Not that he excited hers. At least, not since she'd recovered from the crush she'd had on him when she was nine years old. He'd been thirteen at the time, and very much the big brother she'd never had. Now she thought of him only as a friend. One of her best. Over the years, she'd come to realize she simply couldn't let herself think of him any other way.

Except, like now, when she thought of him in professional terms. In the eight years she'd worked in cardiology, she'd encountered any number of surgeons whose arrogance was exceeded only by their lack of sensitivity. And cardiac surgeons—because the human heart was literally in their hands—could be the most arrogant of the lot. Neither she, nor any of the other nurses in the unit, considered Mike among them. He was exceptionally skilled. *Brilliant* was the word often bandied about by the surgical staff. And he demanded as much of those who worked with him as he did of himself. That was something that intimidated the daylights out of the newer, younger nurses. The rest, those who'd been around for a while, simply stood in awe of him. But Katie knew what many did not. Despite the self-confidence, the drive and the talent, he often found the work he did profoundly humbling.

As she listened to him repeat an explanation to Eva, she also knew he'd put even more demands on himself lately. His bedside manner was changing, too. She rarely saw him touch a patient to offer reassurance or comfort anymore. It was a professional barrier, she was sure. But since his divorce last year, that barrier seemed to be slipping into his personal life as well.

As bad as she was about having no time for a social life, Mike was ten times worse.

"So, how are you feeling now?" Mike asked.

Eva's indomitable spirit fought through her fear. "Like I was hit in the chest with a wrecking ball."

"With or without spikes?"

Eva seemed to consider. "Without."

"That sounds about right." The corners of Mike's eyes crinkled with a faint smile as he glanced toward the monitor again. Just as he did, his pager went off. "You're looking good," he assured her, reaching inside his lab coat to silence the electronic device clipped to his belt. "Almost good enough to start chasing those grandkids of yours." His glance slid to the illuminated digits on the pager. "But we'll have you rest across the hall for a while anyway."

"You know, Katie," the patient whispered, watching her adored doctor check the number he was to call. "You should get yourself a man like this. I know for a fact he's not married. I asked him about every one of the pictures in his office and there wasn't a wife among them."

That was because he'd finally divorced the little gold digger, Katie thought.

"Oh, I'm afraid that really isn't possible," she replied, going along easily with the conversation while removing the telemetry leads from the woman's chest. "The day I graduated from nursing school, two friends and I signed a pact. We agreed never to marry a physician. Ever." Raising the side rail, she shook her head in mock seriousness. "I'm afraid getting involved with someone like Dr. Brennan is out of the question."

Mike's expression was utterly bland. "I think everything's under control here," he announced, having heard—and deliberately ignored—what they were saying. "I'm going to leave you in this nurse's capable hands, Eva. But I'll check on you this evening. You behave yourself.

"Make sure that IV is wide-open," he said to Katie when he turned. "And if I'm not here when you get back from across the hall, page me. I need to talk to you."

Katie was back from the CICU in less than ten minutes. But when she walked back through the unit's double doors, she immediately encountered Dr. Aniston, an opinionated, overbearing cardiologist who still thought of nurses as subservient ladies in starched white hats who dusted patients' rooms and passed out pills. He was imperiously demanding to see the nurse assigned to one of his patients. Since she was that nurse, and since she hadn't been around when he'd come onto the floor, his mood was not good.

"I was about to leave," he informed her, signing off on an order with his flashy gold pen. "I don't have time to wait around for nursing staff."

"I was moving a patient to intensive care."

She'd been doing her job. Since he had no reply for that, he chose to ignore her statement completely.

"This patient can be discharged," he said without so much as a glance toward her. His balding head gleamed like a strobe under the overhead lights. "I'm changing the dosage on his meds. Explain that to him and have him make an appointment with my office in three days."

On the other side of the counter, Alice rocked back in her chair. Catching Katie's eye, she rolled hers toward the ceiling—an antic which would have made Katie smile had Dr. Aniston not been facing her. The cardiologist was a royal pain in the posterior. Even his patients found him abrupt. But he was good and he knew it, and his ego had grown to exceed all five feet eight inches of his banty-legged frame.

He and Mike were so totally opposite, she thought, the comparison unavoidable as the man huffed off. Mike could be in the middle of a crisis, but he'd be like the eye of the storm. Dead calm. Dr. Aniston was the storm. And even if something wasn't a crisis, he turned it into one.

"Is Dr. Brennan still here?" she suddenly asked Alice.

Alice opened her mouth, but it was Jan, of the fantasy-inducing Hawaiian vacation photos, who replied as she approached the desk. "If you're looking for him, he's in the lounge. I just saw him go in."

After a quick "Thanks," Katie headed down the hall, the soft soles of her white sneakers soundless on the polished floor. She'd see what Mike wanted, then distribute meds, check on her new admit and start on her discharge. But if he intended to rope her into some new project now that his old one was nearly complete, the answer would simply have to be no. Friend or not, she had to start asserting herself somewhere.

Since he was the one who'd pointed that out, he shouldn't complain if she decided to practice on him.

The staff lounge was part locker room, part lived-in living room. The old willow-green sofa sagged from years of interns and residents catching a few winks between crises.

The round, white Formica table sported a couple of cigarette burns from the era before smoking had been banned from the building. But the microwave, refrigerator and coffeepot worked, and the tall window at the far end of the room let in daylight—what wasn't blocked by gray clouds and the parking garage, anyway.

Mike was on the far side of the room. Standing by one of the gray lockers, he was trading his lab coat for his suit jacket.

"Heading for your office?" she asked, her gaze skimming over the shoulders of his crisp, white shirt.

"Yeah. I've got appointments this morning. Surgery this afternoon." Looking preoccupied, he flicked a glance across the newspapers cluttering the table, watching her approach. "How's Eva doing?"

"She was stable when I left her. She thinks you walk on water."

She thought he might smile. All he did was shake his head. "She's just feeling grateful right now." He shrugged a beautifully tailored jacket over his broad shoulders, automatically tugging his shirt cuffs from his sleeves. The smile finally formed. Not much of one. But it was there. "I can't believe you told her about that crazy pledge."

"Hey, I'm a woman of my word. I couldn't have her getting her hopes up now, could I?"

Katie's soft smile was infectious. Mike returned it mostly because he couldn't avoid it—even though he knew there was far more to that pledge of hers than she'd ever admit. The old oath she and her buddies had taken sounded like a joke. And it might have been just that at one time. But it wasn't any longer. Not for Katie. He had the nagging feeling she was dead serious about never marrying a doctor, because in her mind, to marry a doctor would be to marry a man like her father.

Most people wouldn't see that as a problem at all. Dr. Randall Sheppard was one of the town's most prominent pediatricians, a man who was incredibly generous with his time and his talents. A true gift to the community. But while, to Mike, he was the inspiration for why he'd become a doctor himself, Katie saw him only as someone who'd taken far more than he ever gave as a husband and father.

Mike grabbed his overcoat, checking the pocket to make sure he still had the ticket for the dry cleaning he kept forgetting to pick up. He couldn't help but think that Katie was cheating herself big-time letting such a prejudice interfere with her prospects, especially since he knew how much she wanted a family of her own. But her hang-ups about her dad were one subject he'd learned to avoid with her.

"Anyway," she continued, reaching into the inside pocket of his overcoat to hand him the slip of paper that was sticking out, "Eva wanted to fix me up with her grandson, but I told her I didn't do blind dates, either. Is this what you're looking for?"

Exasperation lined his brow. "Thanks," he muttered, shoving the ticket into his shirt pocket.

"What did you want to talk to me about?"

"I need a favor."

"I'm not picking up your dry cleaning."

"Cute."

"And I'm not going to coordinate another research study for you. I got roped into the one you're doing by default as it was. Nurses started coming to me with their questions because they knew I knew you, and the next thing *I* knew, I was monitoring half your study patients because no one else 'understood your criteria.'" She mentally stiffened her spine. "I'm sorry, Mike," she added, softening anyway. "Please, don't ask."

"Do I detect a backbone?"

"I mean it," she warned, refusing to soften any further.

"Then I guess it's a good thing it's not another study." He knew the extensive checks and cross-checks in a research project could be a real pain for the nursing staff. He truly appreciated Katie taking his on. "But it's not like you didn't owe me. Didn't I rescue that schizophrenic cat of yours last month?"

The light of triumph turned his blue eyes wicked. He had her there and he knew it. Spike, her chickenhearted guard cat of indeterminate pedigree, had escaped her apartment as she'd dragged in her Christmas tree and headed straight up the twenty-foot pine by her front window. Mike happened to own an extension ladder. It had been left behind by the previous owners of his house.

"Okay. So we're even," she decided. Skeptical anyway, she tipped her head. "What's the favor?"

He had one arm in the sleeve of his overcoat. "It's not that big a deal. I just need a date. For the Heart Ball," he explained, fabric rustling as he tackled the other sleeve. "Dr. MacAllister insists that I go. It's kind of hard to turn down the chief of staff."

Katie blinked at the man looming four feet in front of her. When she looked at Mike, she saw...Mike. But she also knew what other women saw. His hair was a rich shade of sable, thick and worn just casual enough to invite a woman's fingers to test its softness. His features were chiseled, his jaw angular, his nose thin as a blade, and his mouth carved and sensuously full. Then there were his eyes, those incredible, piercing blue eyes that held such intelligence and compassion, and revealed very little of what was actually going on inside the man himself.

All that before she got below his neck.

Under his nicely fitting clothes were a pair of broad shoulders, a set of sinewy biceps, taut pecs and a six-pack of abdominal muscles that would have any woman with an ounce of breath left in her body sighing with pure longing.

Having gone a tad farther than she'd intended to prove her point, she casually glanced back up to meet his eyes, dismissing the faint flutter in her stomach as nothing more than autonomic response.

"You want me to get you a date? Geez, Mike. Look around you. There are a dozen women in this hospital alone who'd kill to go out with you. And what about all those hard little bodies at the gym?" She didn't go to the gym herself. Her ego couldn't take it. But she'd seen him in a tank and jogging shorts. All he'd have to do was walk through the weight room and women would be dropping at his feet. "You could probably have your pick."

"I don't want a real date," he countered, too busy dismissing the idea to be flattered by Katie's certainty. "I don't want to have to call somebody back, or make small talk all night. Then there'd be the expectations and hints about getting together again. Or maybe she'd be bored to death with me and chomping at the bit to go home. I just don't want to deal with any of that right now."

He didn't want to deal with dating, period. Katie was fairly certain of that. Since his divorce following his move from Portland eighteen months ago, he hadn't expressed an interest in going out with anyone at all. At least, he hadn't to her.

"So what is it you want?" she asked, at a loss.

"I want you to go with me."

She stared at the challenge in his jaw.

"You know," she said, wondering if he knew how defensive he looked, "for someone who knows his way around the inside of a chest, you don't know squat about how to touch a girl's heart. But, hey, a free dinner? A chance to wear something someone hasn't thrown up on?" She shrugged. She and Mike always had a good time together. "Why not?"

She was a little surprised by how relieved he looked. "Thanks, sport." He curved his hand over her shoulder and gave her a little squeeze. "I owe you one."

"Yeah, you do," she muttered good-naturedly, and walked with him to the door.

She turned left for the med room.

Mike turned right, heading for the unit's wide double doors. Moments later, he was jogging down the stairwell, preferring movement to waiting for an elevator. Taking all three flights and a short hall to the street in less than a minute, he left the hospital with its familiar sounds and antiseptic smells, and strode into the gray drizzle that was winter in the Northwest. There might be days when that drizzle turned to a downpour or to sleet or, occasionally, to snow, but from October to June, some sort of precipitation invariably seemed to be falling from the cloud-filled sky.

He wanted sunshine. Just a day of it, he thought, then dismissed the wish as a waste of mental energy. Even if the clouds did decide to depart, he wouldn't have time to take advantage of the break.

He had one less concern to deal with at the moment, however. He could forget about having to scrape up a date for the hospital auxiliary's annual charity fund-raiser. The necessity was hardly a priority. The event was a month away, but he'd seen no point in letting the matter nag at him. He'd known it would, too. And the thought of having to spend an evening being attentive to someone he barely knew while mingling with the movers and shakers who could help shape his career, held all the appeal of a tooth-ache. Even if the evening hadn't been important from a career standpoint, he really didn't want to ask someone out and have her think he was interested in pursuing a potential relationship. Since his divorce, he'd had no desire to throw himself back into that briar patch again. There wasn't much of anything he even missed about not having a spe-cial woman in his life. Except sex.

His dark eyebrows jammed together, the thought catch-ing him off guard as he finally reached his car and then jockeyed the black Lexus through the early-morning rush-hour traffic. He'd been so busy he hardly even thought about sex anymore—which should have told him right there that he was working way too hard.

Frowning past the windshield wipers swiping at the rain, he headed toward the complex of modern medical offices eight blocks away. It wasn't that he didn't think about sex at all, he reminded himself. He was a healthy, thirty-four-year-old male who responded predictably to an attractive woman. He just wasn't into casual sexual relationships. Not that he'd found himself tempted by one lately, he had to concede. Or, not so lately, for that matter.

That thought failed to provide the encouragement he was looking for. It also made him consider that there were times, sex aside, when having a girlfriend would be handy. For a nice dinner out. A quiet evening by the fire. For occasions like the Heart Ball. Thanks to Katie, though, he didn't have to concern himself about that last one. Even though she'd given him a hard time about it, he'd known he could count on her. She was like family that way.

Mike didn't question the faint smile that came and went with the thought. His mind was already racing ahead as he turned down the parking ramp under the two-story office complex and pulled into the space marked Michael J. Brennan, MD. He had follow-ups with two bypasses and an atrial defect, and work-ups with three referrals whose records he'd studied until midnight. After a quick lunch, he had a leaky mitral valve to repair.

If all went well, he could check on his other hospitalized patients, hit the gym for a quick workout, run back by the hospital to check on the valve, grab takeout and be home by nine-thirty. Unfortunately, that would be a little late to ask Katie if she'd go over the discrepancies he'd found in the data collection for his research study. Having hit her up for one favor today, he'd been reluctant to mention wanting her help with that, too. Maybe she could do it tomorrow if it wasn't her night at the free clinic. If she balked, he could bribe her with dinner. If that didn't work, he could always bring up the time he'd beat up his kid brother for her, but he liked to save the big guns for when he really needed them.

Chapter Two

"**Y**ou know, Michael, if I wasn't your friend, you'd have waited until we were at work tomorrow to ask me to do this."

"But you are my friend, and I like taking advantage of you."

"At least you're honest."

"So," he said, shutting the door and closing out the steady drum of rain while she shook water droplets from her curls, "are blood pressures being taken at the prescribed intervals after the drug is administered, or is someone getting sloppy? The readings I'm getting are all over the place."

Slipping off her burgundy raincoat, she eyed Mike evenly. He stood with his back to the massive, carved oak entry door, a navy T-shirt hugging his chest and gray, drawstring sweatpants hanging loosely on his narrow hips.

He'd obviously had time to get comfortable. She needed the same.

"First things first." She'd just spent the three hours since she got off work trying to scrape up more volunteers for the free clinic. She needed a break. She needed food. "You said we'd order takeout."

"Already done. I called Wangs. Two orders of mu shu pork and a large house special fried rice are on their way." Taking her coat, he flicked a glance over the long, cocoa-colored sweater and leggings she'd changed into between work and...work. "You get the glasses. I'll get the wine."

Pulling off her wet shoes so she wouldn't track up his parquet-tiled floors, she watched him lay her coat over the long, empty planter that served as a divider between the spacious entry and the more spacious dining room before he headed through the foyer for his kitchen. She knew he couldn't hang the garment in the guest closet. It didn't have any hangers. Like the empty planter, there wasn't much of anything in the obscenely spacious house at all.

Hoping that was about to change, she glanced past a pair of long, black snow skis and a set of poles propped against one of the white entry walls. Her eye was immediately drawn to the cathedral-ceilinged living room. The walls there were mostly glass. Black glass, since it was seven o'clock at night. But the room's focal point was the striated rock fireplace that stretched from floor to ceiling like the side of a narrow, jagged cliff.

The huge room was magnificent, but not a single stick of furniture broke the sweep of neutral wall-to-wall carpeting. The only object in the soaring space was a telescope on a tripod. It stood like a sentry where two of the glass walls met, its long, tubular shape pointed toward infinity.

"Where are the fabric samples?" she asked, entering

the almost equally austere kitchen. This room was blinding white. But at least it sported a few signs of life. A toaster. A gleaming black coffeemaker. The water bottle from Mike's gym bag.

Mike was bent in front of the open refrigerator. From what she could see from where she'd stopped at a cabinet, the pickings inside it were pretty slim.

He reached for the bottle of wine between the orange juice and the milk. "The what?"

"Fabric samples." Crystal clinked as she removed two goblets from his meager collection of glassware. "You didn't cancel your appointment with that interior designer your mom recommended, did you?"

"No," he muttered blandly. "I didn't cancel. I sent her away." The door closed with a nudge from his hip. "The woman had barely walked in when she started talking about how the house was 'speaking to her.' When she got to the dining room and started waxing poetic about how perfect it would be with an Isfahan hunting tapestry on the wall, bowls of pussy willows on a sideboard and chairs with open, vase-form splats, I told her I had an emergency and that we'd have to cancel. I had the feeling she was more interested in how the place would look in a magazine spread than in what I might want."

Katie could tell he expected an argument. Or, possibly, defense of the designer's artistic abilities. He wouldn't get either from her. She might have championed the idea of a designer, but after hearing the part about communicating with the house, she'd have sent the woman packing herself. "With open what?"

"Vase-form splats. Apparently that's designer-speak for a vase-shaped back on a chair. Like the Chippendales at my folks' place."

"I didn't know that."

"I didn't, either. And personally," he added, pulling a corkscrew from a drawer, "I didn't care."

"She obviously doesn't know she's supposed to be working with your tastes, not hers. You should call someone else."

"I'm not calling anyone," he informed her flatly. "The only reason I called to begin with was because you and Mom kept nagging at me. The place is fine the way it is."

"Michael, this house is as sterile as a surgical suite. You've been in here six months—"

"Five," he corrected, refusing to let her exaggerate.

"Fine. You've been in this house five months and the only room you've furnished is your office."

"I have a bed."

"Have you bought a bedroom set yet?"

"I don't need one. The closet has plenty of drawers in it."

She couldn't argue with that. She'd seen his enormous walk-in closet when he'd given her the grand tour after he'd moved in. It had more drawers than she had in her entire duplex.

"Well, you need furniture everywhere else," she insisted, wondering how he kept from going mad in all this echoing space. "You need something comfortable to sit on. You need tables. You need pillows." She motioned behind her. "You need something in that entryway."

"There is something in the entryway."

Katie eyed him patiently. "You need plants. You need art. Those," she said, vaguely indicating the skis propped against the wall, "do not constitute art. They're sporting equipment."

"Those are there because my brother is picking them up sometime this week. I meant the little paper bird my niece made for me. It's sitting in the niche by the front door.'' He gave her a smug look and hoisted the unopened bottle. ''Do you want this now, or do you want to wait until the food gets here? We can eat while we go over the data.''

He was changing the subject. He wasn't being particularly subtle about it, either. Not that he ever was with her.

Katie picked up the glasses. For some reason that totally eluded her, Mike was peculiarly obtuse about furnishing this place. She knew he'd bought it because he couldn't stand the confines of the apartment he and Marla, his ex-wife, had moved into when he'd returned to Honeygrove. Yet, once he'd moved in the few things Marla hadn't taken when she'd left, he'd done nothing else. She didn't know if he simply wasn't into aesthetics, or if making the place more livable had psychological consequences he wasn't sharing. What she did know was that this house was not a home.

Apparently he caught the grinding of her mental wheels. ''This bothers you more than it does me, Katie,'' he informed her, clearly wishing she'd drop the subject. ''Forget it. Okay?''

''I just think you'd be happier if it was more comfortable.''

''I'm not here enough to be uncomfortable. And I'm not *un*happy.''

Moving beside him, she set the goblets on the counter and indicated that he should pour. He might think he wasn't uncomfortable, but she wasn't ready to give up yet. ''Maybe you should ask your mom to do it herself. She'd be thrilled.''

The creases bracketing his mouth deepened with a grimace. The expression spoke volumes.

''You're right,'' she conceded, watching his hands as he deftly worked the corkscrew from the bottle. He had beautiful hands. Strong, capable and far too masculine for the delicate work she knew he did. "I can't picture you living with oriental rugs and gilded mirrors. You're definitely more the natural colors and tactile fabrics sort. Maybe a few pieces of marble sculpture here and there. And a place for your car in your bedroom. Guys love their cars."

"You could always do it for me."

She brightened. "You'd give me carte blanche with your checkbook?"

He was teasing. So was she. Yet his blue eyes suddenly went dead serious.

"You're probably the only woman I would trust with it." He handed her a freshly filled goblet, filled the other for himself and snapped a wine saver onto the bottle before he stuck it back in the fridge to keep it chilled.

"Come on," he murmured, picking up his glass, "we've got a few minutes before dinner gets here. We can get started on that data."

He took two steps before the phone rang. "Please don't let that be the hospital," he said on a sigh, and snatched up the phone under the counter.

Katie could tell immediately that he didn't get his wish. Not wanting to eavesdrop—not once she'd figured out that the patient he was discussing wasn't anyone she knew, anyway—she took her wine and moved into the foyer. For a moment she waited to see if Mike had to go back to the hospital, but then she kept going, stepping into the living room, rather than heading back to his office with its walls of books, photos of rafting and sailing trips and the computer on his desk that linked him to the hospital.

She was thinking of what he'd said moments ago about trusting her, and feeling oddly touched by the thought, when she stopped beside the telescope in his living room.

There was no way to see anything through the powerful scope. Not with the heavy clouds tonight. But she stood by the instrument anyway, trying to judge the direction it was pointed, and trying to figure out what star or constellation Mike had been looking at the last time he'd used it. She wondered if he actually made time to use it anymore. Or if it was only a pastime he resorted to on restless, and cloudless, nights.

Thinking of Mike being restless conjured an image of him leaving his bed and standing where she was, looking out at the night sky. The thought of him being unable to rest was what bothered her, but thinking of him naked except for his briefs or whatever he slept in, disturbed her in other ways entirely. She was sure the image had formed only because of the little inventory she'd taken the other day, anyway—the mind's habit of recalling odd bits of memory. So, she banished the errant thoughts and listened to the muffled rumble of his voice while she sipped her wine and remembered the first time she'd ever looked through a telescope herself.

She'd been nine years old. Mike had just turned thirteen.

"Can I look through your birthday present, Mike? Can I? Please?"

The tall, skinny boy with the unruly dark hair didn't move from his perch on the redwood deck. Keeping his back to her, he sighed with impatience. "It's dark. You're not supposed to be out here."

"Mom said I can be because you are."

The word he muttered was one he wasn't supposed to use. Katie would have told him so, too, but he'd turned around to frown down at her. It wasn't a frown, really. Not the kind his younger brother Tommy gave her. He didn't slug her the way Tommy did, either. But then, Tommy hadn't slugged her all summer. Mike had belted him the last time he'd done it and they both got grounded.

Tommy got grounded yesterday, too. He'd locked her in her dad's garden shed during a game of hide-and-seek, and then forgotten about her. Mike had rescued her. Probably because he'd heard her screaming.

"One look, then you go home."

"I don't have to go home. Mom and Dad are inside with your parents."

The Brennans and the Sheppards lived next door to each other, their Tudor-style homes separated by an expanse of lawn and a low hedge with an iron gate. The adults liked to spend time together on Saturday nights, but Mike and Tommy didn't want her hanging around much anymore—except when they wanted her to watch their baby brother for them so they wouldn't have to do it. It wasn't like it used to be when they'd shared the play pool in their underwear when they were younger. Mike and Tommy had turned into...boys.

Katie could forgive them for that as long as they didn't tease her and make her cry. Since Mike never did, she liked him better. "What are you looking at?"

"A star."

"Which one?" she asked, climbing onto the redwood deck to stand by him.

"The North Star."

"I know where that is."

"Yeah. Right."

"I do!"

He stepped back from the tripod. "Show me."

She did. Not with the telescope, because she didn't know how to use it. She tipped her head to the velvet black summer sky and pointed straight to the Little Dipper and the bright star in the end of its handle. She thought stars were fun because there were stories that went with the constellations—legends of hunters like Orion and pretty ladies like Cassiopeia. She'd learned them from her Aunt Claire, her mom's sister. Aunt Claire had taught her a lot of things, like ballet positions and how to whistle through her teeth.

Mike already knew how to whistle through his teeth, and he thought ballet was for girls, but her knowledge of the constellations kept him from making her go away. He already knew quite a few of the formations himself, and once he showed her how to focus the telescope, something that had her grinning like a Cheshire cat, they took turns looking at the brightest stars in the constellations they knew. She liked that he didn't treat her like a dumb little kid. But then, Mike had always been nice to her. It was almost as if he looked out for her sometimes.

And she'd adored him for it.

Katie touched the cap covering the lens, her thoughts caught in the twenty-year gap between then and now. By the end of that summer, she and Mike had discovered a few of the more obscure star groupings and both had become thoroughly hooked on what the night sky contained. Amazingly, that interest had held despite a disparity in ages that, at that time in their lives, should have left them with nothing in common at all. But that single thread bound them in a comfortable friendship as talk of stars expanded to talk of galaxies and the universe and, ultimately, as they grew older, to their places in it. They never talked of such things anymore—of their dreams, their hopes. They hadn't for a very long time. But the bond remained. For her, anyway.

"Ready?"

Katie turned with a start, nearly spilling her wine. She

caught the drip that ran over the rim with her finger. "Sure. Is everything all right?"

"I don't have to leave, if that's what you mean. The resident can handle it."

She watched his eyes follow her hand as she touched the tip of her finger to her lips. Her movement was natural, completely unconscious. At least, she hadn't been conscious of it until she realized it had drawn his glance to her mouth, and that he wasn't looking away. Even as she lowered her hand, his focus stayed right where it was.

The odd intensity in his eyes caused her heart to bump her ribs, but he was already shifting his attention to the telescope.

"What are you doing?"

She shook her head, shaking off the strange yearning sensation that had come out of nowhere. "Just wondering if you ever use this anymore. I can't remember the last time I looked through one."

"I can't, either. I don't even know why I keep it."

A soft smile touched her mouth as she shrugged. "Maybe it reminds you of a simpler time."

He got that look again. The same one that had turned his eyes so serious when he'd alluded to how much he trusted her. "Maybe," he said, forcing a smile himself. "Life was pretty uncomplicated back then. Come on. I don't want to keep you here until midnight."

Mike kept her in his office until midnight anyway. But that was only because after they'd finished working, she'd asked if Paul, his youngest brother, had made it back to Southern Oregon State all right. Paul had been home for winter break. That inquiry had led to questions about the rest of his family, which led Mike to mention the mountain cabin his other brother, Tom, wanted Mike to buy with him. He'd told her he was considering going in on the cabin, mostly because he knew Tom and his family would use it and raising three kids on social workers' salaries, Tom and his wife couldn't afford it on their own. Then, Katie had reminded him that he'd once wanted a cabin surrounded by pine trees himself, and he'd warmed to the idea even more.

He liked that about Katie; that she could sometimes make him see things he'd overlooked. Or forgotten. She was a good friend, good company. And there were times lately when he really hated to see her go. He just wished she'd lay off him about furnishing the house.

He'd walked her to the door. Now, having waited on the porch until she'd driven off, he headed back inside. The day had been a long one and he automatically turned off lights as he worked his way down the hall to his bedroom. He was tired. His body demanded sleep. But his mind wouldn't shut off. Even after he'd stripped to his briefs, brushed his teeth and pulled back the hunter green comforter on his king-size bed to crawl between the sheets, he could still hear the echo of Katie's quiet concern.

You'd be more comfortable. You'd be happier.

What made her think he wasn't? he wondered, punching his pillow into a ball. He was happy. Downright blissful, damn it. And why shouldn't he be? He was doing the work he loved. He was building his practice and his skills, and he had a roof over his head. Just because there wasn't much under that roof didn't matter to him. The only reason he'd bought the place to begin with was because he'd needed more room, and this particular house had a great view of the woods.

Katie was right. He had always wanted to live surrounded by pines. But just because she was right about that, didn't mean she was right about anything else.

Marla would have hated the place.

The thought of his ex-wife had him whipping the sheets back and dragging his hand down his face. He knew better than to attempt sleep when his mind was revved. He was better off doing something—anything—until his thoughts settled enough to keep him from fighting the blankets all night.

He reached for one of the medical journals piled by his bed, only to toss it back and get up. Had there been a break in the rain, he'd have wandered out to the telescope to see if the clouds had parted enough for him to lose himself in the vastness of space. But he could still hear water dripping from the eaves. So he headed for the kitchen to nuke a mug of milk. There were some remedies modern medicine still couldn't beat without side effects.

Minutes later, mug in hand, he was standing on the thick carpet in his bare living room. With the interior lights off and the exterior security lights on, he could see rain puddled on the deck outside the window. Raindrops landed in the puddles, causing the water to shimmer and dance.

Katie was right. He did need a chair. On nights like this, he could sit and watch the rain. Maybe when his drug study was finished, he'd use that freed-up time to do something about the house. He'd been so busy getting his professional feet under him that he hadn't taken time for anything that wasn't absolutely necessary. He hadn't had a spare minute, it seemed, since he'd finished his residency eighteen months ago. That was when he'd been invited to join the partnership in Honeygrove, and when his marriage had started falling apart.

He hadn't even seen the end coming. But then, he hadn't been looking for problems, and Marla had hidden her agenda well. As beautiful as she was patient, he'd been drawn by her easy smile and seemingly undemanding manner. She'd been enormously understanding of the long hours he'd had to put in as a resident. Being a pharmaceutical rep, she'd been away from home a lot herself. They'd both looked forward to having his residency behind them, to her cutting back on her hours, to building their future. Then, with the move to Honeygrove, Marla's true colors had slowly begun to surface.

They'd agreed that the little apartment they'd moved into was temporary; that a house was a priority. They moved in one day and he had to start work the next, taking over most of a caseload from a retiring partner. Marla didn't go back to work at all. Instead of just cutting back, she quit her job completely and promptly started shopping for an architect to design them a house on a golf course. Her rationale for giving up her job had been that she wouldn't have time to work and oversee the details of having his home built. She'd also said she knew he'd be busy getting himself established, so she'd manage everything for both of them. She also needed to volunteer on the right civic and charitable committees to enhance his standing in the community, and that would take her time, too. Then, there were the hours she needed to spend at the gym and the salon staying beautiful for him.

He didn't want his standing "enhanced." He didn't want to live on a golf course. He didn't want a trophy wife. Most of all, he didn't want his life "managed" by a woman who didn't care about him so much as she did being the wife of a "rich" doctor. She'd wanted the right house, the right car, membership in the right clubs, the right clothes. She'd said she was entitled to it all, because she'd spent the two years of their marriage supporting him. Emotionally, anyway. His parents had paid for his schooling, and he and Marla had paid their living expenses equally, so it wasn't as if she could claim any financial obligation on his part. To add insult to injury, she hadn't wanted to start their family as they'd planned, either.

It had taken two months from the time they'd moved to Honeygrove for all her little plans to come out, two months for him to realize that, from the day they'd married, she'd simply been biding her time.

He turned from the window, from the ghostlike reflection of himself. He didn't know why he was thinking of this tonight. When the divorce had become final last spring, he'd felt relief more than anything else. He hadn't felt any bitterness or pain, either, which had left him wondering if he'd ever loved her at all. It had made him wonder, too, if he really wanted the wife and the kids and the dog. Maybe he didn't need the comforts of a home. As he stood watching the rain, the steam from his mug fogging a streak on the window, he wondered if maybe that was why he didn't care that his house echoed when he walked through it.

The thought settled like a hollow weight in his gut. He didn't like the empty feeling at all. So, he did what he always did when he needed to disassociate himself from something that held the potential to cause discomfort, or to hurt. He pulled back from it, mentally blocking the sensation by focusing objectively on the matter at hand. And, objectively, he knew he wouldn't be thinking of any of this if Katie hadn't originally brought it up. He also knew he needed sleep, and that was his priority at the moment. He was on call for the next five days, so he had to round on all the office's patients, not just his own. Given that one of his colleagues was out with a cold, it could well be one of those weeks.

The week started off badly for Katie, and went downhill from there.

She walked into work the next morning to find the floor short-staffed from a flu bug making the rounds, and every bed filled. There wasn't any staff to float from other units, either, and only one aide was available through an outside service. The bug had been around for a while, and hospitals as far away as Portland and Medford were using up all the temporary help.

The whims of fate being truly perverse, while everyone was running around doing double duty, a staff meeting was called for the next afternoon to explain that the computer program was being changed—just as the *old* new one had finally got up and running. But administration wasn't the only area being unreasonable. Her patients seemed more demanding than usual, too. So did their relatives. Which meant that Katie, who was fighting off a sore throat herself, had to utilize all her skills as psychologist, facilitator and counselor.

As the week went on, stress levels rose. Patience was tested. Dr. Aniston was his usual charming self, which didn't help matters at all, and the nurses, especially the temporaries they did manage to get, balked continually at having to collect extra data each time they administered Mike's study drug when they were barely able to keep up as it was. Rather than having a year's worth of Mike's work skewed, Katie collected most of it herself. On top of that she had a flat tire on the way home from work Wednesday night. On Thursday, her throat was worse and she wound up on an antibiotic so she wouldn't pass anything on to her patients. And Saturday morning, already late because she'd overslept, the hot water handle on her shower broke.

I can do this. Katie repeated the phrase to herself so many times that week that she began to think of it as her personal mantra. She could handle it all simply because it wasn't acceptable to admit that she couldn't. She would cut corners where her own needs were concerned, but she refused to shortchange anyone else. If anyone was counting on her for anything, she would be there.

ϯ That was why she didn't call in sick when no one would have blamed her for doing just that. And it was why she dragged herself to her shift at the free clinic when what she really wanted to do was crawl into bed and sleep for a week. She wasn't a martyr. Far from it. It was just that the thought of letting someone down was anathema to her. She wasn't the only nurse at Honeygrove Memorial who was pulling double shifts when she didn't feel all that great. And the clinic operated with only one nurse and one nurse practitioner or doctor each shift. If she didn't show up when she was scheduled, that left one person to handle an entire evening's worth of indigent patients alone. She knew exactly what it was like to expect someone to be there and not have them show. She knew, too, what it was like to make plans, to count on someone, then have to deal with the inconvenience or the disappointment because one person didn't do what he'd said he would. She simply wouldn't do that to anyone.

ϯ Still, the thought crept into her mind every evening that she really wouldn't mind coming home to someone who would put his strong, supportive arms around her while she talked out her frustrations. Or they talked out his. Or they just held each other while nothing was said at all. But she had no one like that, had no prospect of anyone like that, and the last thing she needed was to dwell on what she lacked.

What she did have were friends. Terrific ones. And it would have helped enormously if she'd been able to unload on them. Not on Mike, however. Aside from the fact that he'd been pressed for time himself the past several days, being a guy, he wouldn't have understood the need for a pair of strong, capable, protective arms to curl up in. Her girlfriends would have certainly related, though. Especially Dana and Lee. Dana Rowan and Lee Murphy, both signers of the now infamous I-will-never-marry-a-doctor pact, were like sisters. The three of them had known each other since ninth grade and, being similarly unattached, would have offered the proper amounts of understanding, sympathy and commiseration. Both worked little more than a stone's throw away. Dana was a surgical nurse. Lee was a nurse practitioner in the outpatient clinic.

With all three of them working in the same building, large and sprawling as it was, it should have been easy for them to get together. It rarely worked that way. Katie couldn't even get away for lunch until the following Monday, and then she had to cancel at the last minute because one of her patients wasn't doing well. She learned from a quick call down to Dana that Lee had canceled, too. The doctor Lee worked for was being his usual impossible self and she couldn't get away, either.

Hours later, reminding herself to try again tomorrow, Katie let herself into her duplex after working her sixth, twelve-hour day in a row. Within five minutes, she'd given Spike his obligatory cuddle, while the fifteen pounds of vibrating fur checked her pockets for treats, traded scrubs for sweats, washed off her makeup and pulled her hair into a ponytail. She was just preparing to see what dietary delight awaited her in her freezer when she remembered the kitty litter and cat food she'd picked up on her way home and left in her car.

Thinking she might as well get it before Spike started getting vocal about being fed, she opened the door to slip out. The cat was right behind her. In a split second, he was between her feet and darting for the twenty-foot pine tree ten feet away.

"Spike! No!" she hollered, and watched him disappear up the trunk.

She couldn't get him down. She coaxed. She cajoled. She tried bribing him with cat food and tuna and a leaf from the fern he loved to destroy when she wasn't around. He didn't budge. He simply sat clinging to a three-inch branch fifteen feet up with his tail wrapped around the orange and black spots on his little white body and a look of abject terror in his eyes. He was a house cat, pure and simple. He might have developed a sudden yen for the great outdoors, but once he got there, he was petrified.

Tired, running out of patience, she coaxed some more. She begged. She told him she was going to wring his furry little neck.

Nothing worked. And the more she tried, the more she realized her throat was tightening up and her eyes were beginning to sting. It was fatigue, she knew. It simply had to be fatigue that was making her stand shivering in the dark wanting to cry because she couldn't get her cat to come to her.

She already knew she couldn't climb the tree herself. She'd tried it the last time the little monster had done this and she'd nearly broken her neck. The couple who lived next door to her were sweethearts, but they were pushing seventy and in no position to offer help. What she needed was a ladder. A big ladder. And the only person she could think to call was Mike.

Chapter Three

"You're lucky you caught me. Two more minutes and I'd have been out the door."

"You weren't on your way to the hospital, were you?"

"Dinner."

"Oh, Mike. I'm sorry."

Muscles shifting under his sweater and jacket, Mike told her not to worry about it and lifted the extension ladder from the ski rack on his black sedan. As anxious as she'd sounded on the phone, he hadn't had the heart to tell her he was already running late. "I begged an extra half an hour. I figured that would give me time for a rescue on my way to the restaurant."

He considered it a fair indication of how concerned she was about her cat that she had no comeback for his faint sarcasm. As she hurried beside him, her breath a puff of vapor in the cool night air, she carried her worry in her eyes. At work, she couched her concerns with professional calm. When it came to friends and family—which she considered her cat to be—she wore every emotion on her sleeve.

"I really appreciate this," she murmured, casting a troubled glance toward the top of the pine. "I really do. I just didn't know who else to call."

"Ever consider the fire department? That's who most people call when their schizophrenic pet gets stuck in a high place."

The look she spared him was laced with tolerance. "Spike's not schizophrenic. He's just a little…hyper. And I couldn't call the fire department," she informed him ever so reasonably. "Not looking like this."

In the merging pools of light from her porch, her carport and the streetlamp on the corner, he watched her push back a long, soft-looking curl that had escaped the tangle of hair anchored atop her head.

"What does how you look have to do with anything?"

"Are you kidding?" Incredulity washed fatigue and worry from her face. "I don't have a scrap of makeup on. My hair's a mess. And nobody but Spike sees me in these sweats." Tugging on the stretched-out neckline of her faded gray sweatshirt, she pulled it back over her shoulder. "Some of those guys are major hunks. What if the man of my dreams was one of them? I'd be mortified if he saw me looking this awful."

For a moment, Mike said nothing. He just stood with the ladder on his shoulder, wondering if he should be insulted. Since it was obviously all right for him to see her as she was, he'd apparently been lumped into the same category as her psycho cat.

Personally, he didn't think she looked so bad. Granted, the old sweats were so loose that a person really couldn't tell how shapely she was. And she did look considerably less polished without makeup and her hair pulled into that high, slightly listing ponytail. But there was an intriguing lack of artifice to her freshly scrubbed face, and a gamine quality about the baggy clothes that was kind of sexy in its own way. Especially with the stretched-out neckline sliding off her shoulder again. It kind of made a guy want to discover just how soft she was under that concealing material. Especially since he already knew she had a great little body. She was curvy and feminine, not sinewy and hard the way some of the women at the gym looked. A man would feel as if he were making love to a marble statue with some of them. But with Katie, he'd know he was holding a woman.

He was wondering if she was wearing a bra, suspecting she wasn't, when he felt a tightening low in his gut. Reminding himself this was Katie he was mentally bedding, he swung the long, aluminum extension ladder upright.

"Why don't you get a ladder from your parents' house?" he muttered, blaming the edginess he suddenly felt on the fact that he hated being late. "You could have your dad throw it in the back of his Suburban and drop it off. Or I'll leave this one," he added, the afterthought occurring as he wedged the ladder between the pine's long branches. "It would make sense to keep one here if your cat's going to keep this up."

His last words were accompanied by an ear-piercing screech and a shower of pine needles as fifteen pounds of skittish feline scrambled higher.

Katie's hand flattened over the knot in her stomach. The thought of imposing on her father had put the knot there. Her panicking cat doubled it. "The ladder scared him," Katie explained, her tone caught between admonishment and sympathy. "Try not to make any sudden moves. Okay?"

A vision of her precious kitty clinging like an ornament to the top of the tree vied with the guilt aroused by Mike's narrowed glance. Having interrupted his evening, she had no business criticizing his rescue effort. Especially since he was going out of his way to help her. That was something her father never would have done. She'd grown up hearing how important her father was, how important was his work, and being told that she shouldn't interrupt him unless it was absolutely necessary. This man shoving a bough out of the way as he started up the ladder was no less important, his work no less significant, yet there he was, six feet up in her tree making kissy noises at her cat.

The thoughts were the sort guaranteed to produce a headache if she let herself dwell on them, so she focused only on Mike's ascent and held the ladder to steady it. The fresh scent of pine enveloped her, but she couldn't see a thing. The instant she'd glanced up, pine needles and droplets of water cascaded in a mist, forcing her head back down.

The cat hissed.

"Hey!"

Her head jerked right back up again. "What happened?"

"He tried to scratch me."

"Spike! Knock it off."

"That's effective," Mike muttered, moving higher.

"Are you okay?" she asked him, thinking of his hands. A cat scratch wouldn't keep him out of surgery, but unless he wore a bandage, a cut or scratch against latex gloves could be awfully irritating.

"Yeah, I'm fine. But he's on the edge of the limb now."

"Maybe I should get him."

Mike clearly refused to be defeated by something one-twenty-fifth his size. He didn't even acknowledge her suggestion before he moved up another rung and his arm shot out.

The tearing sound was the sleeve of his jacket catching on the end of a broken branch. The screech was Spike when Mike clamped his hand around the cat's ruff. Pine cones bouncing through the branches, he dragged Spike along the limb.

"Be careful!"

"I'm not going to hurt him. Ow! Damn it," Mike growled, pulling back with the animal clinging like a barnacle to the underside of his sleeve. "What do you do to his claws? File them to points?"

"That's just the way they grow. Here, sweetie," she cooed, reaching up as Mike pried off the cat and held him out to her. "You're not hurt, are you?"

"You talking to him or me?"

Mimicking Mike's droll glance, Katie tucked Spike's little head under her chin, holding him like a baby while she whispered to the little monster that she'd take his stuffed mouse away for a week if he pulled a stunt like that again. To Mike, she merely said, "Come here," and reached for his arm when he hit the ground so she could pull him into better light.

"Oh, geez," she murmured, when she saw the back of his jacket. Shivering from the cold night air, she hugged the cat tighter. "It did rip."

Something low and succinct preceded his cautious, "Great. How bad?"

"Just a couple of inches. Right along the shoulder seam," she expanded, feeling worse by the second for imposing on him. "It won't take but a minute for me to fix it."

"Then let's go. You need to get inside before you get pneumonia, anyway."

Katie wasn't fooled by the disgusted scowl Mike aimed at Spike before he turned to grab the ladder. She knew for a fact that he liked the cat better than he let on. As she retrieved the grocery sack from her car—since that was what she'd originally started to do—she didn't think that right now was a good time to point that out, or to mention that having a cat of his own might be good for him. Having a pet would put another heartbeat in that mausoleum he lived in, give him companionship, provide a little diversion from his work.

"Take off your jacket," she told him when he followed her in the door that opened to her cozy dining area and kitchen. The low drone of a television newscast immediately greeted them, along with the faint scent of cinnamon from the potpourri on her front entry table. "I'll get a needle and thread and be right back."

"I need to wash up."

"Go ahead."

Spike leapt from her arms as she reached the oatmeal-colored sofa that divided the comfortable space, promptly perching on the matching chair. The walls of her living room were lined with art prints, all Monet and all of his gardens with their verdant greens and splashes of soft color. With her view restricted to the back of a neighbor's garage in one direction and another duplex in the other, the colorful prints and the plants she kept in brass pots on the bookcase and by the windows, were the only way she had of bringing the outdoors in.

It took less than a minute for her to dig her sewing basket from between the quilt she'd started four years ago and never completed and an unfinished cross-stitch project of geese with holly wreaths around their necks. Promising herself she'd have that project done by *next* Christmas, she headed back down the short hall—and found Mike on her telephone. He had the portable unit tucked under his chin and was drying his hands on a paper towel while he paced between the country French canisters on the beige counter by her stove and the bunches of dried flowers and herbs hanging above her sink. Without missing a step, he nodded to where he'd left the jacket on a chair back.

She was at her kitchen table, searching the small basket for the right shade of brown, when she heard him order a string of medications meant to stabilize a dysrhythmic heart. She'd assumed he was just calling whoever he was meeting for dinner.

His pager must have gone off, she thought. Listening, because it was impossible not to, she sat down and snipped off the torn threads from the shoulder seam. When that was done, she began stitching the small rip. Mike paced past her a dozen times, his slow, measured steps more a way to expend energy than a sign of impatience.

"A double bypass was just readmitted through emergency. Eva Horton," he added, hitting the off button on the phone with his thumb.

Katie glanced up midstitch. Mike had his broad back to her as he returned the phone to the end table by the sofa.

"What happened?"

"She was having trouble breathing. Her niece brought her in."

His deep voice rumbled with terminology that Katie understood all too well as he went on to say what the EKG and blood tests had shown. The news wasn't good, but Mike was so accustomed to dealing with such situations that, when his glance fell to the jacket bunched in her lap, he revealed nothing but mild surprise.

With the tear no longer visible, his dark eyebrow winged upward. "You're finished?"

His expression would have amused Katie had she not

been so busy scrambling to keep up. A double bypass, he'd said, identifying the problem first, then the patient. She did that herself sometimes. And she knew it undoubtedly sounded cold and callous to anyone who'd never worked with pain and suffering; to anyone who'd never had to guard against becoming too involved because the emotional drain over the years could be so devastating. It was simply an occupational form of protection. But separating patient from problem didn't always work for her. Not as well as it seemed to for Mike.

Now was not the time to ask him how he did it; how he kept from worrying when he cared.

"I'm finished," she said, making the last, neat stitch so he could be on his way. "I'm not going to make you any later for dinner than you already are. Who're you meeting, anyway?"

"Claire Griffen."

"*Dr.* Griffen?"

"Why do you say it like that?" he asked, watching her bite off the thread and hand him back his jacket. "She wants a consult on a patient. We've been trying to get together for three days, but something keeps coming up. Lately, it seems as if everyone's going in eight directions at once."

"Must be a full moon," Katie muttered. "Just a consult?" Caught by a twinge of something she preferred not to define, she cocked her head and smiled. "You sure that's all it is?"

"Of course, I'm sure." He scowled at her teasing, looking as if he couldn't imagine why else he'd be having dinner with the woman. "We need to talk, and we both need to eat. It's the two-birds-with-one-stone method of time management."

"Have you been out with her before?"

"What for?"

"Well, for starters," she drawled, amazed at the total lack of comprehension in his normally intelligent blue eyes, "she's pretty, she's nice, she's single and you have a lot in common."

"You know I don't have time to date."

Which was why you asked me to the Heart Ball, she thought, but she kept the faintly chiding thought to herself. He didn't have time because he wasn't making time. He didn't *want* a relationship. That knowledge should have worried her. It probably would have, too, if his disinterest in his very eligible, female colleague hadn't just relieved her somehow.

Not caring to consider what the attractive internist might have on her own menu for the night, she moved to where Mike shrugged on his jacket by the door.

"Are you going to get a ladder from your folks, or do you want me to leave mine?"

Checking the back of his jacket to make sure her handiwork didn't show, she considered her alternatives. "Well, there's no way for me to get one over here in my car," she said, thinking out loud. "And Mom's car certainly wouldn't work." The miniscule size of the car alone precluded any further consideration there, but the thought of petite, perfectly groomed Karen Sheppard driving down the road with a twenty-foot extension ladder poked through the windows of her little Mercedes made Katie smile. "If you don't mind," she began, but Mike cut her off as she moved around to face him.

"Ask your dad to drop it off. This is practically on the way to his office."

The knot she'd felt before reasserted itself. "I'm not going to ask for his help with something like this."

"Did you ever consider that he might like you to ask for his help?"

"Frankly? No. And there's really no point in discussing this further," she insisted, holding up her hand to cut him off before he could get started. He'd never been able to understand her relationship with her father—or, rather, the lack of one. And since he knew her dad quite well, he couldn't comprehend how she, who'd lived in her father's house for eighteen years, scarcely knew him at all. "Thanks for your help. Really," she added, her voice softening with apology and fatigue. "I appreciate it."

"Why do you have to be so stubborn?"

"Mike, please. Why can't you just accept that my father and I don't have the same sort of relationship that you and your dad do? Or the same sort of relationship *you* have with him for that matter." She drew a deep breath, and pinched the headache threatening behind the bridge of her nose. Mike made her absolutely crazy when he started in on this particular subject. He simply didn't—couldn't—seem to understand that she did not want to discuss it with him. It wasn't worth the anger and hurt she felt every time they did.

"You're going to be late," she said, her patience straining. She couldn't do this. Not now. She was running on reserve as it was. "I'll keep your ladder for a while, if you don't mind."

The defeat in her tone silenced him. For a moment, he just stood there looking big and solid and strong, and seeing far too much.

"You know I don't mind," he finally said, and absently pushed back the curl that had fallen against her cheek.

The gesture was one of conciliation, and it forced the corner of her mouth to curve. He matched her weak smile with one of his own.

"You're looking a little flushed," he murmured. "Is your throat still bothering you?"

She shook her head, her fingers lingering on the spot he'd just touched when she pushed the curl back again herself. "It's a lot better. Really," she insisted since he looked as if he didn't quite believe her.

"You push yourself too hard."

"You have no room to talk. I'm not the one heading off to a consultation after working all day."

"Yeah, but I'm not sick."

"I'm not either. I'm better." Almost.

His lips thinned, but more in exasperation than doubt. Shaking his head at her, he reached out again and brushed his knuckles over her cheek. "Get some rest."

It had to be the craziness of the day—the week—that made her reach toward him as he turned to the door. He didn't see what she'd done, though. With his back to her as he let himself out, he didn't notice, either, how she drew her hand back to cross her arms, or see how tightly she held herself as she listened to the heavy click of the latch when the door closed.

It was just as well she hadn't caught his attention. She didn't know what she'd have said she wanted if he had. There were just so many times lately when she'd wanted a pair of arms around her. Not just any arms, either. But it didn't seem wise to think about how good it would feel to have Mike hold her, even though there were times she wanted that more than she dared admit.

Three days later, all Katie wanted was to walk out the front door of the hospital and never go back. Eva Horton coded that morning. They'd worked on her for over an hour before she passed away in CICU.

The desire to simply chuck it all didn't last. There were

too many other patients to attend, too much else to be done for Katie to indulge herself in something so easy. The reaction was knee-jerk, anyway; a response that occasionally came when circumstances made her question her skills, her judgment, her choice of occupation. With other patients needing her attention, she couldn't dwell on how unfair it was for Eva's fire and spark to be snuffed out when there had been so much the woman had wanted to do. But Katie couldn't ignore the tugs of sadness that told her she'd failed once again to keep professional compassion from getting personal. Being the pro she was, however, she continued efficiently about her duties, soothing anxious patients, practicing patience with imbecilic insurance red tape, and working around the odd little ache such a loss always left.

Still, she didn't think she'd ever been so glad to leave a place when, having logged in only two extra hours of overtime, she finally left to join Dana and Lee at Granetti's for a drink after work.

Granetti's Pub was something of an institution among the hospital crowd. The cozy trattoria and bar was only a block away, a short dash through the parking garage. Its owners, an Italian chef and his Irish wife, took pride in the fact that much of the hospital's staff thought of the place as they would a friend's kitchen.

When Katie hurried in from the rain, her friends were already there, occupying one of the green-clothed tables under a trellis of faux grapevines and a Guinness beer sign that proclaimed the brand was good for one's health. Dana, looking chic as always with her stylishly short blond hair, held up a glass of white wine to indicate she'd already ordered for her. Across from her, Lee raked her fingers through the dark strands of her wind-tousled shag. With her warm, easy smile, she motioned to the chair beside her.

"Can you believe she actually applied for that promotion?" Lee asked, picking up the conversation as if it hadn't been hours since she'd called about getting together that afternoon.

Katie eyed the basket of warm garlic cheese bread on the table, struggling between the lure of the bread's heavenly scent and the need to shed the last of her holiday weight. The only drawback to having finally shaken her sore throat was that her appetite had returned.

"It's about time," she replied. Inhaling the intoxicating blend of garlic, parsley and Parmesan, she smiled at Dana. "You waffled about it long enough. How long before you hear?"

Dana was an excellent nurse, and her organizational abilities made her the perfect choice for nurse manager of the surgery department. It had just taken a little arm-twisting on their part to get her to see her potential. But then, arm-twisting was what friends were for.

"It'll be weeks. They've just started taking applications. But enough about that." A shining wedge of her hair swung forward as she leaned closer, her blue eyes sparkling like the sapphire studs in her ears. She still looked as fresh and crisp as she undoubtedly had that morning. Even her dewy peach lipstick was perfect. "I want to know what you're wearing to the Heart Ball."

Lee, who rarely bothered with mascara, much less anything with color in it, paused midbite. "What?" She swallowed, nearly choking. "You're going to the Heart Ball? With who? Whom?" she corrected, dropping the bread to the plate in front of her.

"Just Mike," Dana said before Katie could. "But it's

the idea that she gets to go. It's like Cinderella night. She gets to wear panty hose and everything.''

''I can get into the Cinderella part,'' Lee admitted, not at all opposed to indulging in a little fantasy. ''But you had me worried there, Katie. For a minute I thought you were actually going on a date with a doctor.''

Katie's expression turned chiding. ''Bite your tongue.''

''Look, you two.'' Dana sighed in exasperation. ''There's no harm in enjoying a doctor's company if one asks you out. As long as he's single, anyway. Just because you date someone doesn't mean you have to marry him.''

''You can take chances if you want,'' Lee informed their reckless friend. ''I'm not interested. When it comes to personal relationships, any man with an MD behind his name is a lousy risk. So,'' she continued, blatantly changing the subject as she turned back to Katie, ''what *are* you going to wear?''

Though Katie quietly shared the conviction, Lee was definitely the most militant of the three when it came to the old pledge they'd signed. Despite Dana's somewhat looser stance, Katie knew that Dana shared it, too. Her mom had regarded doctors as white knights, perfect marriage material for herself and her daughter. But Dana wasn't about to waste her life the way her mother had, waiting to be rescued. Katie and Lee, however, had seen up close and personal what involvement with a doctor meant. Lee's father had also been a physician. But he'd abandoned his daughter in a more profound way. He'd used her mother for comfort, companionship and sex, then refused to marry her when she became pregnant, leaving her to raise a child alone.

Bad risks, indeed. And no one knew better than they did that life was precarious enough without deliberately setting yourself up for a fall.

The thought of just how precarious life was tugged at the lingering thoughts of what had happened in CICU that morning. But Dana and Lee unwittingly rescued her, demanding her attention as they debated the kind of gown she should wear, and whether she should stick with basic black, or throw caution to the wind and go for red. Something arterial rather than venous. Bright red, rather than burgundy. It had to be long, of course. And clinging.

That decision, made by Dana, had Katie wishing she hadn't reached for the bread, even though she'd only nibbled through half of the piece she'd taken. Once she'd thought of Eva, she found she had less of an appetite than she'd thought.

"Are you okay?" Dana asked, eyeing her suspiciously. "You haven't said a dozen words since you got here."

She could have told them what was on her mind. They would have understood. But her friends were having a good time. Rather than put a damper on the evening by telling them she'd lost a patient, she kept it to herself, much the way she did a lot of things that had no solution. "That's because I can't get a word in edgewise."

"You could always interrupt," Lee murmured.

"So what's it going to be?" Dana asked. "Something dramatic or something bold?"

"I'd say that depends on what either one of you have hanging in your closet. The only things even remotely formal in mine are a memento from our last prom and that gold lamé sausage casing you two talked me into buying during a clearance sale a couple of years ago. The sausage casing is out, and I can't afford to buy 'dramatic' or 'bold.'"

"The gold lamé looked stunning," Dana defended. "It's just out of style now is all. But you wouldn't want anything in my closet, either. The only formal wear in there are bridesmaid's dresses.''

"Ditto," replied Lee. "In fact, I think we all have a couple of the same ones. Hey! What about that royal blue number we wore in Candy Schumacher's wedding last year? You could take off the big bow and the lace from around the neckline.''

"And get rid of the ruffle on the cuffs," Dana added, apparently seeing the possibilities. "And lose that flippy little train thing in the back.''

"I think the flippy, train thing *is* the back," Katie observed. "The only thing that dress had going for it was the color.''

"You're right." Lee propped her elbow on the table and plopped her chin into her hand. "You're going to have to buy something, kiddo. No way around it. Maybe we can hit a sale.''

"Sale?" a female voice asked from behind Katie. "Where's a sale?''

All three women glanced up to see Melba Martin, one of the OR nurses Dana worked with, drop her coat over a chair at the next table. Right behind Melba was Alice from Katie's unit and the impossibly young-looking resident she'd taken under her wing.

Granetti's was not a place for privacy. It was where people went to wind down, or to connect. Unless heads were together in serious conversation, anyone was free to pull up a chair, which was exactly what the newcomers did. More bread was ordered, along with fresh drinks for everyone—except for Katie who, within minutes, was searching desperately for a graceful way to leave without looking as if she were bolting. Everyone's spirits were up, laughter prevalent as conversation shifted from shopping to a quick round of the jokes that had circulated through the hospital that day. She tried her best to get into the party mood, but her best just wasn't good enough.

"What's going on?"

She didn't have to turn around to know who'd come up behind her. Mike's voice was as familiar to her as the feel of her own heartbeat.

"Want to join us?" Dana asked, scooting over to make room for another chair.

"There's room here, too," Melba quickly offered, smiling hopefully at the darkly attractive surgeon.

"Thanks. I just came in to pick up some dinner, but I'll hang around until it's ready."

He wedged a chair into the open space by Dana, since she'd offered first, tactfully avoiding the other nurse's obvious invitation. Though he kept his overcoat on, open over his suit jacket, he immediately loosened his tie. Lines of fatigue etched the corners of his eyes, deepening with his quiet smile when he told the waitress who appeared at his elbow that he wouldn't be staying.

The topic presently under discussion was the Trailblazers' chances at the Western Conference title. Basketball was a passion in Honeygrove. And during basketball season, signs rooting the Blazers could be seen in store and car windows all over town.

Katie was a fan herself, but tonight her enthusiasm simply wasn't there. She wasn't even saying much, which wasn't like her at all.

Mike caught her eye, his own narrowing in question at her silence.

Are you all right? that glance seemed to ask.

Her only response was a shrug and a halfhearted smile.

She hadn't seen him since Eva had coded. He'd been in surgery when his patient had turned critical. And once Eva had been sent to CICU, Katie had no longer been involved in her care. She hadn't even known Eva had died until she'd called over to CICU a couple of hours later to see how the patient was doing.

By now, Mike would have reviewed the chart and talked with the family. She knew he'd gone back to his office to see patients that afternoon, too. One of the nurses in the telemetry unit had called him there to verify a change of medication.

"Here you go, Dr. Brennan." A waiter set a white paper bag on the table in front of Mike. "You have a nice evening, sir."

The arrival of Mike's dinner-to-go jerked Katie from her thoughts. Lee and Dana were engaged in a hot debate with Alice over the Blazers' new coach. Melba and the bespectacled resident, both eyeing Mike's takeout, were trying to figure out which appetizers to order. Behind her, all around her, customers were filling tables and bellying up to the long, mahogany bar with its gleaming brass rail. The drone of conversation was turning to a din.

"Are you sticking around for dinner?" Mike asked her.

"No. No," she repeated, realizing just how far removed from the program she was. Seeing the out she was looking for, she murmured, "I have other plans. I should be going, too."

"If you're ready now, I'll walk you out."

She gave him a nod, turning a quick smile to Alice. Interrupting the animated conversation only long enough to sneak in quick goodbyes to everyone, she promised Dana and Lee that she'd call and gathered her purse and coat. The debate was back in full swing within seconds. The only lull came a moment after she heard the resident's quiet inquiry about what was going on with Katie and Dr. Brennan as Mike guided her between the rapidly filling tables.

Katie heard Lee casually dismiss the speculation with a flat, "Not a thing. They're just friends."

The warmth of the restaurant gave way to damp night air; the animated clatter to the drone of tires on wet pavement and the honk of a horn. It wasn't raining at the moment, but it hadn't been long since it had stopped. Droplets dripped from the building's awning and lights gleamed in streaks on the wet, black street.

"So…" Mike began, pulling his overcoat closed as they headed for the parking lot. "What are your plans? Meeting? Joining someone else?"

"Video. I thought I'd get one on the way home and veg in front of the TV for a while."

He tipped his head, studying her face in the yellow light of the street lamps. "You weren't having a good time in there."

"Not really."

"Any particular reason?"

She lifted her shoulder in a shrug. "It's just been a long day."

Katie kept her glance on the ground, listening to the soft slap of leather on the wet sidewalk. As long as Mike's legs were, he could have easily outpaced her. But he checked his long, athletic stride, deliberately matching his footfall to hers.

"Want to try again?" he asked.

"What?"

"To tell me what's bothering you. It's obvious something is."

She made a face. "I hate being obvious."

Her attempt at lightness didn't quite work. He touched her arm, stopping her when she would have stopped anyway because they'd just reached her car. "You can't let it get to you, Katie."

His dark eyebrows were drawn in a disapproving line, his expression part admonishment, part understanding. "It" was death. The enemy. The demon they fought at all costs—sometimes long after they should have given up the battle. But that was another debate, another thorn that festered on occasion. That he knew her well enough to understand the reason for her mood didn't surprise her. What did was how grateful she felt that no explanation was necessary.

"You've told me that before. And I'm working on it," she assured him. Apparently, she was just slow. But then, she'd always been a late bloomer. She'd been the last of her friends to need a bra, the last to get a first date, the last to have a serious relationship. Apparently, she was going to be the last to develop the armor necessary to insulate herself from certain experiences at the hospital, too.

"I don't know how you block it so well," she murmured.

"Sure you do. I do it the same way we all do." He nudged the hair back from her face, and chucked her under the chin. Despite the encouragement in his touch, his voice held very little. "You just shut that part of yourself down."

She glanced from the regret in his eyes to the sack in his hand. The trick was to keep from shutting down too much. "And go home to eat takeout alone?"

The smile tugging at his mouth conceded nothing.

"Tell you what." Settling his arm companionably over her shoulders, he steered her to the driver's side of her little red Altima. "You share your video," he said, holding up the bag. "And I'll share my dinner."

Her spirits kicked up a notch. "What are we having?"

"Chicken picatta and grilled vegetables. What are we watching?"

"Whatever I can find at the video store by my place."

"Make it a thriller. That'll get your mind off the day." Dropping his arm, he pulled his keys from his pocket and headed for his own car. "Guaranteed."

Chapter Four

Had Mike gone home as he'd planned, he would have changed into sweats, dumped the takeout on a plate, and headed for his study to consume the meal while watching the news, then going over Eva Horton's chart.

Since they were at Katie's place, which he had to concede was far more comfortable than his, she was the one who headed off to change clothes. After a minute of obligatory kiss and cuddle with her cat when they arrived at her duplex, she left him to shed his coat and jacket and ditch his tie while he searched her cabinets for the bottle of wine she'd said was there somewhere.

He couldn't say it bothered him to have his plans altered. Even before he'd run into Katie, even before he'd guessed why she wasn't enjoying the evening with her friends, he'd decided to call her tonight.

He'd already known she'd called the code when Eva had gone into respiratory arrest that morning. He'd known from studying the patient's chart—that precise, unemotional detailing of readings, drugs administered, actions taken—that the staff's brisk efficiency had kept the patient alive long enough to get her to intensive care and call the family to the bedside. He also knew that nothing more could have been done for Eva. She had simply been too sick to survive.

That was what his logic told him. That was what medical school, seven years of training in thoracic surgery, a year and a half in private practice, the patient's chart and her test results would tell a prudent man to believe. And he was a prudent man. He just hated like hell to lose a patient.

He didn't take the loss personally, as if it were an affront to his skill. There were powers infinitely greater than his own. But he wouldn't simply accept her death, either. He would study Eva's charts again, along with the results of her postmortem, and learn what he could from her. Then, he would silently thank her for whatever knowledge she shared by her passing and he would move on, using what he'd learned or confirmed for the benefit of another patient down the line.

He found the bottle he was looking for—a gift from Alice, Katie's unit secretary, according to the Christmas tag on it—just as Katie padded into the kitchen in navy leggings and an old University of Oregon Health Sciences Center sweatshirt. After handing him a corkscrew, she bent down to scoop cat food into a dish, then turned her attention to collecting plates from a cupboard and silverware from a drawer.

Moving around her to get glasses, he skimmed over her delicate profile, and watched her give him a soft smile as she slipped behind him to put the plates on the coffee table in the living room. She looked far more at ease than she had at Granetti's, her smile less strained. But he suspected from the way she muttered to herself when she doubled back to get place mats, that she was still as preoccupied as she'd been at the restaurant. As preoccupied as he was himself.

They'd each been through such days before. Though, thank God, they didn't happen often. And they'd both been around long enough to know that there was nothing for either of them to say. They'd acknowledged the loss. It was enough for him now just to know that there was understanding in silence; to know they could empathize without the words. So, while she set the coffee table, he sidestepped the cat winding itself between his legs, tossed the foam containers in the microwave to heat their cooling contents and took a measure of comfort in knowing that while they both saw Eva Horton differently, each was thinking of her. To him, she was a seventy-four-year-old, female, open-heart with cholesterol readings that went through the roof. Katie, he was fairly certain, would be more likely to remember the woman by the way she'd gripped her hand when she'd been frightened, and to recall the little jokes, whatever they were, the two seemed to have shared. Because of that, she would hurt for the family, and for the temporary friend she'd let the patient become.

She knew better than to get too close, he thought, picking up the fur ball meowing at his feet. She just couldn't always help it. Any more than he could help wanting to make sure she was all right tonight. He never questioned his concern for Katie. Because she'd been part of his life forever, he could let himself feel things with her that he needed to steel himself against with everyone else. A man—a physician—only had so much emotional energy. If he didn't channel it, he'd burn out faster than a sparkler on the Fourth of July.

Spike pawed his way up his chest, seeking a hug. Obliging the shameless little beggar, Mike was rewarded with a sandpaper lick on the side of his neck. The cat smelled like Katie, he thought, like her perfume or soap or whatever it was that hinted of sunshine and softness and always reminded him of her. The spoiled little animal must have picked up the scent from her clothes and her skin when she held it.

He didn't know why the thought made him smile.

"Better?" she asked, her glance moving from the open collar of his shirt and rolled-up sleeves to the way he cuddled her pet.

"It always helps to ditch the tie."

"I was referring to what you're doing."

She didn't look smug. Not exactly. As she reached up and scratched behind the cat's ear, her expression was more like quietly pleased.

"Are you trying to get me to admit there's something to be said for holding something soft and warm?"

Her eyes met his, gentle and knowing. "The only thing that keeps you from admitting it is stubbornness."

She was right, of course. He firmly believed there were physiological benefits to owning a pet. He even recommended them to some of his elderly patients; especially the ones who lived alone. He just liked giving her a hard time about her cat. He wasn't sure why, exactly. Maybe it was because she couldn't tell if he was serious or not, and he liked the look she got when she was trying to figure him out. Maybe it was because she was fun to tease and it wasn't often that he had fun anymore. She was right, though. In a way. He did feel the need to hold something soft and warm. Her pet just wasn't it.

"I need food." With one hand, he scooped the cat to the floor. "I didn't get any lunch."

She didn't question the change of subject. She simply held his glance long enough for him to know she knew exactly why he'd had no time for the meal, then turned on her heel to head for the microwave.

"Food," she announced, wrestling out the steaming containers with a hot pad. "I'll dish up. You load the VCR. Do you want a salad?"

He told her he wanted anything she put on the table. Since she was sharing his dinner, she contributed a loaf of French bread and a salad she created in thirty seconds by emptying a bag of mixed greens into a bowl, adding what was left of a bag of croutons and tossing the lot with bottled dressing.

Within two minutes, she and Mike were passing the bread, the wine and watching the opening credits of the movie. Within twenty minutes, the meal was history and each had claimed a spot at opposite ends of the sofa.

Any other night, the psychological thriller the woman at the video store had recommended would have easily occupied Katie's mind. The plot was full of twists and turns. The pace was breakneck. Yet, an hour into the video, Katie had completely lost track of the story line. Even as she dutifully attempted to concentrate on the images flickering over the screen, her thoughts restively wandered.

While the attorney on-screen passionately argued his client's case, Katie thought about Eva, about the pacemaker implant in 318, and about how she was never going to get the hang of the new computer program that had been installed that morning. Telling herself to stop thinking about work, she shifted her thoughts to Dana and about the new position her friend had applied for, wishing she had the guts to make some sort of a change herself, but not sure what she'd do if she did find the courage.

Not liking the direction her thoughts had taken there, either, she shifted her glance from the thread she was picking on the cuff of her sock to where Mike lounged on the opposite end of the sofa. What she really wanted was to shut out distractions the way he seemed to be able to do. He was totally, completely, one hundred and ten percent absorbed in the movie. He always had been able to focus when he wanted to. When he had that intent, intense look on his face, nothing short of an explosion could get his attention.

She curled up a little tighter in her corner, wondering as she did if he was conscious at all of what he was doing. Somewhere along the line, he'd toed off his shoes and slumped down to rest his head against the back cushions. His long legs were crossed and stretched out ahead of him. Beside him, stretched the length of his thigh and jammed as tight as he could get, was Spike.

The cat lay on his back, his white belly exposed, eyes closed and clearly relishing the gentle, distracted way Mike's long, elegant fingers slowly stroked his thick fur.

She wasn't sure what it was about hands that fascinated her. But they did. Her grandma Sheppard's were old and withered, but her fingers were as straight as her spine and her nails always perfectly polished in pale mauve. Her Grandpa Hancock's were gnarled and spotted, his middle finger enlarged with a callus where he held his brush to paint. Her mom's were dainty and soft. Her dad's were blunt. Alice's were always beringed and her nails brightly colored.

Maybe that was what it was, she thought, Spike's little chest disappearing as Mike's palm covered it. Maybe she found hands interesting because they said so much about a person. Mike's spoke volumes about him. Sinewy and strong, his were incredibly masculine, yet so skilled, so capable of the most delicate, minute motions. His hands held the power to heal, to cure.

As she watched him idly slip his fingers through the velvety fur, she couldn't help considering what other powers they might hold. A woman couldn't look at hands like that and not wonder how they would feel on her body. At least she hadn't been able to look at his lately without the thought occurring. As patient as he could be, she didn't doubt he'd be an incredible lover. But he could be demanding, too, and that thought was even more provocative.

With a typical feline change of heart, Spike decided he'd had enough just about the time Katie figured she had, too, and he silently leapt to the floor. Mike, his focus glued on the set and blessedly oblivious to her little flight of fancy, didn't move a muscle. His hand lay exactly where it had fallen when the cat slid from under it.

Curious to know what held him so rapt, anxious for something—anything—else to occupy her mind, she glanced at the television.

The images on the screen didn't quite provide the distraction she was looking for. The action had moved from the courtroom to a bedroom. Fifteen feet away, across the coffee table that held their empty plates and half the bottle of wine, the attorney on the screen was relieving his seductive female client of her blouse. He was also engaged in a rather long, decidedly thorough exploration of her tonsils.

Katie's first thought was that the actress had been surgically enhanced. Her second was that she doubted Mike was considering the surgical technique such enhancement required. But thinking about what was going on in Mike's mind when the woman had been stripped to her garter belt didn't seem like such a good idea. Especially since he was beginning to shift rather uncomfortably on his end of the sofa.

When the man pushed the woman onto a bed and she clawed his back with her nails, Katie swore she heard Mike groan.

''I think we should have picked something with a few

good chase scenes," he muttered, his attention still riveted on the screen.

"It started out with one," she offered helpfully.

"Yeah, well, that was more the sort of action I was in the mood for. All this does is remind me of what I'm missing." The muscle in his jaw jerked as he reached for his glass of wine on the end table. His deep voice dropped like a rock in a well. "If it weren't for the diseases out there, I'd can the celibacy routine."

More surprised by the admission than the topic, she murmured, "I know what you mean. It's been so long since I made love I'm sure I've forgotten how."

"Keep watching." Sitting back, he raised his glass toward the couple on the screen. "I think you're going to be reminded."

Sure enough. The camera panned down. The man rose up. A female hand clutched the sheet.

Katie slowly blew out a breath. "Sex is highly overrated."

"Spoken like one of the deprived."

"It is," she defended, her attention, like Mike's, fixed on the screen.

"So's the need for oxygen."

"Humans can survive without sex."

The hand clenched again. "Not as a species," he countered.

"I mean, we can survive longer." An artful closeup of a naked hip—or maybe it was a shoulder—filled the screen. "You can live a whole life without sex, but only minutes without oxygen."

"Exist," he corrected, over the sounds of heavy breathing and violins. "Some people would say you can *exist* a whole life without sex."

Did he feel that he was simply existing? she wondered,

not liking the thought at all. "Tell me. Is this discussion we're having practical, or philosophical?"

"Diversionary."

"I see. Well, as long as we're diverting ourselves, would you mind answering something for me about the male mind?"

"Is this going to get me into trouble?"

"It shouldn't." Pulling her glance from a shot of an arched back, she plucked at the loose thread on her sock again. "I just wondered if men are always after the finish, or if they ever just want to be held, too."

He hesitated, consideration entering his voice. "It depends on the man. And the woman."

"That's very diplomatic."

"Thank you." He shifted again. "More wine?"

"I'm fine. Thanks." Contemplating the thread, she gave it a tug. "Mike?"

"Yeah?"

"You mentioned the diseases out there." A quarter inch of cuff unraveled from her sock. "What do you say to a woman when you want to know if she's okay? If she doesn't have anything communicable, I mean. Some of that stuff is so scary."

Because she was busy stuffing the thread under her cuff, she didn't know when he glanced from the entwined limbs on the screen. But after several seconds passed and he hadn't answered, she looked over to find him quietly watching her.

"It hasn't come up," he admitted, clearly curious. "I meant what I said before. I haven't been with anyone since Marla and I split. Before that, the partners I'd had brought it up, and I made sure I used protection. Why? Have you met someone you're getting serious about?"

She gave a little smile, her hair brushing her shoulders as she shook her head. "Hardly. I've only been out with a couple of guys since Jim and I broke up. They never got past the peck-at-the-front-door stage.''

It had been nearly two years since she and Jim Mitchell had parted ways, which was about how long the two of them had been together. He'd been a nice guy, an architect with a terrific future ahead of him, one he'd wanted to share with her. She'd seriously considered it, too, until she'd faced the fact that while she cared for him, she didn't love him. She didn't expect fireworks out of a relationship, but she wanted—needed—something more than what they'd had. Even as badly as she wanted a family and children of her own, marriage wouldn't have been fair to either one of them.

The only light in the room came from the flickering images on the television and the lamp on the end table beside Mike. With that lamp on low, his shadowed expression looked almost…protective. ''The only one I knew about was the guy you met at the Octoberfest in Mount Angel. The investment broker. Who was the other one?''

''Your cousin. Brandon. Remember? Your mom fixed me up with him when he was visiting from Medford.''

''He doesn't count. He's family.''

''He wasn't *my* family.''

Mike didn't look any more pleased with her rationale than he had when she'd mentioned Jim. She wasn't exactly sure why that was, either. He'd only met Jim once. That had been back when he and Marla had been married and living in Portland and Katie was already working at Honeygrove Memorial. There had been a four-year period after she'd graduated and moved back from Portland herself, when she and Mike had sort of drifted apart, the way friends sometimes do when marriage and relocation enter the picture. But, even though Mike had never said a word against Jim, she'd sensed that he hadn't cared much for him. That was fair enough. She hadn't cared much for Marla, either.

"Maybe I will have a refill."

"You can have mine. I have to drive."

She didn't really want the wine. She just wanted something to concentrate on other than the odd jealousy she'd felt toward his ex-wife. But she reached for the glass anyway, thinking to take a sip and set it on the coffee table. The glass didn't make it that far. When Mike held it out, her hand collided with his, pale liquid sloshing over her thigh.

Katie gasped.

Mike swore.

Reaching past her, he snatched a napkin from the coffee table. Katie, trying not to spill the few remaining drops in the glass, leaned toward the table with him to set down the glass. Angled as she was with her legs tucked under her, she had to lean sideways. To keep from tipping over, she also had to grab his shoulder.

"Hold it!" Stifling a giggle, she gripped harder, trying to keep her balance when he moved closer. "I'm going to wind up on the floor."

"Then give me the glass. You're going to drop it."

"Am not."

"Are to."

She was. Slipping one arm behind her back to keep her steady, Mike plucked the stemmed goblet from her fingers with his other hand. "You dope," he muttered, grinning himself. "You're going to break the glass and your neck, too."

He'd placed the glass on the table and her knee had jammed against his hip when he finally met her eyes. Warm brown, flecked with gold, they sparkled with humor. Beneath the hand supporting her back, he could feel the delicate bones of her spine and the edges of her shoulder blades as she shifted to keep her balance. The enticing fullness of her breast pressed to his side.

He felt his own smile fade. The breath he drew brought her scent, that combination of spring and warm female that suddenly didn't seem as innocent as it had before. Close up, there was a seductive edge to it that played utter havoc with the nerves at the base of his spine.

This is *Katie,* he chastized himself.

Repeating the admonition, he steeled himself and prepared to move back. He would pull her upright, drop his hands and ignore the raw, unexpected hunger burning low in his gut. Or so he was thinking as he watched her smile slowly die.

In the space of a heartbeat, she'd gone utterly still. He didn't know what she saw in his expression, but there was no mistaking what he saw move through hers. Confusion. Hesitation. Considering that he was holding her as intimately as a lover, neither surprised him. What caught him totally unprepared was the awareness that darkened her eyes, turning the gold flecks molten.

That awareness jolted through him like lightning, frying his logic on the way. This was Katie, and somewhere in the back of his mind, sanity was telling him he should let her go. At the moment, he just couldn't think of why that was necessary. His glance skimmed her face, moving over her clear, poreless skin to the wild tangle of tawny hair brushing her shoulders. She wore it loose tonight, and it looked so sensuously soft that it fairly begged him to sink his fingers into its spirals and curls.

The sensations elicited by the eroticism in the movie had been nothing more than physiological reaction to visual stimulus. Predictable, uncomplicated, undirected. The desires stirring inside him now were infinitely stronger and screaming with complications. As his glance dropped to the inviting fullness of her mouth, there was no mistaking their direction at all.

He gave her every chance in the world to pull away. But she didn't move. As he slowly lowered his head, he wasn't sure she even breathed.

He wasn't sure he was breathing himself when his mouth touched hers. The contact was tentative, testing, an experiment driven by opportunity as much as long-standing curiosity. That curiosity seemed to be there for her, too. Or maybe she was just curious to see what he would do. When she still didn't move, he cupped his hand to the side of her neck and slipped his fingers into the silk of her hair. With his thumb on her cheek, he angled her head the way he wanted it, coaxing her open to him, and touched his tongue to hers.

He didn't expect the heat. The fire. The warm, sweet taste of her strafed through him like a flame set to dry tinder, incinerating any intention he had of ending the kiss right there. He drew her closer, drinking deeper. If she'd given him any indication at all that she wanted him to stop, he would have found a way to let her go. Somehow. But the small sound that caught in her throat hinted far more at longing than protest.

The next sound he heard was his own, the moan torn from deep within his chest when she started kissing him back. Shifting her curvy little body in his arms, digging her fingers into his shoulders, she mated her tongue with his. Her breathing quickened, her heartbeat racing against his chest.

She wants this.

A fist of pure need slammed into his gut.

This is Katie, he repeated, only this time, the phrase held more realization than warning.

Her unexpected impact on him would have had him pulling back himself, if he hadn't just felt her stiffen. As if suddenly aware of what she was doing, she lowered her head, turning away to hide the confusion he'd glimpsed in her eyes.

With his hand still on her neck, he traced the line of her jaw with his thumb. "Should I have done that?"

She shook her head, her loose curls caressing the back of his hand. "I'm not sure."

She dropped her hands from his shoulders. He let her go, watching as she pushed her trembling fingers through her hair and rose from the sofa. She didn't pace, as he'd thought she might do. Or start clearing the coffee table or straightening and fussing as she tended to do when she was agitated. She just stood there, looking as if she didn't quite know which way to turn.

She was trying for distance. But, apparently, not from him since she stayed right where she was.

Reaching for the remote on the coffee table, he punched the mute button, instantly killing the squeal of tires, and rose beside her. When she didn't look up, he turned her face to him and cupped her cheek with his palm.

"I can't say I haven't thought about kissing you before, Katie. You've just never given me any reason to think you wanted me to touch you."

She'd given him plenty of reason now. "I know."

"Then you've thought about it before, too?"

The play of emotions on her face was fascinating. Guilt and caution collided with need. She didn't have to say a word for him to have his answer.

With the edge of his thumb he traced the corner of her mouth. "What we were talking about before," he prefaced, drawn by the almost unconscious way she moved her head toward his hand, "was there a reason we were talking about safe sex, or were we just making idle conversation?"

Katie's heart jerked against her ribs. "I thought we were

just talking. To divert ourselves from the movie," she explained, finding his earlier analysis as good as any. "We talk about a lot of things."

His fingers traced her collarbone, slipping up to curve at the side of her face. "It seems there are few things we don't talk about, too."

Obviously, she thought, but the word lodged in her throat. He was turning her to putty with nothing more than the brush of his thumb over her mouth, scrambling her mind with the realization that he'd actually thought about kissing her.

The thought of what else he might have considered pooled heat low in her stomach.

"For instance," he said, his deep voice quiet and faintly accusing, "you never told me you needed to be held. If you had, I'm sure we could have reciprocated on occasion. Especially after days like today."

"It didn't seem like something I should ask." She swallowed, at a total loss over which was more disarming— the fact that he'd sensed her need for a pair of arms and the knowledge that he sometimes shared the feeling, or the compelling, almost proprietary way he touched her. "'Would you hold me?' isn't quite the same as 'Would you donate supplies to the clinic, or rescue my cat?'"

"But the need is there," he countered easily. "And I'd do anything I could for you, Katie. You know that." His eyes locked on hers, darkly, beautifully intent. "Is there anything else you haven't mentioned that you'd care to share?"

Like the fact that I'm scared to death of what I feel for you? she wondered. *Or, how very much I'd like you to shut up and kiss me again because I'm afraid to think right now?* "I'd better plead the fifth."

The admission made the gleam in his eyes turn feral. "Then answer one question for me." He stepped closer, though he was already so close she could feel the heat of his big body. "If you're not sure how you feel about what just happened," he murmured, tracing her lower lip with the tip of his finger, "what would happen if I do it again?"

Twenty minutes ago, her mind had been churning. Now, it didn't seem to be functioning at all. There were reasons she should put an end to this delicious torture. Reasons she should ignore the incredible yearning he unleashed inside her. She just couldn't think of what they were. Not when he was touching her. She'd been right about his hands. They were magic. And his voice was pure seduction. Deep, rich, quiet—it flowed over her like warm honey, soothing nerves even as his touch enlivened them.

The combination was positively lethal.

Splaying her hand on his chest, she whispered, "Maybe we should see."

It wasn't the wine that made her head spin. She hadn't had that much. It was the feel of his mouth playing over hers and of his arms closing around her. She wasn't even sure if it was his heartbeat she felt, or her own, knocking against her ribs when his hand drifted down her back and he pulled her closer. But she could feel him hard against her, his hunger fueling hers when, long, breathless moments later, his free hand slipped under her sweatshirt and skimmed toward her breast.

She was sure her knees would have buckled if he hadn't been holding her. The sensations he elicited rocked her to her core.

"Katie," he whispered, his voice strained. "There was one thing we didn't talk about. Are you on anything?"

"The Pill," she murmured, not even questioning why he would ask. "I never went off them." At the moment, she couldn't remember why that was, or what she'd been hoping for. It didn't matter. Mike was kissing her again, drugging her with his taste and the heat of his breath against her skin. With his hands on her hips, his mouth making delicious forays from her lips to her neck, he backed her toward the little hallway.

It didn't occur to her to slow them down, much less stop what they were doing. When she bumped the corner of the wall and he took her by the shoulders to get her on a straighter path, her only thought was that Mike wanted her as badly as she wanted him. Beyond that, she simply couldn't think.

Still guiding her backward, his hands skimmed her sides, dipping under her sweatshirt to pull the fleecy fabric over her head. She was halfway down the hall when the shirt hit the floor. By the time he unfastened the clasp of her bra and slid the lacy straps down her arms, they'd reached the doorway to her bedroom.

He tossed the bra on her dresser. Without taking his mouth from hers, he pulled back far enough for her to unbutton his shirt while he pushed her leggings over her hips. His shirt landed on the bra and her leggings over her antique rocker just as she felt the edge of her bed bump against the backs of her legs.

"Put your arms around me."

His breath feathered hot against her ear at the command. Slipping her arms around his neck, she felt his rock solid chest brush her softer flesh. Fire raced through her at the contact. But fire was racing through her everywhere he touched. His lips traced a line of heat up her throat to her jaw, finally claiming her mouth when he cupped her breasts with his palms, taunting her nipples with the slow strokes of his thumbs. Then, his mouth replaced his hands and the only thing that kept her upright was her grip on his beautifully muscled shoulders.

She'd never felt passion before. The realization was as stunning as the white-hot need he fed as his hands shaped her waist, her hips, her stomach. She'd never known what it was like to be slowly robbed of her sanity by the feel of a man. She'd known arousal and the warmly pleasant feelings lovemaking could bring. But she'd never known she could be driven mad. She'd never known either, that she could be driven to beg. There was hunger in his touch, a raw, aching urgency that had her sinking her fingers into his hair, urging him closer still. She wanted him, all of him.

She didn't realize she'd voiced the thought until she felt him pull away. But the sharp sting of disappointment was salved by the realization that he'd only stopped to finish unzipping his pants. Within moments, slacks, briefs and socks had gone the way of the rest of their clothing, and he was drinking the moan that caught in her throat when he pulled her fully against him.

The feel of him, hot and hard against her stomach, nearly undid her. But it was the feel of him pressing her back to the bed, his big body covering hers, that nearly turned her blood to steam.

Contrasts flooded her senses. The delicious smoothness of his back, the coarse, masculine feel of his heavy, hair-roughened leg as he wedged hers apart. She felt his hand skim along the back of her thigh, the warmth of his hand on her cool skin burning like a brand as he drew her leg over his. She murmured his name. At least she thought she did. His fingers stole through her hair to hold her head between his hands, his mouth coming down hard on hers as he entered her, filled her, consumed her.

There was no holding back. No pretext of slowing down. She met his smooth thrusts, sucking in his breath as he stole hers and felt herself fly into a thousand pieces. Within seconds, his hands tightened their hold and he was flying with her.

Katie wasn't sure how long it was before their breathing quieted. It could have been seconds, or minutes. But the sensual fog finally, inevitably began to lift. As the haze cleared, rationality leaked in, as unwanted as a disruptive guest and just as disconcerting. But just as she started to remember a couple of the more glaring reasons she should have pulled back from Mike while she'd still been capable of logic, he lifted himself off of her and rolled her over with him.

"Don't think."

His words were a low rasp, but there was no mistaking their insistence when he threw his leg over hers and tugged her eyelet comforter over their cooling bodies. They hadn't bothered to turn on a light, much less to pull the covers back. "Just let me hold you," he murmured, coaxing her head to his shoulder. "Just for a while."

Nothing else he could have said just then would have blunted the edge of panic so effectively. He wanted to hold her. Whether he wanted that for himself or for her, she didn't know. But either way, the motion of his hand kept her where she was. With slow, easy strokes, he traced a path from her back to her thigh, the movement seeming as soothing to him as it was to her.

"Just for a while," he repeated, his voice dropping to a whisper.

She knew exactly what he was doing. He knew as well as she did that once they moved from each other's arms, nothing would be quite the same. But as long as they stayed where they were, they could postpone the moment they would have to face what they'd done. More than willing to avoid that moment for as long as possible, she curled into the protection of his arms, and let herself think only of how she'd always wanted to be exactly where she was.

Mike hadn't intended to fall asleep. He especially hadn't planned to spend the night. When he opened his eyes and saw the clock on the nightstand glowing 5:42, he realized he'd done both. He'd also overslept. The only reason he'd awakened now was because a cat had just curled up by his head.

In the space of seconds, it occurred to him that he couldn't remember the last time he'd slept so soundly. But the realization that he'd just had the best night's sleep he'd experienced in ages was ruined by the fact that he was late. It didn't help matters, either, that Katie lay curled in his arms, her back to his chest and her sweet body creating all manner of havoc in his.

He knew the instant her consciousness returned. Even before he began to ease his arm from beneath her head, he felt tension seeping into her supple muscles, and heard the faint shift of her breathing from deep to shallow.

"It's a quarter to six," he whispered, the need to hurry forcing him from the bed. "What time do you usually get up?"

Her muffled, "Six," sounded oddly strained.

"Then stay put. I'm going to be late if I don't leave now." He didn't consider it a very good sign that she hadn't moved. But he had no time now to worry about why she wouldn't turn to face him. "I have a seven-o'clock surgery." He could make it home in ten minutes. Less than that since there would be no traffic and if he hit the lights right. It would take him twenty minutes to shave, shower, dress. Another thirty to get to the hospital, change again, and scrub in. They'd just have to start late. No way would he go into a surgery rushed. Talking more to himself than to her, he murmured, "I'll have to do rounds after."

The room was dark, mostly shapes and shadows. He wasn't familiar with the space, but he managed to collect his clothes and pull on his pants without stumbling over anything. What he couldn't find were his shoes.

"You left your shoes in the living room."

She was sitting up now, and pushing back the tangle of hair he'd buried his fingers in last night. With one hand clutching the comforter to her throat, her slender shoulders bare, and one long, shapely leg visible in the light spilling through the doorway, she looked as tempting as sin itself.

"Right." In the shadows, he saw her grip the thick material tighter. "Thanks."

"Mike?"

The uneasy sound of his name stopped him in the doorway. He didn't know if it was regret he sensed in her, or caution. He had no idea what she was feeling. He didn't even know what he was feeling himself. Self-recrimination and embarrassment were high on the list, though. Never in his life had he allowed his physical needs to control him. Yet, with Katie, he'd kissed her once and promptly kissed his control goodbye.

Now he was acting as if he couldn't get away from her fast enough.

"You know I have to go, Katie." He had no idea what she wanted him to do; what he wanted to do. Reassure her? Kiss her? Keep his hands to himself? Drop dead? All he did know was that until he had time to figure it out, he didn't want to do anything to make the situation worse. "I'll see you at the hospital. Okay?"

She gave him a nod, the motion as tentative as the feelings churning inside them both.

A moment later, hating the way he was leaving, he found his shoes and coat and headed out the door.

Chapter Five

When a surgeon was late for surgery, it wasted the time of the entire surgical team and backed up every case scheduled behind it for the rest of the day. Knowing how conscientious Mike was, and having a friend in OR who occasionally grumbled about such backups, Katie could hardly fault Mike for his abrupt departure. There was just something about having a man race from her bed and bolt for the door, no matter what his reason or excuse, that added a touch of humiliation to the varying degrees of embarrassment and anxiety she was already dealing with.

She'd never had a one-night stand in her entire life. And the fact that she'd just had one with Mike had kept her vacillating between total disbelief and abject panic all morning. It was a fair indication of her mental distress that she was wishing he'd been a total stranger.

What in heaven's name had she *done?*

"There you are." Cindy, the copper-haired RN with the

cinnamon freckles who'd joined the team last month, hurried toward her as Katie left a patient's room. "Dr. Brennan just put my patient on this," she said, holding up a clear vial. "What is it I'm supposed to do for his study? All he said was that the instructions are on the forms, but I can't find them and Alice isn't here."

"Take the patient's blood pressure every fifteen minutes for two hours after it's administered," Katie replied, hating the way her heart had hitched knowing Mike was on the floor, "and do an arterial line draw every thirty minutes for three hours."

Cindy rolled her brown eyes toward the ceiling. "Like I don't have enough to do around here. I've still got lines to pull on the angiogram in 309 and I'm supposed to pick up my daughter at dance class at four." The exasperated look she aimed at her watch said she'd barely make it. "These drug studies are such a nuisance sometimes."

"If you're running behind, I'll do it. All I have left to do is chart."

The older woman's expression immediately turned quizzical. "I wasn't hinting for you to do it for me," she said, sounding surprised that Katie didn't know that. "I'm just whining."

"It's okay." The smile she offered was a tad weak, but it served the purpose. "Go ahead and administer it. I'll get the readings."

Too grateful for the assist to question it any further, the petite redhead told Katie which patient it was, turned on her rubber-soled heel and headed around an empty gurney. Sidestepping the same gurney, Katie disposed of the empty IV bag she'd just replaced and turned into the med room for the supplies she would need. Most of the staff pitched in and helped each other when they could, but her offer now had little to do with team support. She just wanted to stay busy. It was the only way she could avoid dwelling on what had happened last night. Every time she thought about it, which was roughly every other minute, she felt sick.

She had totally jeopardized her relationship with Mike; allowed feelings she should have kept locked away to break free. She knew better. She was thirty years old, for Pete's sake. Old enough to know that sex changed everything between a man and a woman. Feelings. Expectations. The roles they played in each other's lives.

What had happened last night could easily ruin what they had, but she couldn't let that happen. Even if he felt something beyond friendship for her, which she seriously doubted, there was no future for them. Not as a couple. He didn't want to be bothered with a relationship, and she had no intention of living the way her mother had, raising a child with a husband who had no time for family dinners or school plays or going for walks in the snow—and that was if he stayed around long enough to get past the first couple of years. Half the doctors on staff had been divorced at one time or another—Mike included. Not that she blamed him for the demise of his marriage. But the statistics did point out that doctors were simply a bad risk. Logic aside, she and Mike weren't lovers. They were *friends*. And she would do everything in her power to make sure that was what they remained.

If he was still speaking to her.

Since she'd been tied up with the same patient for the last twenty minutes, she had no idea how long he'd been in the unit. Considering that he'd already spoken with one of the nurses about a patient, it was apparent that he hadn't felt compelled to find her as soon as he'd arrived.

"Hi."

The sound of Mike's deep voice sent her heart to her toes.

Totally disquieted at the thought of facing him, she

slowly turned from the counter. He stood still as stone in the doorway of the cabinet-lined room, his blue eyes fixed like lasers on hers and his expression as guarded as she felt. He looked terribly intimidating standing there in his white shirt and navy sport coat. Very big. Very male. And very capable of making a woman kiss her common sense goodbye.

Recalling all too well that he'd done precisely that last night, her glance faltered.

"Hi," she echoed, finding the tray in her hand the safest place to look. "Checking on your patients?"

"Just finished."

"How did your surgery go?"

"Fine. Do you have a minute?"

He clearly wasn't interested in small talk, or in wasting time. As soon as she murmured, "Sure," he glanced over his shoulder to see who was behind him in the hall, then stepped into the crowded little room. A moment later, he closed the windowed door with a quiet click. He looked uncertain, which wasn't like Mike at all. And a little edgy, which wasn't like him, either.

"I know this isn't the place to talk. I just didn't know when else I'd get a chance to see you today." A muscle in his jaw jerked as he cautiously scanned her face. "Are you all right?"

Katie opened her mouth, and promptly shut it again. She'd never had trouble talking to Mike before. Ever. Yet she had no idea how to answer him now.

"Maybe this would be easier if I hadn't left the way I did this morning."

"You were late. I know you had to go."

"Thanks for the understanding," he murmured, self-deprecation heavy in his tone, "but I still don't think it helped. You didn't deserve that."

She tried to smile, if for no other reason than to ease

some of the bridled tension radiating from his body and fraying the ends of her nerves.

"Don't worry about it." The smile never materialized. Regret wouldn't allow it. "Your oversleeping isn't the problem. I mean, it didn't matter as much as…well, not like…"

"Having slept together?" he suggested.

She pulled a breath, and slowly blew it out. Something about the way he said the words, the hint of memory in his eyes, pooled heat low in her stomach. "Yeah. That," she agreed, wanting to pace but having nowhere to go. "I'm just not totally sure how that happened."

Mike said nothing for a moment. He just stood with his hands in his pockets, the way he sometimes did when he was with a patient. He watched her—much as he might a patient, too—as if he needed to hear what she had to say about where the discomfort was before he could decide the best way to proceed.

"Does it matter?"

"No," she quietly replied, unwilling to expose any more of herself than she already had. She didn't want him digging too much. She didn't want to dig much more herself, for that matter. "It doesn't."

"Then maybe you shouldn't worry about it."

She gave a little nod, clutching at the advice. He didn't seem to think it mattered why things had gotten so out of hand. Either that, or he'd already figured out the reason on his end and he was too much of a gentleman to tell her there wasn't anything all that complicated about the human sex drive.

The problem now was where they went from here.

He seemed to be trying to figure that out, too, as his glance skimmed her mouth, then immediately jerked to her eyes.

He cleared his throat. "Are we all right? With each other, I mean?"

As questions went, that one was loaded. It asked everything from *Do you hate me?* to *What do you expect from me now?* But, with the hospital operator paging an orderly over the PA, and a parade of people constantly passing the window behind him, he didn't seem any more comfortable with getting specific than she did. He was only performing triage—a quick assessment of the damages to determine how serious the problem was, and what needed to be done immediately to keep the situation from getting worse. All she cared about just then was that he didn't seem to want things screwed up between them, either.

"I'm okay...if you are." She pushed her fingers through her hair, the motion showing more agitation than she'd wanted him to see. "Why don't we just chalk last night up to a brief moment of insanity. Or the movie. Or the wine," she quickly added, though they both knew that hadn't been the case at all. "Okay?"

With anyone else, Mike would have breathed a sigh of relief at her willingness to dismiss the incident as of no consequence. He thought he should have with Katie, too. And he did. In a way. As close as he could figure, what had happened last night had simply been the result of two people who'd been deprived too long and who'd trusted each other with their physical needs.

He could live with that explanation. It was honest, neat and as uncomplicated as he could make it, under the circumstances. And Katie seemed all right with her own rationalizations, despite the fact that they rang more of "excuse" than explanation. Still, if she was willing to go on as if nothing had happened, then that was what he'd do, too, even though making love with her had done nothing but make him want more. The mere thought of how she'd responded to him, of the mindless passion that had erupted between them, made him want to back her up against the counter and lose himself completely in her heat. But she clearly wasn't comfortable with the idea of a repeat performance. And the last thing he wanted to do was ruin the best relationship he'd ever had by pushing for something she didn't want.

There was no mistaking the faint tension filling the air in the moments before he finally said, "Okay," and reached for the door. But they were saved having to let that tension escalate by the abrupt rap of Cindy's knuckles against the window.

Pulling the door open, Mike stepped back.

"Excuse me," Cindy said to him, slipping past. Soles squeaking on the beige linoleum, she headed for a box on the end of the counter, grabbed a handful of alcohol pads and dropped them into her pocket. "Are you tied up now?" she asked Katie.

Pretending she was only smoothing the front of her scrub top, Katie pressed a hand to the knot of nerves in her stomach. "No. I can help. I was just getting some tubes."

"She's taking readings for me for your study," Cindy pointed out good-naturedly, oblivious to the strain snaking between the attractive surgeon by the door and the woman he cautiously watched. "I just heard Dr. Carlisle tell Dr. Chapman that you may be asked to present a preliminary paper on it at a conference.

"They did dozens of drug studies at the hospital I worked for in Salem," she continued, opening and closing doors in her search for whatever she was looking for now, "but this is the first one I ever heard of that actually has doctors excited."

"Thanks," Mike murmured, since she obviously intended her remarks as a compliment. "It's nice to know it might have some merit."

Mike had mentioned the possibility of the conference to Katie the evening she'd helped him input his data, and being asked to present to one's colleagues was an enormous compliment. But she was fairly sure he wasn't really thinking about his paper at the moment. If he had been, she was certain he would have reminded her that she'd promised to help him organize his materials, and asked what nights she was free this week. All he did was give her a lingering look she couldn't decipher at all before he told them both he had to go and headed out the door.

Cindy wasn't as slow on the uptake as she'd first appeared. Watching Katie release a long, low breath, her glance bounced to the door and back again. "Is everything okay?"

"Yeah. Sure." Avoiding the curiosity etched in the other nurse's face, she asked, "Why?"

"Because I have a strange feeling I just interrupted something."

"Not at all," Katie assured her, trying for nonchalance as she picked up the tray of supplies she'd come in for. "We were just talking."

"You and Dr. Brennan are friends, right? Old friends from what I hear."

"We lived next door to each other when we were kids."

"Oh."

"Ready?"

Skepticism ran rampant over the woman's freckled face, but Cindy was too busy to indulge in any further speculation. Katie didn't doubt, however, that had the woman had time, she'd have poked a little more. There was nothing certain members of the staff liked more than gossip, and Cindy fit right in with that crowd. Katie, however, wasn't about to give her any grist for the mill. Once the hospital grapevine started feeding a rumor, it took forever for it to die. She and Mike would get past this. They simply had to.

Some decisions were a snap to make. It was the execution that posed the problem.

Because Katie finally had some time off, she didn't see Mike for the next couple of days. She didn't hear from him, either. Neither was unusual. They could go weeks seeing each other only at work or at Granetti's. But the unease that had hung between them like a wall when they'd parted in the med room wouldn't allow her to shake the feeling that his silence wasn't a good sign. She didn't think it a good sign, either, that her heart skipped every time the phone did ring. Until she'd gone to bed with him, she wouldn't have even thought about him calling—much less lain awake at night trying to figure out why he wasn't.

Her next day back at the hospital was Sunday. Since Mike didn't work weekends unless he was on call, which he wasn't, she didn't see him then, either. But Monday morning, as she hurried into the nearly deserted cafeteria to grab a bagel, he was standing at the beverage counter next to the cold sandwich station.

He was in green surgical scrubs, the tucked-in top and drawstring pants doing more for his wide shoulders and impossibly narrow hips than a custom suit would do for most men. Judging from the snug green surgical cap covering his hair, it seemed that he was between procedures.

Her first thought when her footsteps faltered was that she could leave before he saw her. Her second thought was that the first was ridiculous.

Determined to act as normal as…normal, she strolled over to the tall, silver urns and snagged a foam cup for herself from the stack. On the outside, she was fine. Inside, the sudden, anxious knot in her stomach had effectively canceled the need for solid food.

"Did you do anything exciting this weekend?" she asked, watching him fill his cup with strong black coffee.

He'd been preoccupied, totally unaware that anyone had come up beside him. At the sound of her voice, he hesitated an instant before he cut a glance toward her. Eyes the color of a fathomless lake scanned her face, quick and assessing, before he turned his attention back to his cup.

Despite the quirk of a smile that had come too late to be anything but an afterthought, there was infinitely more caution than welcome in his expression.

"I wired new speakers to my stereo," he replied, moving farther down the line for a white plastic lid. "And I went up to Mount Hood with my brother," he added, hitting the highlights.

"To ski or to look at the cabin he wants to buy?"

"To look at the cabin."

"What did you think?"

"It needs work." The lid snapped on with a quiet click. "You were out late last night."

His tone was remarkably conversational. It was the observation itself that threw her.

"Not really. I got in about eight-thirty," she told him, wondering how he'd known she hadn't been home. "Did you come over?"

"I called. I take it you didn't check your messages."

"There weren't any."

"Well, I left one. I asked you to call me back if you got in before ten."

Frowning, she held her cup under the hot cocoa dispenser. "Spike must have erased it."

She halfway expected Mike to give her one of his tolerant looks and mutter something like, "That's original." Or to give her a bad time about blaming her cat. All he did was give her a sidelong glance that said she'd have to do better than that.

"I mean it," she insisted, wondering if he thought she'd purposely ignored his call. Until three days ago, he never would have doubted her. But then, until three days ago, she wouldn't have hesitated when she'd first seen him—or felt such ambivalence over the fact that he'd tried to reach her.

"Sometimes he steps on the Play Messages bar when he's walking across the end table and the messages play back. He does," she stressed when he said nothing, hating that she felt she had to defend herself. "Was it something important?"

"Nothing that couldn't wait," he conceded. "Cameron is selling Girl Scout cookies. She wanted me to ask if you'd buy some."

Cameron was his niece, his brother Tom's daughter. Katie didn't doubt for a minute that the diminutive seven-year-old with the dark hair and Brennan blue eyes had asked her Uncle Mike to hit her up for a sale. The little girl had already unloaded a calendar, a magazine subscription and six chocolate almond bars on her this school year alone. But the question was one Mike could have posed the next time he saw her—which made Katie wonder if there hadn't been another reason he'd wanted to talk.

"That kid's going to break me," she informed him, trying for their old ease. "It's too bad you didn't call before I left. I could have taken orders from everyone at the meeting."

"The meeting?"

"For the free clinic. That's where I was. I'm on the expansion committee."

Like lightning, his dark eyebrows bolted together. "You said you were cutting back on your hours there."

"I did. On the hours I work in the clinic, anyway. I'm only giving them one night a week instead of two. And this expansion thing will only last a couple of months, so it's not like it'll take much more time than it has in the past.''

She didn't believe for a minute that her tendency to overextend herself mattered that much to Mike. He'd just been the person who'd listened to her complain for months now about how she felt she was working herself into a rut, stagnating, turning into an old maid with a cat. After listening to her moan and complain, he was the one who'd encouraged her to cut back on her volunteer hours and use the time to take a class, or smell the flowers, or do whatever it was she wanted to do that would expose her to new people and new experiences. He'd even pointed out that when a person spent all day and a couple evenings a week taking care of others, she didn't have to feel guilty about taking a little time for herself.

Because he'd been so supportive was precisely why she'd avoided mentioning how she'd wound up with this commitment a couple of weeks ago. She simply hadn't wanted to hear another lecture about how she would never have time for herself if she didn't say no once in a while. At the moment, however, she would gladly welcome his logic, practicality and exasperation. They would be familiar, comfortable, and those were things she wanted badly to feel with him again.

"It's only for a couple of months," she defended, deliberately encouraging criticism. He said she rationalized more than anyone he'd ever known. "I wasn't all that keen on the yoga class it's too late to sign up for now, anyway."

There was no lecture. Mike didn't even comment on the lack of steel in her spine, much less get that faintly annoyed frown that said her logic completely escaped him. He just gave her a steady look she couldn't read at all.

"You'd better move," he advised a moment later.

"What?"

She was wondering if he'd given up on her, her heart

sinking at the thought, when she felt his hand slip under the edge of her short sleeve. With his fingers circled firmly above her elbow, he moved her out of the way so the woman behind them could get to the sugar.

She thought he'd let her go. Instead, he pulled her a little closer so the woman's companion could move past, too. His palm seemed to burn into her cool flesh, his heat searing into her in a grip that suddenly felt more possessive than perfunctory. But it was the motion of his thumb moving slowly up and over her bicep that sensitized her nerves. With nothing more than that tiny concealed caress, he demanded a response from her body that she wanted badly to deny.

Thinking it would have been easier to deny her next breath, she cautiously met his eyes. Now that she was intimately familiar with the feel of his hands, it seemed all he had to do was touch her to create instant havoc.

He seemed to have felt that same, unnerving jolt. There was no mistaking the tension etched in his compelling features—or his quick displeasure. His jaw locked and his hand fell. Just as it did, someone dropped a metal tray. The reverberating clang jolted her so badly she jumped.

"Watch it." His hand darted out again, steadying the cup in her hand. Seeing that it was secure, he immediately pulled away. "You don't want to burn yourself."

Unnerved, she managed to say something appropriately inane in agreement. They were in a place where any of a dozen people could see their every move. That alone would have caused him to let go of her as quickly as he had. But Katie was dead certain he'd have broken that evocative contact just as fast had they been alone. The fact that they were not alone was what took some of the sting from his abruptness.

"Hey, Mike." A tall, reed-thin anesthesiologist in surgical greens walked past with a plate of toast. "Rumor has it you're on the shortlist to present at the cardiovascular conference in Seattle. Prestige like that can't hurt when it comes to funding a new surgical wing around here.'' He lifted his toast in a salute. ''I sure hope they ask you.''

Mike's smile was easy, his manner remarkably unaffected as he accepted his colleague's good wishes. From what the other doctor was saying, Katie gathered it wouldn't be long before the medical conference panel decided which new studies and procedures merited exposure through their enormously respected forum. That he was even under consideration had truly surprised Mike. All he'd planned to do with his study results, if they proved worth writing about, was submit them for publication, something that was often done to share information. But Dr. MacAllister, the chief of staff, had brought the study to the attention of the panel and now it held the potential to make Mike widely known among his peers—and bring the reflected glory to the hospital.

''You never expected it to get this big, did you?''

Katie posed the observation quietly as the other doctor walked off. She wanted nothing more than to get beyond the awkwardness of the past several moments, and the subject the interruption raised had provided the perfect diversion.

Already uncomfortable with the notoriety, Mike turned back to her with a shrug. ''I think we know by now that some things just have a way of getting out of hand.'' He motioned her ahead of him, stepping back as if to keep from taking her arm again. ''Let's get out of here. There was another reason I called you last night.''

If it was his intention to keep her off guard, he succeeded beautifully. In the space of a minute, he'd gone from sensitizing her nerves to knotting them. He didn't looked pleased. He also looked as if he were now in a hurry as they dealt with the cashier and then headed for the exit.

The wide, brightly lit corridor outside the cafeteria branched in three directions. A middle-age couple—visitors, Katie assumed—looked around as if uncertain where they were going. Two women in white lab coats walked past, pushing their way through the cafeteria's doors. A nurse from pediatrics, identifiable by the teddy bears on her scrub top, ambled behind them, her nose already buried in the romance novel she apparently intended to read on her break.

Mike motioned Katie toward the stairwell door and pushed it open for her to pass. They'd both be taking the stairs to get to their respective floors. But right now, the bright, beige-walled space with its long flights of brown, skid-proofed stairs would also provide a modicum of privacy. And privacy was what he was after.

He didn't like feeling at a disadvantage. It made him defensive. And he liked that feeling even less. What he really didn't care for, however, was the unease he sensed in Katie when he'd touched her.

That discomfort was still there when she turned to face him. He could see it in her body language as she held her cup close to her stomach, her opposite hand worrying the plastic tab on the lid. He could see it in her eyes, by the way they refused to meet his for longer than a couple of seconds.

As the heavy door closed with a solid thud behind him, he focused on the hot pink stethoscope draped around her neck. She'd taped a tiny, golden guardian angel pin above the bell. He started to touch it, to touch her, only to fist his hand and drop it to his side.

"About the Heart Ball," he began.

Katie's glance immediately faltered. "You don't want me to go."

"Of course I do." A frown sliced through his features. "I just wanted to make sure you didn't want to back out."

It wasn't necessary for her to ask why he thought she might do such a thing. With the reason fairly screaming between them, the question would have been a tad redundant.

"I said I'd go."

"I know what you said." Defensiveness gave way to caution. She'd also implied that she intended to forget what had happened between them. But if the past few minutes were any indication, she was having as difficult a time doing that as he was. "I just wanted to make sure you hadn't reconsidered. Or, if you had reconsidered, that you hadn't changed your mind."

"I haven't."

"Good." He gave her a tight little nod. "Thanks."

"No problem," she said quietly, still feeling his tension snake toward her. "So, I'll see you later...."

Her last words were muffled by the echoing bang of a door being thrown open above them. Hurried footsteps, of the high-heel variety, sounded on the upper landing.

Catching Katie as she started down the stairs, Mike called, "Wait a second. What do I tell Cameron? About the cookies. She's calling me tonight."

Katie opened her mouth, but it wasn't her soft voice he heard. The throaty, "Good morning, Dr. Brennan," came from the owner of the high heels, a strawberry blonde in a brown suit that fairly shouted "accounting department." Bouncing her way down the last couple of steps, she smiled her way past, wiggling her fingers at him on the way. He hadn't a clue who she was. Nor did he care. Since she'd barely acknowledged Katie, his only thought was that her cheerfulness was obviously gender-specific.

Watching her sway out the door, Katie muttered, "I'll take a box of whatever has the least fat in it."

The response was typical Katie, which would have relieved him enormously had he time to think about it. The door swung open again, the rattle of glass tubes in a plastic carrier identifying the young man toting it as someone from the lab. Thinking it a miracle that people actually managed private conversations in this place, Mike hurried down the stairs, purposefully ignoring the odd twinge in his gut when he heard Katie laughing with the lab guy as she headed up.

The break Katie had taken that morning was the only one she had all day, which meant she didn't eat until she came flying in the door of her duplex late that afternoon. With the flu continuing to play havoc with the nursing staff, those who'd already survived it were still running themselves ragged. Katie was no longer thinking about work, though. All she cared about as she changed into fresh scrubs while apologizing to Spike for not being able to play, then shoveled down a carton of yogurt while wrapping a baby gift she'd bought for a young woman she'd befriended at the free clinic, was that Mike wasn't avoiding her.

She hadn't been at all sure what to expect when she'd seen him in the cafeteria that morning, but he hadn't acted at all as if he were trying to distance himself. That had been her biggest fear. That he would decide for whatever reason that he didn't want anything to do with her. But she knew Mike didn't play games. He hated them, in fact. So she knew without a doubt that he wouldn't still want her to go to the Heart Ball with him if he didn't want her around.

Curling a pile of pink and blue ribbons on top of the square white package, she told herself she should simply accept that it would take a while for their former comfort level to return and let it go at that. She shouldn't worry about why it had been so important to Mike that she wasn't backing out. But she obviously had far less willpower than she'd thought she had where Mike was concerned. She simply couldn't help wondering if it was because he wanted assurance that they hadn't done anything irreparable to their friendship. Or because he didn't want to have to scrape up another date. A "real" one this time.

Thinking some questions were best left unanswered, she tried to ignore the faint sting that came with that last thought. She knew Mike didn't want an emotionally involved relationship. That was why he'd asked her to go to the obligatory affair in the first place. Yet the need to know his rationale tugged at feelings she very much wanted to protect.

She set the package by her purse and grabbed her coat. She was due at the clinic at six o'clock, which gave her exactly fourteen minutes to make the ten-minute trip. Considering her tendency to be tearing out the door without a minute to spare, she was way ahead of time.

Or so she was thinking when the phone rang, catching her with one arm in the sleeve of her burgundy raincoat.

It was nearing the dinner hour. That being the case, odds were that the caller was a solicitor wanting to sell her something she didn't need or want, or some charity seeking a donation to the cause du jour. Deciding to let the answering machine get it, she pulled her coat on the rest of the way, picked up her purse and the package and waited to see who it was in case Spike erased the message before she got back.

It was Mike. He asked if she was there.

She cut him off just as he asked again.

"I haven't left yet. I'm about to," she hurried to add, glancing at her watch while she listened to the sounds on the other end of the line. "Are you in your car?"

He was. And he was ten blocks away.

"Wait for me," he insisted. "I have to tell you something."

There was no mistaking the unusual excitement in his voice, or the gleam of it in his eyes moments later after he pulled his black sedan up to the curb and strode up to her door.

Holding Spike so the straining feline wouldn't bolt, Katie stepped back when Mike came in and watched him close the door. His raincoat hung open over his jacket and slacks, and his dark hair had been ruffled by the late January wind. His big body seemed to fill the room, raw energy radiating from him in waves.

She could have sworn she felt that elemental power when his eyes met hers. It seemed to tug at her midsection, drawing her toward him even though she knew she never moved.

"I was on my way to the gym when I got a call from Robert Thornton," he began, seeming oblivious to the disconcerting sensation himself. "He's on the panel for the Seattle conference. The chairman," he explained, ignoring the way the cat leapt from Katie's arms and started purring against his leg. "They want me, Katie. They want me," he repeated, his voice quiet with awe. "But that's not all."

Looking somewhere between stunned and wanting to grin, he settled for pushing his hand through his hair. Most of it fell more or less into place.

He took a step toward her, one dark lock promptly falling back over his forehead. "All I did when I started this study was modify a standard surgical procedure and tweak a drug protocol. Now they want me to present my preliminary findings. And," he stressed softly, "they want me to demonstrate my technique at the medical school."

His gaze danced over her face, years seeming to wash away with his smile. Katie knew he'd changed. She'd even worried about how he seemed to be closing himself off, losing bits of his personality the more he buried himself in his work. Yet, until she witnessed his transformation now, she truly hadn't realized how much of himself he'd locked away.

He didn't appear to be holding anything back at the moment, however, and the pleasure she felt for him overrode her concerns. He had earned an honor many doctors labored years to achieve, if they ever won such recognition at all.

"That's wonderful! Have you told your parents?" she asked, throwing her arms around his neck to give him a hug. Had she not been so thrilled for him, she might have considered what she was doing. As it was, she could only react as she would have a week, a month or a year ago. "And your brothers?"

Telling her he hadn't had a chance to share the news with anyone but her, he lifted her, hugging her back. Had he been with anyone else, he would have been far more circumspect in his delivery of the news. For one thing, he wouldn't have been battling a grin. It would be considered bad form among his peers to act like a kid who couldn't believe he'd hit a home run. Understated pride was the accepted way to deal with this sort of professional stroke. That was what the rest of the world would see once he walked out Katie's door, his family included. But with Katie, he could share this first blush of excitement and know she would be as pleased for him as anyone could be. That was why he'd had to see her.

It was only a matter of seconds, however, before he began to think seeing her might not have been a good idea after all. Actually, seeing her was okay. Holding her was the problem. The scent of her, the feel of her in his arms, jolted him with a swiftness that nearly stole his breath.

His body was hardening in response even before he lowered her to the floor. The same thing had happened to him in the cafeteria that morning; that swift, gut-tightening awareness that threatened to scramble his senses. He'd felt the smoothness of her skin beneath his hand and his mind had flooded with memories of how she'd tasted, the shape of her breasts when he'd peeled off the amazingly provocative scraps of lace she'd worn. The feel of her body now brought those memories back with a vengeance—along with a few others that were playing utter havoc with certain parts of his anatomy.

Now that he'd been intimate with her, all he had to do was touch her to want her. Hell, he thought, all he had to do was think about her.

With anyone other than Katie, he'd have seen no problem with that. Considering how long it had been since any woman had affected him even half as strongly, he should have been relieved by the phenomenon. Now he considered it a curse, the Fates' idea of some perverse joke.

Tension flowed into her muscles even as she slowly slipped her arms from around his neck. Stifling the urge to tangle his fingers in her hair and turn her face to his, he locked his hands loosely at the back of her waist, curious to know what she would do. By the time her hands were flat on his chest, he could tell by the wariness shadowing her expressive eyes that she was going to pull back.

Not ready to risk a lifelong friendship by pushing, wishing he'd never touched her at all, he made it easy on them both and dropped his arms to his sides.

Her glance moved over the five-o'clock stubble shadowing his jaw, not quite meeting his eyes. "This is great news," she began, her voice thready. "It really is, Mike. If I wasn't on at the clinic tonight, I'd like to help you celebrate."

He watched her back up, his eyes narrowing at the way she touched her fingers to her lips and trailed them to her throat. The motion had to be subconscious, a behavior triggered by her own memories of how they'd responded to each other. It was too enticing to have been deliberate. And too telling for him to ignore.

The thought that she might be struggling with the same feelings he battled did nothing to cool him down. "I think I'll just head to the gym." A workout definitely held merit. So did the cold plunge pool. "That's where I was going, anyway."

"But that was before," she reminded him, referring to the call that had brought him there. "You can't just do the gym, then go home to that empty house. You should celebrate. Call friends and go out.

"That's what you should do." Warming to the idea, or the diversion, she motioned to the phone. "Call Jerry and Sue," she suggested, referring to the radiologist he sometimes jogged with and the man's wife. "I bet they'd love to—"

"I don't want to call Jerry."

"Then call your mom and dad," she hurried on, undaunted. "I'm sure they'll want you over for dinner. Or they'll take you to the club."

"I'll call them later."

"But if you call now, they can get a table."

"I don't want to go to the club," he muttered.

"I'm sure they'll make reservations wherever you want to go."

Since he seemed intent on ignoring her practicality, she started punching in numbers herself. The senior Brennans had had the same phone number for as long as she could remember. She knew it as well as she knew her own. "This isn't your mom's bridge night, is it?"

He took the phone from her hand, careful not to snatch it, and dropped it back on its base. "I have no idea if it is or not."

Just because he probably would wind up at the club with

his folks didn't matter at the moment. He didn't need Katie making sure he had someone to be with tonight. He didn't need her reminding him that his house was so damn empty. What he really didn't need was the disappointment he felt knowing she wouldn't be part of his evening. "I'm not in the mood to go out." His voice sounded tight and just a little edgy. "I want to go to the gym."

That really wasn't what he wanted, and he knew it. What he wanted to do was take her to dinner. And to bed. Not necessarily in that order. That he was suddenly feeling as frustrated as hell about it didn't help, either. Neither did the fact that Katie looked even more wary than she had moments ago.

"I'm making you late," he muttered, hardly able to blame her for the way she crossed her arms as she backed away. He was being ridiculous. He knew it. But he couldn't seem to help it.

Digging in his pocket for his keys, he took a step away himself, giving her even more space. "Are you working tomorrow?"

She eyed him uncertainly, her hair shimmering with shades of dark honey and gold as she gave him a nod. "I'm scheduled for the next seven days."

"You have to work this weekend, too?"

She nodded again, clearly bewildered by his scowl. But she went along with him the way she might a confused, agitated patient, watching him just as closely. "One of the nurses wanted to get away this weekend with her husband. I traded days off with her."

All Mike had wanted to know was if she'd be at the hospital tomorrow, thinking he'd tell her he'd see her then. Now he felt exasperation join the annoyance he was trying to curb. Not only had she worked last weekend and spent that Sunday evening at a meeting of the organization she was presently on her way to help, she had now committed herself to working a week straight so someone else could get away to relax. Considering that the free clinic attracted mostly pregnant, indigent women and that she had a sack of diapers and formula and what looked like a baby gift parked by the back door, he wouldn't hazard a guess as to who she was rescuing now, or what else she'd committed herself to.

It was no wonder she'd gotten sick a couple of weeks ago. The woman took care of everyone but herself.

Not trusting himself to share his theory about why she did that, not sure he trusted why it mattered, he turned to the door.

"I'll see you tomorrow," was all he said before he pulled it open.

Katie's response was just as guarded. "Sure," she replied, her tone faint and decidedly puzzled. "You have a good evening."

Oh, he and the free weights would have a great time. "Thanks," he mumbled, thinking he might as well add a few dozen laps to the night's routine. "You, too."

Chapter Six

"That's the one." Dana stepped back, critically eyeing Katie's image in the dressing room mirrors. "Definitely."

"It certainly has more potential than that last one." From where Lee sat in the corner of the multi-mirrored fitting room, she gave a dismissing wave toward the black crepe, halter-style gown hanging on the louvered door. "At least it has part of a back. You'd freeze in that other thing."

Katie glanced from her friends, who were both still in uniform since they'd hit the mall straight from work, to the strapless, black velvet gown Dana had just zipped her into. With its long, slim skirt and fitted bodice, it was very understated, very elegant and, most important, on sale. It just didn't have a lot of material on top. "Don't you think it's a little low?"

Dana made a tsking sound. "You only think it's low because you're usually buttoned up to your neck. It barely shows your cleavage."

"That's because this is all I've got."

"Not to worry. We'll get you more in lingerie."

"More what?"

"More cleavage. We'll get you one of those push-up bras that make mountains out of molehills, so to speak."

"I don't *want* mountains."

"We're not talking the Andes here," Dana muttered. "Just a little something to make it more interesting while still being subtle."

Katie eyed her friend evenly. "I believe 'interesting' and 'subtle' are a contradiction in terms."

"That depends entirely on the wearer. With your hair up and those long, drop pearl earrings of yours, you'll look smashing." Enormously pleased with what she was creating, Dana tugged on the wide strip of velvet that skimmed the top of Katie's breasts. "What I have in mind is to play up your feminine allure. You know, be subtly sexy."

"She'd need 'subtly sexy' if she was going with someone who'd notice. Like she keeps reminding us," Lee said, "this isn't a real date. Mike asked her to go with him because he needs a warm presentable body to occupy a chair next to him at dinner."

Dana refused to let her creative balloon be robbed of its air. "You're being entirely too practical, Lee. Who she's going with is a mere technicality. This is her Cinderella night, remember? For one evening, she'll just have to pretend Mike Brennan is her knight in shining armor."

"You're mixing your metaphors." Far more anxious about the impending evening than she wanted to admit, Katie gave the top of the gown a yank herself. No way was she adding more cleavage. With her arms, shoulders and the top of her chest completely bare, she was exposing enough skin as it was. "The knight goes with Guinevere. Cinderella got a prince."

"You're missing the point. He can be whoever you want him to be. When the clock strikes twelve or whatever hour it is when he feels he's schmoozed enough, he can go back to being himself again."

"Ah," Lee murmured, smiling as she let herself get into the fantasy. "But before that happens, we'll have transformed her into this alluring creature who...what? Captivates him? Bends him to her will?"

Dana gave a sage nod. "Bending his will works."

"I see." Lee's eyes sparkled. "So, she'll have him on his knees begging at her feet while he offers her champagne in her crystal slipper."

"Now you've got it."

"And feeding her caviar with a silver spoon by a fountain in the moonlight with a ginger-scented breeze bringing strains of Strauss from the orchestra inside."

"Exactly."

"And when he offers his hand for a dance, she finds the champagne has gone to her head and he lifts her in his arms to cradle her against his chest. And with the music playing and her resistance shot, he proceeds to steal her breath with his kisses."

Lee was clearly waiting for an indication she was still on the right track. But Dana was suddenly silent. So was Katie. Neither moved a muscle as they stared at the pretty-but-decidedly-unassuming woman staring back at them.

"I was just trying to get into the spirit of things," Lee defended.

"You were doing just fine, too." Dana, intrigued, quietly encouraged her. "Keep going."

"That's okay," Katie interjected. "You really don't have to."

"Why not? She's finally getting into this. Go on, Lee. What happens after the stealing-her-breath part?"

"Nothing," Katie replied, though "nothing" wasn't

what had happened at all. After stealing her breath, the "prince" had backed her down her hall while systematically removing her clothing. He'd also reduced her to a mass of quivering nerve endings, which somehow resulted in her hesitating only slightly before she'd unzipped his pants.

"He does nothing," she hastily repeated, turning away to hoist the heavy skirt past her white socks. "Now, what kind of fool—shoes, I mean. What kind of shoes," she repeated, "do I wear with this? Can I get away with my black leather slings?"

For a moment, the only sound in the dressing room was the rustle of Lee's rumpled uniform as she slowly rose to stand beside Dana. Turning away had accomplished nothing. All Katie had done was face the mirror, which gave her friends an excellent view of the consternation shadowing her face. Reflected back in the features of a striking blonde and a slightly frayed-looking brunette was both confusion and concern.

"Hey." Dana touched her shoulder, sympathy heavy in her voice. "What's wrong?"

"Yeah," Lee agreed, giving Katie's too-emphatic reaction priority over her little lapse into fantasyland. "What's going on?"

Katie shook her head. It wasn't like her to get rattled so easily. And it certainly wasn't like her to rain on a parade. Her friends were just letting their hair down after a day in the trenches. She'd had no business taking the good-natured banter so seriously.

"PMS?" she offered, wondering precisely when she'd lost her sense of perspective.

"Ah," Lee murmured knowingly.

"That would explain it," Dana agreed. "Try exercise. It works wonders."

"Or herb teas," Lee suggested. "If you don't have a list of what to use, I'll give you one. Very soothing."

Contrite, Katie smiled. "Thanks, guys."

Smiling back, Dana spread her hands. "What are friends for?"

The question made Katie feel like a fraud. There was precious little she hadn't shared over the years with these two wonderful women. But her consternation over Mike wasn't something she could bring up without getting into the reason she was such a mental mess to begin with— and that wasn't something she was willing to mention at all. Dana would want details. Lee would think her a traitor. Beyond that, what had happened between her and Mike needed to stay between the two of them, if for no other reason than they were both trying to get past it. It was only a matter of time before she would stop being reminded of how shamelessly she'd responded to him every time she saw him. In time, too, her body would stop craving his touch. She didn't know if her rationale made any sense or not, but if she couldn't make sense of how she felt to herself, she had no hope of explaining it to anyone else.

Unfortunately, the one person she could have talked with to straighten it all out was also the same person she wanted to talk about. Seeing no earthly way to separate the two, she sought less complicated ground.

"Friends are for turning me into Cinderella." She glanced down at the white socks poking from under the deep hem and wiggled her toes. "Come on, you guys," she coaxed, making it sound as if she were simply anxious to get on with her transformation, rather than desperate to change the subject. "Shoes?"

By the time her friends declared her properly outfitted and accessorized and they'd headed home after annihilating a pizza, the evening was shot. They hadn't shopped only for Katie. Dana bought a going-away present for a neighbor who was moving, and Lee purchased a slinky red teddy. They'd also looked for something for Katie to give her dad for his birthday next month, but he was nearly impossible to buy for and they'd come up with zip. Since her mom hadn't been any help in the idea department so far, Katie was taking suggestions from everyone.

Dana had suggested that she ask Mike since he would know exactly what to get him.

That was true enough and, normally, he was exactly who Katie would have turned to. She wouldn't have even hesitated. Mike would know of some obscure book or odd little collectible that even her mom, the woman who had been married to the man for thirty-three years, probably wouldn't have known to consider. But she couldn't just pick up the phone and call Mike anymore. There were no conversations, quick or otherwise, that didn't leave her painfully aware of the strain in their relationship.

On the surface, their interaction at the hospital seemed quite normal. To anyone watching them, anyway. During rounds, Mike's professional manner was the same as always—efficient, pleasant, precise. He even greeted her with the same casual smile he offered everyone else, when he wasn't preoccupied. But to Katie, it was apparent that he weighed his words when they spoke, much as she had found herself doing with him. And the spontaneity that had once allowed them to spend a moment talking about whatever the other was up to was completely missing. Their former ease with each other had taken a hike. Gone the way of the dodo. Vanished. Valiant as their efforts were to pretend that what had happened didn't matter, they were miserably ineffective. She hated the guarded way she felt. More than anything, she hated that he so clearly felt the same way.

He wouldn't even touch her.

She'd never realized before how often or how casually

Mike used to initiate physical contact. Now, every time he'd reach toward her to get her attention, he would deliberately check his motion, curling his fingers to stuff his hand in the pocket of his lab coat or his jacket or his slacks. As for the way he used to drape his arm companionably over her shoulders to walk her to the elevator or her car, that behavior was history. But what she missed most was the habit he'd developed in the past few months of nudging her hair back from her cheek.

She had never let herself believe there was any significance to the gesture beyond brotherly affection. Yet, being deprived of his touch had become as significant to her as being deprived of his friendship. And even though they continued to work together surprisingly well, their friendship was definitely suffering. When a week passed and he'd yet to ask for her help with his presentation, she bit the proverbial bullet and brought it up herself after he'd written orders one morning.

"I posted your memo about the end of your drug study," she said, coming up beside him at the nurses' station. "It was nice of you to thank the nurses for their help."

"I couldn't have done it without them. Or you," he added, pocketing his pen. "I know it was a lot of extra work."

"You have all the data you need, then?"

"Enough to form a conclusion." His smile deceptively easy, he handed her the chart he'd just closed. "How's the new computer program working out?"

He wasn't all that interested in the computer. She was sure of it. All he wanted to do was change the subject, and because there were a half a dozen other people within earshot, Katie simply said, "Not," and turned her attention to the orders he'd left for his patient. Even if they had been alone, a circumstance he seemed to be avoiding, there wasn't much she could say anyway. She'd given him the perfect opportunity to ask for her help. It didn't take a rocket scientist to figure out that he didn't want it.

He still wanted her to go to the Heart Ball, though. He reminded her of it a moment later, and again, two days before the event. It was almost as if he was afraid she'd forget.

As if she could.

The date was marked prominently on her calendar, and she was quite aware of just which day fell where. By the Saturday morning of the ball, it had been exactly thirty-one days since she'd last drawn the little witch's hat on her calendar that marked the first day of her period. The people in Greenwich could practically set their to-the-nth-of-a-second, international time clock by her cycle. She was that regular. Normally. And no matter how she counted, she was three days late.

The delay could be caused by fatigue. It could be nerves. After all, heaven knew her nerves had had their little neurons tested, frayed and stretched considerably over the past three weeks. And she was on birth control, she reminded herself. Maybe she was just coming down with something. Again.

The knot in her stomach doubled at the thought. The fact that she'd had something in the first place—the sore throat that had dragged her down during the week from hell last month—could be the problem. She'd been on an antibiotic, and certain antibiotics rendered birth control pills ineffective.

But they'd only done it *once,* she mentally argued, pacing between her closet and the bathroom while she got ready for work. Pulling on her uniform, Spike trotting faithfully at her heels, she also reminded herself that that particular argument held about as much water as the brass colander on her kitchen counter. How many young girls had she talked with at the free clinic who'd only had sex once—or so they'd claimed—and were now hugely pregnant?

She whipped her wildly curling hair into a scrunchee at her nape. Wondering how she was ever going to tame it for tonight, she added mousse to the mental list of items she needed to pick up on her way home this afternoon—and told herself it was way too soon to panic. She had been pretty upset lately and when she got upset her system did get a little out of whack. She'd skipped an entire period the month she'd taken her nursing boards. Stress could do that. So just because there was a possibility she could be pregnant didn't mean she was. The fact that she was a couple of days late meant nothing. It was rather like watching a pot, waiting for it to boil. Her period would start if she'd just stop worrying about it.

Still, just to be sure, she added pregnancy test to the list. After all, she was stopping at the drugstore, anyway. If she left work at the exact moment her shift ended, she could make her stop and be home by four-thirty. That would give her exactly two hours to take the test to put her mind at ease, shower, and transform herself into something resembling a vision.

The plan was sound. It was her timing that was off.

She left work right on time, but it took longer at the drugstore than she'd thought it would because she decided to go to one she didn't usually frequent so she wouldn't run into anyone she knew. Then, since the store stocked three brands of home pregnancy tests, she had to read them all because she wanted the one that would give her the fastest, most accurate results. Even with those little delays, she figured she could have accomplished everything on time—if Spike hadn't decided he'd been ignored just a little too much lately and unearthed the four-foot fern atop her bookcase. He'd dragged it, rootball and all, over her pale beige carpet and stuffed it under her bed. By the time she had what she could salvage of the listless plant recovering in a milk carton atop her fireplace mantel—the one place Spike couldn't leap on—and the mess vacuumed up, she'd was left with sixty-two minutes to perform a miracle.

Mike was there in sixty-one.

She seemed harried.

That was Mike's first impression when Katie opened the door and stepped back to hustle Spike onto the sofa so the cat wouldn't make for the pine tree out front. His second thought, as he watched her clip on a long, dangling pearl earring and open the closet for her coat, was that she looked exquisite.

"I'm almost ready," she said, pulling her long, burgundy raincoat from a hanger. "I can put my lipstick on in the car."

He reached for the coat. "Slow down."

"I don't want to make you late."

"You won't." His appreciative glance moved from the soft curls cascading from the pearl clips that held her hair up and away from her flushed face, past the dangling earrings, and skimmed the satiny expanse of shoulders and arms. Her skin looked as soft as the midnight black velvet clinging faithfully to her high breasts, narrow waist and enticing swell of her hips. The gown was classic, elegant. And Katie filled it out in a way that nearly made his mouth water. "How long can it take to put on lipstick?"

"With liner? About thirty seconds."

"I think we can spare that. Go."

He took her coat when she handed it to him and watched her hurry down the short hall, his glance roving shamelessly over bare skin and the rich-looking fabric that reached from the middle of her back to the floor. He was so accustomed to seeing her in scrubs or a sweater and leggings, that he'd forgotten how stunning she could be. Or had he even known? he wondered. He'd seen her dressed up on any number of occasions over the years. It was just that none of them had been since he'd moved back to Honeygrove.

Or maybe, he thought, turning away when she disappeared though the bedroom door he'd backed her through three weeks ago, he was just looking at her differently now. And seeing far more than he once had.

Preferring to avoid the thoughts complicating his life, he turned to face a bedraggled plant in a milk carton on the mantel.

"That's interesting," he murmured, when the rustle of heavy fabric caught his attention. "New art?"

Preoccupied, still rushing, confusion shifted through her dark eyes. Clutching a small, beaded bag, she reached to take her coat, and finally noticed where he was looking. "Oh, that. That's why I'm running late. Spike decided to rearrange the bookcase."

"Were you ignoring him again?"

For the first time since he'd arrived, she didn't simply brush a glance past his shoulders or his chin. The faint smile curving her lush, rose-tinted mouth was fleeting, but there was enough of that soft expression in her eyes for him to feel the connection that had been missing the past few weeks. Insignificant as the subject was, he'd immediately suspected why her cat had decided to punish her. And without words she'd confessed to the transgression. There was something nice about being that attuned to someone.

He hadn't realized how often they communicated in that once comfortable, companionable way. At least, he hadn't until communication between them had become so strained. Before, they could speak without words. Now, they were so busy not talking about the thing that loomed as large as an elephant between them that when they spoke, they actually said very little that mattered.

"I'm ready." Since it was apparent he wasn't going to simply hand over her coat, she turned to let him help her on with it. "I hope I haven't forgotten anything."

A shining strand of hair spiraled from her nape. He didn't know if it had escaped the clip holding up the rest of her hair, or if she'd left it down on purpose. But he lifted her coat over her shoulders, then untucked the intriguing lock to keep it from being crushed.

"I can't imagine what else you'd need. You look great."

He didn't know if she was surprised by the flattery or not. With her back to him, he was aware only of the way she'd tensed when he'd slipped his finger under her collar to rescue the curl. Or maybe it was the weight of his hand on her shoulder that had made her go still.

Dropping his hand, he let the other slide from her shoulder.

"Thank you."

Her hesitant thanks could have been for the compliment, or for letting her go. Had they not been on the way out the door, he might have asked her to get more specific. But discretion truly was the better part of valor and now was not the time to rock their boat. It was more like a leaky canoe, anyway. An extremely narrow one in rough water. The only thing that had kept it from tipping so far was their tacit agreement to ignore what had happened. As they hurried out to his car a few moments later, then spent the fifteen-minute drive in a stimulating conversation about the weather and the road construction they encountered, he knew that wasn't going to be possible much longer.

The grand ballroom of the Westridge Country Club was an enormous space lined with gilded mirrors, hung with massive chandeliers and set with round tables sporting red linens, white china and sparkling stemmed crystal. The Heart Ball was considered one of the main social and charitable events of the season, which meant the women—mostly wives or girlfriends of the various doctors, lawyers and corporate types in attendance, if not doctors, lawyers and corporate types themselves—were all properly gowned and coiffed. There were black gowns, of course, and every jewel-tone imaginable. But with the heart theme, many of the women had opted for shimmering red taffeta or satin. Even a few of the men sported red ties and cummerbunds with their tuxedos.

With the strains of a classic concerto filling the air, compliments of the ensemble near the dance floor, Katie couldn't help thinking that the overall mood would have fit right in with the little fantasy Lee had been working on in the dressing room. Unfortunately, Katie couldn't appreciate the ambiance as much as she would under other circumstances. Apprehensive and anxious, she just wished it were midnight and the ball were over. Mike was trying as hard as she to keep things pleasant, but there was an unfamiliar tension in him tonight that had her nerves jumping like the tracings of an EKG.

She stood near a set of the ballroom's huge, open doors, watching the crowd while Mike dealt with their coats. By being his nondate, she'd tacitly agreed to support him by putting up a good appearance. That was exactly what she'd do, too. As important as it was for him to maintain the right connections, and keep his chief of staff happy, she couldn't let him down. Aside from that, her parents were in there somewhere, along with many of their friends and acquaintances. So were Mike's colleagues. And some of the doctors she worked with. It wouldn't do any good at all to let the strain between her and Mike show.

There was one other little matter preying on her mind.

She hadn't taken the test. She'd simply been too rushed. So now she had to spend the evening pretending everything was fine between her and Mike while trying not to obsess over whether or not she was carrying his child.

"Show time."

Mike drawled the words from beside her. Feeling his hand on her elbow, she looked up, her glance skimming the row of black studs on his white pleated shirt and the satin stripe edging the lapel of his black jacket. The last time she'd seen him in a tuxedo had been at his wedding. She'd thought he looked incredibly handsome then. Tonight, when she needed him to look comfortable and ordinary, when she needed him to look like her friend, he looked devastating.

"Start looking for Dr. MacAllister," he said, leading her into the crowd. "We're at his table." He nodded to a couple who smiled and nodded back. "It's number twenty-something."

Grateful for the diversion, her glance swept over the numbers in the silver holders on the nearby tables. They were in the forties. "Do you know who else we'll be with?"

"Aniston and Chapman and their wives.

"What?" he asked, when she wrinkled her nose.

"We have to sit with Dr. Aniston?"

"What's wrong with him?"

"Other than the fact that he's a short, bald, ill-tempered egotist?"

With his hand on her elbow, Mike steered her in the direction of a white-coated waiter bearing a tray of champagne. "You forgot opinionated. But that's just between you and me. Anyway, you know how to deal with difficult people. You do it all the time. And Aniston's all right," he said, clearly seeing no cause for concern. "He's just got a Napoleon complex. Do you want champagne? Or would you rather have something from the bar?''

Considering that another minor stress had just been added to the evening, she didn't just want a drink, she wanted general anesthesia. Unfortunately, there was a little possibility she needed to consider. And considering it had her looking everywhere but at him. "I'll just have water. Or a soft drink."

Mike's eyebrow shot up. "You sure?"

"I'm sure." If she was pregnant, she wasn't going to take any chance of harming her...their...baby. "Ginger ale would be fine," she expanded, not sure she hadn't paled as the idea became more real.

Their baby. Hers and Mike's. A little dark-haired, blue-eyed Brennan, she thought, her hand flattening on her stomach.

"Are you all right?" Mike's glance followed her unconscious motion, then sharpened on her face. "You're not fighting something off again, are you?"

"No! No. I'm —"

"Katie! There you are. And Michael! It's so good to see you."

Katie's mom enveloped first Katie, then Mike in a Chanel-scented hug. Unaware of her daughter's relief at the interruption, she stood back, smiling fondly at them both. With her smooth, ash blond hair tucked in a shining chignon and her petite frame encased in a long, red beaded sheath and jacket, Karen Sheppard looked perfect, as always. Which made Katie, as always, feel as if she'd just stepped from a wind tunnel.

Self-consciously tucking back a strand of the hair that had survived her every effort to tame it, she straightened her shoulders and smiled back.

"You look charming," Karen pronounced, scanning the earrings and black velvet gown. "The dress is even prettier than you described. You should have borrowed my pearls, though. They would have looked perfect. But never mind that," she hurried on, looking chagrined at having been unable to resist the suggestion. "Your way is lovely. Where are you sitting?"

"Table twenty-something." Suddenly self-conscious about her bare throat, wondering if maybe she should have borrowed the pearls, she covered the offending spot with her hand. "Hi, Dad."

Like Mike, Dr. Randall Sheppard looked as comfortable in a tuxedo as he did a lab coat. He did not, however, look like a man about to turn sixty. If not for his thick, silver hair, he could have easily passed for a man ten years his junior. His personality and reputation gave a person the impression that he was a large man, though he was actually as lean as a runner, and easily an inch or two shorter than Mike's six feet.

Hearing his daughter's greeting, he glanced toward her, his hand falling from where he'd clapped Mike on the shoulder. His patrician features folding in puzzlement, he stepped forward to place a quick kiss on her cheek.

"This is a surprise, Kathleen," he said, his use of her formal name creating a certain distance even as he smiled. "I expected to see Mike, but what are you doing here?"

"Oh, Randy," Karen murmured, sounding more conciliatory than exasperated. "I told you she was coming with him." She shook her head, the rubies in her ears catching the light from the chandeliers. "I must have mentioned it while he was preoccupied with something," she explained to Katie with a dismissing little laugh. "I can't hold him responsible for what I tell him unless I'm sure I have his attention. You know how your father always has a million things on his mind."

The picture of amused tolerance, she skimmed her smile to Mike, avoiding her daughter's subdued expression as she tactfully changed the subject. Katie was so accustomed to the way her dad seemed to forget she existed, and her mom's excuses for him, that her own responses were just as automatic. Having been so subtly dismissed, however unintentionally, she simply crossed her arms and told herself she didn't care.

"I do wish your parents could have come tonight, Michael," her mother was saying, "but they wouldn't miss Paul's tournament. Imagine. He could be state swimming champion."

The murmur of other conversations drifted between them. Over the high-pitched enthusiasm of two ladies who apparently hadn't seen each other in a while, Mike responded to Mrs. Sheppard with an oldest brother's pride in his youngest sibling, and replied with ease to Dr. Sheppard's inquiry about how his practice was going. There was no mistaking the genuine interest in the older man's question, or the sincerity in his response when he said he was glad Mike was doing so well. Dr. Sheppard had been interested in him for as long as he could remember, and Mike had always found him willing to listen and explain. But even as they spoke, he could see Katie withdrawing from the brief conversation.

He'd seen her smile slip while she'd talked with her mom. Now, as she stood with one hand covering her throat, her other arm banding her waist, she'd grown quieter, her expression losing what little animation she'd managed. She'd seemed preoccupied since he'd picked her up, but this was different. This had to do with her parents. She was always more subdued around her mom, but with her dad, she nearly turned mute. She couldn't be around her father for sixty seconds without seeming to shrink into the background.

"And we really shouldn't hold you two up any longer,"

Mrs. Sheppard concluded a minute later. "I see Angie Baker coming now."

A woman Katie recognized from her parents' church was moving in on them like a heat-seeking missile. Having caught the woman's eye herself, Mrs. Sheppard leaned forward and dropped a quick kiss on Katie's cheek.

"Have fun tonight, sweetie. And you, Mike," she added, smiling up at the man she'd known since he was in diapers. "Mark the fifth of next month on your calendar. It's Randy's birthday. His sixtieth. We'll need you to help celebrate."

Mike assured her that he'd be there if he could, but he was more aware of Katie than whatever else it was her mother said, as a woman in a dress the shade of bile, but what he supposed would be called "lime," tugged her away. The stunning woman at his side seemed to visibly relax as her parents were whisked off, her slender, enticingly bare shoulders falling as if some of the air had just leaked out of her.

"You don't need a necklace."

Surprise registered in her eyes, just before appreciation settled in. Her hand fell from her throat. "Thank you."

"Are you sure you don't want that wine?"

Though her smile faltered, she murmured, "I'm sure. Listen, Mike. About dad's birthday," she began, only to find the rest of what she wanted to say stuck in her throat.

His hand had settled on her bare back, right between her shoulder blades.

"What about it?" he asked, letting his hand slip down to the soft velvet as he guided her to the bar.

"I have no idea what to get him." His fingers were now splayed at the small of her back, his thumb moving in a slow caress. Thinking he might just like the feel of the fabric, she tried to dismiss the motion. "If you can think of anything, will you let me know?"

"I'll see what I can come up with. There's Dr. Mac-Allister." Looking as innocent as an altar boy, he increased the pressure of his hand, slipping it just a bit lower. It was almost as if he were testing her, challenging her to question the contact. "It looks like the Anistons are with him."

Chapter Seven

"You're Randy Sheppard's daughter?" Dr. Aniston posed the question over a forkful of Chicken Oscar, his attention momentarily diverted from the conversation taking place to his right. "I've known Randy for years. He was our children's pediatrician. You and I have met before, haven't we?"

Dr. Aniston's beady little eyes narrowed. Had she been in scrubs and standing by the nurses' station at the hospital, Katie was sure he'd have had no trouble placing her at all.

"At Memorial," she politely replied. Seated between him and Mike at the table of eight, she rearranged her asparagus, pretending to look as if she, too, was enjoying what was probably a delicious dinner. "I'm on the cardiac floor."

"I knew you looked familiar." Chewing thoughtfully on chicken, crab and béarnaise, he stabbed the air with his empty fork. "I remember. You work day shift. Right?"

"Right."

"Of course, I'm right," he insisted, going for the crab again. "I know exactly who you are now. You're one of the efficient ones.

"Murleen," he mumbled, oblivious to Katie's surprise at the compliment as he nudged the woman seated to his left. "Did you know Randy Sheppard's daughter works at Memorial? She takes care of some of my patients."

Mrs. Aniston, a matronly woman in billowing black taffeta, turned her attention from Dr. MacAllister. "I know, dear. Dr. Brennan mentioned it when she was introduced. Maggie, Gwen and I had a delightful conversation with her while you men were discussing arterial plaque.

"Speaking of which..." Her voice trailed off meaningfully as she frowned at his plate. "Stay away from the crab and the sauce and eat your vegetables. You're a cardiologist, Clark. How do you expect your patients to watch their cholesterol when you won't watch yours?"

Mrs. Aniston cast a beneficent smile at Katie and returned her attention to the discussion her husband had just joined. Gwen Chapman, the forty-something wife of Dr. Samuel Chapman, and Dr. Chapman himself, a pleasant, wiry fellow with a receding hairline and silver-rimmed glasses, were laughing at something Dr. MacAllister had said to Mike. Finally turning his own attention back to his chief of staff, Dr. Aniston dutifully traded another bite of crab for a baby carrot.

If there was anything redeeming about the evening, it was seeing the usually overbearing Dr. Aniston with his wife. The woman easily matched his five-foot-eight-inch height, but she had to outweigh him by thirty pounds, a difference that might have seemed less disproportionate had she not been wearing huge, puffed sleeves. He deferred to the woman as if she were either adored or feared, something Katie would have found as amusing as she did interesting, had she been in a mood to feel amused at all.

The topic under discussion was the large number of doctors and nurses at Memorial who were natives of Honeygrove. It had been Maggie MacAllister's observation about Katie being a native—and who her parents were—that had elicited Dr. Aniston's question to Katie moments ago.

The man didn't seem willing to let the subject of her father go, either.

"Does Dr. Sheppard send any patients to Memorial?"

"Most of his go to Children's," Dr. MacAllister replied, speaking of another hospital not far away. "He uses us for his adolescent orthopedics, but we don't see him that often."

"Tell me," Dr. Aniston continued, turning to Katie. "With Randy Sheppard for a father, how is it that you didn't become a doctor yourself? Did you try medical school?"

"Clark, really," Mrs. Aniston scolded under her breath.

"No, I didn't," Katie replied with an ease that totally belied her discomfort with the subject. She'd never even considered medical school. With her father's prominent reputation, she would have lived her life constantly in his shadow. In some ways, she did anyhow. "Nursing appealed to me more."

Another carrot was skewered. "I'll bet he tried to talk you into medical school, though."

"Not really." Her father had actually talked more to Mike about Mike's aspirations than he ever had hers. Wondering as she often had if her father would have shown more interest in her if she'd been a son instead of a daughter, she murmured, "The choice was mine." With a little nudging from my friends, she had to silently add. It had actually been Dana and Lee who'd talked her into nursing school. They'd insisted she was a "natural."

"And an excellent choice it was." The rescue came from Mike. "Her other option was to be an astronaut, but she doesn't like to fly. She gets airsick."

"I can see where that would pose a problem." Mrs. MacAllister offered the observation with a smile. "So, did you always plan on coming back to Honeygrove after nursing school?" she asked, returning the conversation to its former topic.

"Always. I can't imagine living anywhere else."

"That's what our son says. He's moving back here next month, you know. It'll be so good to have him close again. And having him on staff will be such a pleasure for his father."

It won't be a pleasure for Dana, Katie thought, keeping her smile frozen in place. Trevor MacAllister might be a terrific surgeon and his parents might be delighted to have him home, but he had exercised his considerable charm on Dana in high school, then totally trashed her reputation. Ever since Dana had heard he was coming back, she'd been making noises about a transfer.

"It is a wonderful place to settle down, isn't it?" Maggie went on, oblivious to the pain her son had caused. "Perfect for raising a family. I'm sure that's why the young people return. Don't you think, Dr. Brennan?"

"It's probably one of them." With the grace of a man not easily cornered, he gave her a disarming smile. "But I don't think that's its only appeal. We have the river for sailing and windsurfing in the summer. We're only a couple of hours to skiing in one direction and an hour and a half to the beach in the other. We have great medical facilities, a high school football team that's always in the finals." The crease at the side of his mouth deepened with his obvious affection for the place. "There are a lot of reasons why a person would want to come back here to live."

"But isn't having a family something you think about?"

"Actually, no." Despite the obviousness of the woman's question, Mike remained remarkably at ease. "I barely have time to take advantage of the river or the mountains or the beach."

"But that's only right now." With a dismissing wave, her speculative glance shifted to Katie, who'd just slowly set down her fork. "Once you get yourself established, you'll have far more time...."

Dr. MacAllister laid his hand over his wife's.

"I'm not sure what it is," he said to Mike, "but women seem convinced that people just aren't happy unless they're married and going to Little League. You're the only bachelor at this table. That makes you fair game." He gave his wife an affectionate smile. "Leave him alone, Maggie. He's a busy man.

"Speaking of which," he continued, deftly changing the subject as he reached for his wine. "We have a toast in order here.

"To Dr. Brennan," he declared, after everyone had picked up their glasses, "and his presentation at the cardiovascular conference in Seattle next week. His work is brilliant, but it would have taken the world far longer to discover it if it hadn't been for me."

Dutiful chuckles accompanied the clinks of crystal, along with murmurs of congratulations and well wishes. Katie raised her water glass, her smile a ghost of what it had been when she'd first heard Mike's news. It was inevitable that someone would bring up his presentation, but all it had done was remind her that Mike no longer wanted her help. Between that and his very decisive response to Mrs. MacAllister's question about family, she was amazed she managed a smile at all.

She was thinking that the evening had turned into little more than an exercise in stress management when the orchestra geared up for dancing. They made it halfway through dessert and coffee before Dr. Chapman asked his wife to join him on the floor. Dr. Aniston, not to be outshone, held his hand out to his wife and escorted her off to the rustle of heavy taffeta.

"Well, Doctor," Dr. MacAllister said to Mike as he rose and pulled out his wife's chair. "I suppose we'd best join them. Save one for me, Katie."

There was no graceful way for them to refuse. But Mike was fairly certain Katie was trying to think of a way to do just that when he turned to find her reluctantly removing her napkin from her lap.

He doubted anyone who'd met her tonight had a clue that she was strung tight as a bow. She'd charmed the partners in his practice when he'd introduced her to them earlier, and she'd held up her end of the conversation beautifully during dinner. She hadn't even flinched when Dr. Aniston had stepped on the emotionally sore issue of her father. But her usual animation was history, and the tension between the two of them suddenly seemed thick enough to cut with a scalpel.

"This won't last much longer." He pulled her chair out, taking her hand rather than offering his. "I promise."

By "this" Katie thought that he meant the evening. But the edge in his voice robbed her of any certainty. She wasn't sure of much of anything where Mike was concerned anymore. The sense of command he exuded at the hospital, his tendency to simply take over, had never slipped into their personal dealings before. They did just then, however. He didn't guide her through the tables to the floor with his hand politely at her back. He led her there by the hand, refusing her any chance to think about whether or not she wanted to dance with him.

Or maybe, she thought when they reached the floor, his decisiveness was simply a way to keep himself from balking. The orchestra had just started the chorus of "Strangers in the Night" when he slipped his arm around her waist and drew her toward him.

The feel of his big, hard body seared her from her breasts to her knees.

"We're just going to dance, Katie." His voice was a tight whisper, a feathery brush of warm breath against the pulse pounding in her ear. "Relax."

With his muscular thigh flexing against hers, she'd have had a better chance of relaxing in an electric chair. But the censure in his tone had her consciously dropping her shoulders and untensing her arms.

"That's better," he murmured, easing her into the slow rhythm of the music. "I figure we have to stick around for an hour or so, then we can leave. Can you manage that?"

"I think Dr. MacAllister regards you as his guest of honor tonight. We'll stay as long as you need."

The heels she wore made her taller. When he'd held her before, the top of her head had just reached his chin. Now, she barely had to tip her head to meet his eyes.

For a moment, he said nothing. He just let his hooded glance stray over her face, the chiseled lines of his features totally unreadable. Behind her, all around her, couples swayed and turned, the music underscoring conversations and muffled laughter. They were moving, too. Barely.

"If you want to say good-night to your parents before we leave, you might want to do it soon."

"Even if we could find them, it's not necessary." She could feel his hipbone against her stomach, his thigh brushing hers. Without thinking, her arm inched higher on his shoulder, bringing her closer still. "Mom isn't expecting it and Dad won't care. Is there anyone you need to see?"

"I think I covered all my bases earlier," he said, preparing to challenge her statement about her dad. The feel of her body flowing toward his vaporized the thought as soon as it formed. Breathing her scent, wondering what she had on under the gown—it was all he could do to concentrate. The black velvet was so soft it begged to be touched. Like her skin. Her hair. "Once we leave the table, if we don't make eye contact with anyone, we should be safe."

"We sound like we're desperate to escape."

"Aren't we?" Steeling himself, he nudged her closer, picking up their pace so they could dance and talk without being overheard. His breath ruffled a curl near her ear. "Two more minutes of Aniston's theory on the moral decline of the country, or Mrs. MacAllister's veiled remarks about how man wasn't meant to live alone, and I'll be begging for a lobotomy."

"She means well. Family is important to her, so she thinks it should be for everyone."

"It is important," he muttered, nodding to Dr. Claire Griffen as she spun by with her date. "I just don't know that I need one of my own."

He spoke easily, the conclusion sounding no more important to him than the need to buy stools for the breakfast bar in his kitchen.

"Ever?"

"I won't say ever. I just can't see it in the near future." He gave a mirthless chuckle. "Or the distant future, for that matter."

Katie lowered her head, everything disappearing from view but the fine black fabric of his tuxedo jacket. Her voice, already quiet, lowered even more. "I didn't realize Marla had hurt you that much. I'm really sorry, Mike."

Her words, like the sympathy they conveyed, set him aback.

"Hurt has nothing to do with it, Katie. Not everyone wants what Mrs. MacAllister does. What *you* want," he emphasized, because he knew how badly Katie wanted children someday. Even as a child herself, she'd been in her element baby-sitting his little brother and the other kids in the neighborhood. He was pretty sure, too, that one of the reasons she worked at the free clinic was so she could hold the babies when their moms brought them in.

"It's not that I don't like children," he defended. "You know I'm crazy about my brother's kids. I just don't feel the need to commit to any more obligations. I don't see how I could even if I wanted to. Despite what everyone else seems to think, I'm happy with my life just the way it is."

There was enough defense in his tone for even Mike to question the conviction. But that defense was there because he was tired of everyone from his office manager to his mom and Katie trying to fix his life for him. He was fine with what he had. With the invitation to the conference, what he had was better than fine. In fact, as far as he was concerned, the only problem in his life was the woman in his arms.

If he could just move beyond the fact that their bodies seemed made for each other and get his old friend back, even that part of his life would be all right. He hadn't wanted to risk his relationship with her by pushing for something she didn't want. But he didn't want to go on this way any longer, either. Their relationship was *already* in trouble, and she seemed no more happy than he was. The fact that their bodies did fit so well wasn't something he could ignore, either. His own body wouldn't allow it.

"Sorry," he murmured, wishing to heaven that he knew what was going through her mind. Torn between pleasure and torture at the feel of her moving with him, he pulled her a little closer. "I didn't mean to take that out on you."

Katie's soft, "It's okay," was barely a whisper. Under the circumstances, it was the best she could manage. She knew he was just unloading on her in a way that he couldn't with their dinner companions. And there had been a time when she'd have thought nothing more of his claims than how incredibly sad it was that he was denying himself so much.

She still felt that sadness. Only it felt far more personal now. He didn't need, nor did he want, anything in his life that he didn't already have. He couldn't have made that any clearer if he'd written it out on a banner and strung it across the room. No matter how much she wanted to believe everything would be all right between the two of them, what he'd just said proved it might well never be.

She hadn't realized how easily she'd settled into his arms until she let her hand slip from his shoulder. Despite the warmth low in her stomach, or perhaps because of it, her body had fitted itself to his, her movements effortless as she'd followed his lead. Now, with his arms feeling a little too necessary, she had to back away. If sleeping together had stressed their relationship, she couldn't bear the thought of what would happen if that test in her bathroom turned out positive.

"Katie? What's the matter?"

All she could think to say was, "The music stopped."

The last strains of the piece were fading even as she spoke. But Mike was dead certain it hadn't been the end of the music that had pulled her out of his arms. Baffled by why she suddenly looked so lost, he stepped closer. His hand settled on her shoulder. "Do you want to leave now?"

She looked as if she wanted nothing more. He even thought that was what she was going to say when someone's beeper went off, causing half the people around them to start patting at their pockets.

"The next one's mine, Dr. Brennan." Dr. MacAllister's voice came from behind Katie. "And you may dance with my bride. Who, by the way,'' he added, winking at his wife as Mike reluctantly broke contact with the subdued woman stepping back from him, ''has promised not to ask anything too personal.''

Well versed in keeping up appearances, since she'd done it all her life, Katie gathered her composure around her like a cloak and graciously accepted Dr. MacAllister's hand. Offering his own hand to an extremely curious Mrs. MacAllister, Mike watched the younger woman charm his chief of staff with her soft smile.

"Lovely girl, isn't she?" Maggie MacAllister asked, a speculative twinkle in her eyes.

"Yes. She is."

"I know you're old friends, but you two make a very nice-looking couple."

He didn't know how he was supposed to reply to that. So he just said, "Thanks," and thwarted her fishing expedition by asking when her son was to start at Memorial. Yet, even as they talked, his thoughts remained on Katie.

He wasn't sure why she'd gone so still and so silent moments ago. He didn't even know if she'd have told him had he pressed. He didn't know, either, why she'd become so quiet during dinner when his study had been mentioned. But enough was enough. When presented with a problem, he diagnosed it and fixed it if he possibly could. He did not ignore it, hoping it would go away.

No, he and Katie needed to talk. Tonight.

It was nearly midnight when Mike finally climbed behind the wheel of his black Lexus and the valet closed Katie's door. Slipping the sleek car into gear, he guided it from beneath the brightly lit portico into the dark and the rain. The rhythmic slap of windshield wipers underscored the rush of air from the heater and the defrosters.

Those droning, constant sounds did nothing but intensify the silence stretching between them.

"I owe you big-time for this one, Katie."

She turned from her window. "You don't owe me anything."

"Sure I do. You were miserable in there, but you stuck it out. Considering how uptight we've been with each other lately, I'd say you went above and beyond this time."

The lights from the dashboard provided only enough illumination to see shapes and shadows. Glancing at her profile to check her reaction, he caught the glint of an earring when she looked down at her lap.

He bit back a sigh. "That won't work. Ignoring what happened isn't going to make it go away." The frown in his brow revealed itself in his voice. "You won't even acknowledge how messed up things are getting, will you? And they are messed up," he said before she could deny it. "You can't even be happy for me anymore."

Katie blinked at him in the flash of passing streetlights. Though all she could see was the tense set of his shadowed profile, it was enormously apparent he had as much preying on his mind as she did on hers.

"What are you talking about? My not being happy for you, I mean."

"My study."

"I am pleased for you about that." She shook her head, at a loss. Of everything that seemed to be changing between them, her pride and pleasure over the acceptance of his work was definitely not one of them. "What makes you think I'm not?"

"Katie," he said patiently. "I've known you forever. I think I can read your expressions by now. When Dr. MacAllister offered that toast, you couldn't have looked more unenthused if you'd tried."

"If I looked unenthused," she replied, not sure she liked

being read so easily, "it's because I thought you wanted me to help you with the data."

There was more defeat in the admission than she'd intended, along with something that sounded suspiciously like hurt. Hating that it was there, afraid of what it might reveal, she did what she always did when something stung and tried to convince herself it simply did not matter.

She was still working on it when she heard his heavy sigh.

"Do you know why I haven't asked you to help me with that paper? I haven't asked," he continued, his voice a low rumble of resignation, "because I didn't want to listen to you make up excuses about why you couldn't come over. I didn't think you'd want to be alone with me."

His last remark brought her head up again. All along, she'd been thinking he didn't want to be alone with her. "I told you I'd help you," she murmured.

"I know you did. But that was before we slept together. Nothing's been the same with us since."

Katie's mouth was open, ready to counter whatever excuse he'd deigned to offer. She promptly closed it, and turned her glance to her own side of the windshield. With his quietly spoken conclusion echoing in the air, she had no defense at all.

"We can't ignore it anymore, Katie. Not talking about it isn't working. Pretending it didn't happen isn't working, either." His hand clenched on the wheel, the tension there echoed in the smoky tones of his voice. "I can't even figure out whether or not you want me to touch you."

They were even. She couldn't figure it out, either.

He didn't seem to expect a response, anyway. He cast a glance toward her, his expression unreadable, then returned his attention to the road.

It was only a matter of minutes before he pulled up to the curb in front of her duplex. He killed the engine, leaving them in a silence so heavy it seemed to press the oxygen out of the air. Even the rain had stopped, robbing them of its beat on the roof. The only sound Katie heard was the anxious beat of her heart in her ears and the bark of a neighbor's dog. After a moment even the dog fell silent.

Unlatching her seatbelt, she watched Mike reach toward the dashboard. He hesitated, his arm outstretched, then he turned off the car's lights. Though his expression was shadowed, it was easy to see he was making no move to get out.

Unhooking his own seat belt, he angled his big body toward her.

"Answer one question for me."

"If I can."

"You can," he assured her, his glance moving slowly over her face. "And no evading."

She pulled a breath, then blew it out. "What's the question?"

"Are you uncomfortable with me because you're embarrassed about what happened, or because you can't forget about it?"

No evading, he'd said. But he didn't say she couldn't hesitate. "Both," she finally replied.

"Okay," he murmured, his voice growing quieter with her admission. "Then let's deal with the embarrassment factor. Is it as bad now as it was at first?"

Thinking he sounded as if he were going through a checklist to diagnose a defect, she shook her head. "Not quite."

"What about the other? The not being able to forget part." The deep tone of his voice turned velvet soft. "Is it on your mind a little less every day, or a little more?"

In the shadows, he watched her lift her glance from his

shirt. Her eyes glittered in the dim light, and her skin looked as pale as marble.

"Yeah," he agreed, hearing the answer in her silence. "It's on my mind all the time, too."

It seemed natural to touch her, necessary in a way he didn't care to question. That was why he didn't stop himself when he reached to tuck her hair behind her ear. If she pulled back, if she stiffened, he might have reconsidered what he was about to propose. But she made no attempt to break the contact.

"Maybe we should just give it more time," she suggested quietly.

"Until what? We've stopped speaking to each other? We've tried your way and it hasn't worked."

"I know," she conceded. "I just don't know what else to do."

"Try mine."

There was no mistaking the possession in his touch when he cupped her jaw in his hand and tipped her face to his. It had been possession she'd felt when he'd skimmed his hands over nearly every inch of her flesh, and it had been possession he'd claimed when he'd stripped her to her soul and entered her body.

With her eyes locked on his, it was that knowledge charging the air between them. The thought that he wanted to capitalize on the claim he'd staked shook Katie to her core.

He brushed his mouth over hers, the caress so light it felt like the touch of satin on silk. It amazed her how something that looked so sculpted and hard could be so incredibly soft. He did it again, the sensations he elicited sending signals through her body that had her melting in some places, tensing in others. He'd made love with her only once, yet he had her body responding to his as if they'd been lovers forever.

"See," he whispered, the faint sound vibrating against her cheek as he traced a path to her ear. "It's working already." He slipped one hand inside her coat and drew his hand from her waist to her breast. Her nipple bloomed shamelessly against his palm. "We want each other, Katie. We know each other. If we're careful, there's no reason we shouldn't take up where we left off a few weeks ago."

His mouth brushed hers again, the tenderness of his kiss seducing her as surely as the carefully banked hunger behind it. He wasn't going to put any demands on her that she didn't want. And he wasn't going to let himself lose control with her again. He couldn't have made that more apparent had he tried. But his words echoed in her head, tearing at her heart, and when she found herself thinking she didn't want him exercising control with her, she grabbed hold of what little good sense she still possessed and turned her head away.

Fisting her fingers in the fabric of his jacket, she pushed herself back. She was scared to death of losing her friend. And she wanted him more than anything she'd ever wanted in her life. But not the way he was proposing.

"Being careful isn't always enough." If it were, she wouldn't have a pregnancy test sitting in her bathroom at that very moment. "And I won't sleep with you just because we don't have anyone else."

"It wouldn't be like that," he said, stopping her when she turned away.

"It would be exactly like that," she countered, weary, disappointed. Hurt. And when it was over, she thought, they'd be left with nothing.

"It's late," she whispered, before she reached blindly for the door handle. "You don't have to walk me to the door." Catching his arm when he started to get out anyway, she managed what almost passed for a smile. "I'm not a real date, remember?"

She had the door open and was halfway up the walk before Mike could decide whether or not to follow her. By the time he sank back in his seat, she'd opened her front door, slipped inside and turned out the light.

There was something wrong. Something more than just the mess their relationship had turned into. He wasn't certain how he knew that. He just did. The same way he sometimes knew that he couldn't believe the results of tests just because they were pointing toward a particular diagnosis. It was an instinct he'd learned to trust implicitly over the years.

He looked down at his hands, feeling as if something precious was slipping through them, and finally reached for the ignition. He knew now why she'd wanted to pretend nothing had happened. There was nothing to say that didn't just make the situation worse.

Chapter Eight

"Should I keep these or toss 'em? Toss 'em? Fine."

A pair of jeans that had never fit well but had been a heck of a buy landed on the pile of clothing on Katie's bed.

"How about these?" She held up a pair of pants that had never gone with anything, not sure why she'd bought them, either. "Should they go, too?"

The white cat with the Halloween colors marking his back lay curled like a spoiled sultan on her pillow. He eyed the pants with disdain.

"Good decision."

The pants joined the pile. So did a half-dozen shirts, a jacket she'd worn to death and an assortment of belts, purses and shoes that should have been culled years ago. She rarely got rid of anything. Her old Girl Scout badge sash was stowed in a box on the shelf above her collection of dead corsages and every letter and birthday card she'd

ever received. She had her grade school set of encyclo-
pedias and mementos from vacations up there, too—which
was why there was no room for anything else in her closet.
But this cleaning was symbolic. She'd started it at 6:00
a.m. because she hadn't been able to go back to sleep.
Two hours later, she was still at it.

"Have a slipper," she said to Spike, tossing him a mate-
less, pink bunny-bootie to bat around.

Spike's ears immediately perked up, but he ignored the
offering that landed on the white eyelet comforter. Green
eyes alert, he sprang from a coil to leap onto the floor.
One more surge of feline muscle and he was perched on
her windowsill, his dark tail slowly swaying.

Katie had barely turned to see what had caught his attention when she heard a car door close. The sharp report
hit her like a jolt to the chest. She'd opened the eyelet
curtains to let in the morning light. Between the open slats
of her blue miniblinds, she could see the front fender of a
black sedan.

Catching a glimpse of herself in her dresser mirror, she
shoved her hopeless hair back from her face and tugged
at the stretched-out neckline of her baggy gray sweats. It
was totally unfair of Mike to show up when she looked
like the aftermath of a storm. Especially when, inside, she
felt the same way.

When she opened the front door to let him in, she noticed he looked only marginally better than she did.

"Morning," he murmured, a mountain of hesitation in
a cabled burgundy sweater and jeans. He had a shaving
nick on his jaw, and his hair looked as if he'd combed it
with his fingers a dozen times on the way over. "I come
bearing bagels."

He held up a sack, his blue eyes steady on hers. Even
in an uncertain situation, he exuded confidence. She used
to admire that about him, tried to fake it herself. Faced

with his quiet determination as he stepped inside, she simply found it unsettling.

Preferring he didn't know that, she closed the door and turned her attention to the cat mauling her shirt to get down.

"I wasn't expecting you."

"I know."

Without waiting for an invitation, he headed for her kitchen, tension radiating from him in waves as his glance moved from the boxes by her open front closet to the tennis rackets, hand weights and collapsible rowing machine between her dining table and the sofa.

"I would have called, but I didn't want to give you a chance to come up with an excuse not to see me." Paper rustled as he set the sack on the table. "What are you doing?"

His frown darted to the hallway and the mess visible on the end of her bed. The narrow slash of black velvet she'd worn last night hung on her bedroom door. Next to the door was another box. "Are you moving?"

Had Katie not been so busy trying to figure out why he'd shown up so early, she might have paid more attention to the concern behind the question. She wasn't into subtleties at the moment. All she could consider as his agitation crept toward her, was that less than nine hours ago, he'd made it quite clear that he wouldn't mind a little sex along with their friendship.

"I'm just cleaning," she replied, still shaken by his very practical logic. They wanted each other. They liked each other.

She was convenient.

He hadn't exactly said that last one, but the implication had been there. With her, he wouldn't have to go through the dating routine, the hassle of getting to know someone.

He didn't want a real relationship. How many times had he told her that?

"I figured it was time I started doing some of the things I said I want to do instead of just talking about them. Cleaning closets was on my list of New Year's resolutions."

"This year's, or last?"

"This."

She hadn't even tried to smile.

Neither had Mike. He stood six feet away, his jaw working as he studied her face. When Katie was under strain, the natural blush faded from her cheeks and shadows beneath her eyes dimmed their usual spark. He'd always been able to tell how good or bad things were with her simply by looking at her. He'd never consciously considered that before. But he did now. And from the shadows marring her translucent skin as she began fiddling with the fringe on a sofa pillow, he doubted she'd slept well lately at all.

Being careful isn't always enough.

Her softly spoken words still echoed in his head. He'd been staring at his bedroom ceiling, trying to figure out just where he stood with her, when those words had first drifted into his thoughts. Piling on top of them like cars of a crashing train were thoughts of how preoccupied she'd seemed most of the evening, how she'd declined anything alcoholic to drink, her strange silence after he'd unloaded on her about wanting his life to stay as it was.

He'd sat bolt upright, feeling as if he'd been kicked in the gut. The same feeling was there now as he walked over to where she continued fussing with the fringe.

He started to touch her, partly to make her look at him, partly because he ached for the contact. Not trusting the latter, he kept his hands to himself.

"Katie?" he began, his voice raw. "Are you pregnant?"

Her head snapped up. "No." The denial came too quickly for the question to have surprised her. "No," she repeated, abandoning the pillow to cross her arms tightly beneath her breasts.

"I thought I might be. I'd had that sore throat, and antibiotics can interfere with birth control pills," she explained, figuring he could fill in the blanks in her explanation. "But I took a test last night." She hugged herself tighter. "It was negative."

Expert that he was at concealing his thoughts, she couldn't begin to read Mike's reaction. And her own had thrown her completely. She'd expected to feel relieved by the results as she'd stood in her bathroom staring at the little white stick that had come in the box. But what she'd felt hadn't been relief at all. Just the possibility that she could have been pregnant had fully awakened the yearning she'd always had for a child. That the child could have been Mike's only compounded the totally unexpected, totally irrational sense of loss that filled her even now.

Rational or not, the disappointment had left a void she could almost hate him for creating.

Staring at the toes of her socks, she forced a disbelieving little laugh. "I can't believe how disappointed I am over something that would have totally upended both of our lives. But being realistic, we're lucky we didn't get caught. We were never meant to be lovers," she continued, her voice softening with regret. "We have too many differences."

"We didn't have them before."

"Sure we did. They just didn't matter."

She thought it odd that he still looked every bit as tense as he had when he'd arrived. She'd told him he was off the hook. Yet, there was no mistaking his disquiet as his glance moved over her face, and settled below her crossed arms.

The handsome lines of his face were devoid of expression, his thoughts shuttered as he drew a deep breath and slowly let it out.

His glance flicked back to hers. "What would you have done had the result been positive?"

The quiet question knitted her brow. "What difference does it make? It wasn't."

"Humor me. What would you have done had you been pregnant?"

"The only thing I could do," she replied, wondering what alternatives he thought there were for someone who'd picked out her children's names when she was ten. "I'd have had the baby."

"Then what?"

"I don't know what you want, Mike. There isn't any point—"

"Just answer me. You'd have had the baby. Then what?"

"If you're asking if I would have expected anything from you, the answer is no. You don't want a family. I do. I'd have raised it by myself." She lifted one hand as if to ask what other reasonable alternative she would have had, and immediately crossed her arms again. "I didn't let myself think about it beyond that."

It seemed to him that she'd thought it through well enough. "You surprise me," he said mildly, wondering at how little she must think of him. He might not have sought such a commitment, but he'd never turn his back on his own child, let alone on her. "You're the one who blames her dad for never being around, yet you'd deliberately deprive a child of his father."

"There's a difference between depriving a child of your time and protecting him from being hurt." They were talking hypotheticals. Katie forcibly reminded herself of that even as his veiled attack fed the knot in her stomach. "You said yourself you don't have time for any more commitments. You're a doctor, Mike. Half the time even your free time isn't your own. And most of your free time," she pointed out, "you spend on clinical research. You don't have any more time for a child than he did."

"Are you saying I'm like your father?"

Something had shifted. Katie wasn't sure what it was, but she suddenly felt as if she were standing on an ice floe with a giant crack racing toward her, not knowing which way to jump. As much as Mike admired her father, it would hardly be an insult to admit there were a few similarities between the men. Dedication. A love of medicine. Veiled dispassion in his dealings with certain people. But Mike also knew how much distance there was between sire and offspring.

It was the distance between her and Mike that concerned Katie, though. Like the crack in that floe, it seemed to be growing wider by the second.

"I don't know why we're even discussing this," she said, wishing desperately for the ease with him that she could scarcely remember. "We're talking about a situation that doesn't exist and things that don't matter."

"You said they do now."

"What matters is that we want different things. The rest of it would only make a difference if we were involved with each other. But we can't be. Not that way," she said, her eyes begging him to understand. She couldn't invest herself like that, then just walk away when it was over. And it would be over, too. Sooner or later. She needed more than a strained friendship and incredible sex from him. She wanted the family he didn't seem to need and the commitment he didn't want. She needed the whole package. He only wanted parts.

He held her glance while he reached to the back of the sofa to scratch Spike behind his pointed little ears. The gesture was deceptive in its ease. As he considered what she'd said, defensiveness stole over him like a shadow.

"You're right," he finally said, the simple phrase somehow encompassing everything she'd said. "This isn't getting us anywhere."

He blew a breath, looking very much as if he wished he'd never raised his questions. Or, perhaps, his wish was that he hadn't pushed for the answers. "I'm sorry. About all of it. About last night, and about what happened a few weeks ago. We both know it was a mistake." Shoving his hand into his pocket for his keys, he headed across the room. "I promise, it won't happen again."

She whirled around to follow him, the need to protect herself colliding with the need to keep him from slamming the door between them. "Mike, please. You were the one who said we should be able to figure out a way around all this. We just need to…"

"To what?" he prodded, when her voice trailed off. "Fix it?"

"Yes."

"How?"

At the demand, she went silent. Her delicate features were shadowed with the same sense of hopelessness he felt. She had no answers.

He had only one. "I think on this particular consultation we'll have to go with your first course of treatment. The only one I could come up with nearly killed the patient."

His dark head dipped toward the mess behind her. "I'll let you get back to your cleaning," he said, the corner of his mouth twitching in a parody of a smile. "You don't want to lose your momentum."

Avoiding Katie's eyes, he looked back to make sure the cat stayed put and let himself out. He'd known exactly what he wanted when he'd walked up to the door. Answers. Well, he had them. In spades.

She wasn't pregnant. There were thanks to be offered for that, he was sure. And gratitude to the patron saint of disastrous complications, whoever she was, sat high on his list at the moment. So did relief. As alienated as he and Katie were becoming, he couldn't imagine the pressure a pregnancy would put on their relationship. Yet the thought that Katie could have been carrying his child had caused him to feel something far less definable than relief or gratitude.

Taunted by the feeling now, he deliberately blocked it. He'd wanted her in his bed, as well as in his life, but it was as clear as a specimen slide that a physical relationship with him held no interest for her at all.

Wanting to think the hurt in his chest was only a bruised ego, he felt another bolt of self-protection kick into place. He had his paper to finish and then he had the rest of the afternoon free. He would ignore the fact that he'd wanted to spend it with Katie.

"I knew I should have stayed in bed this morning. I can't believe I did this. He thinks I'm an idiot."

Jan, the thirty-something nurse who'd turned the staff green with her pictures of Hawaii, peeled off her gloves, her waist-length auburn hair flying as she hurried past the nurses' station.

"What's that all about?" Alice wondered aloud.

From the computer behind the counter, Katie swallowed her own agitation and watched Alice's ebony eyes narrow behind her glasses. The frames were pumpkin orange today. So was her pantsuit.

Having noticed the other nurse's distress herself, Katie cleared the screen. "I'll go see."

Jan was headed for the med room.

Holding the bell of her hot pink stethoscope so it

wouldn't bounce, Katie jogged up behind her. "Are you okay?"

"I've only assisted with that procedure once before," the distraught nurse stressed, still hurrying. "It's not like we have the same kind of experience up here that they do downstairs. But he made it clear he didn't want me back in there after I get him another setup. He looked at me as if I didn't have an active cell in my brain."

"Dr. Aniston?"

"Dr. Brennan."

"Mike?"

"He's in 306 putting in a central line."

"Why's he upset with you?"

"I contaminated his field."

Ouch, Katie thought, rounding the corner into the med room behind Jan. "That might frustrate him a little, but Dr. Brennan doesn't get upset about—"

"I did it twice."

Grabbing the phone, the pretty young nurse punched the number for Central Supply and ordered another central line tray. Stat. A supply runner would have it there in two minutes, but when a surgeon was standing at a patient's bedside waiting for something that should already be there, those two minutes could feel like eternity.

"He needs another pair of sterile gloves, too. After my hair brushed the tray, I bumped his glove with mine."

Katie eyed the fabulous length of enviably straight hair cascading down the back of the woman's blue scrub top. Jan always wore it clipped back from her cherubic face and, usually, well out of the way. But Katie had seen it slide from her shoulder sometimes when the woman bent over, and she could easily imagine it causing a problem if the sterile field was over a hospital bed. There were reasons operating tables were narrow, just as there were reasons surgical personnel covered their hair and their bodies with caps and gowns. They didn't perform that many sterile procedures in the unit. Still, it didn't matter if only one strand had touched the corner of only one instrument. Contaminated was just that.

"My tray should be up by the time I give him these."

Jan headed into the hall with the gloves in her pocket and her hands twisting her heavy hair into a knot so she could drop it down the back of her top.

From the med room door, Katie watched her disappear into the room halfway down the long hall. Fifteen seconds later, just as Katie returned to the computer to finish inputting diet changes, Jan was back out, her eyes trained on the floor as she shook her head.

"What?" Katie asked as she hurried past her again.

"I took him a pair of sevens."

"He wears nines."

"I know," she mumbled, skirting a nursing assistant before disappearing into the med room again.

The woman looked as if she were on the verge of tears. Katie had been there herself. There were simply some days when nothing went right, and Jan seemed to be having one of them. Though Katie couldn't imagine Mike deliberately upsetting a nurse, his quiet censure could be devastating.

She should know. She'd been on the receiving end of it herself a while ago.

"Your tray should be here any second. I'll go check on it for you."

The threat of tears mingled with faint hope. "Would you mind taking it in to him? All you have to do is drop it off and go. He said he could do the procedure himself."

To Katie, it was a fair indication of Mike's frustration level—and his lack of confidence in Jan at that point—that he'd sent her packing. For a number of reasons, everything from having the extra pair of hands, to having someone available to get more supplies, a doctor always liked to have a nurse handy when he was performing such a procedure.

No one was more aware of that at the moment than Jan, and it was painfully evident that she'd rather stand naked in a hailstorm than walk back into that room.

Having been in that awful, awkward position herself before, too, Katie snatched a tan packet marked Sterile Gloves Size 9 from a box and gave Jan's shoulder a sympathetic squeeze. She had her own reasons for not wanting to face Mike at the moment, but she murmured, "No problem," and bravely headed into the hall.

The runner was coming through the unit's double doors with the blue cloth-wrapped tray when, seconds later, she left Jan banging her head softly against the med room wall.

Katie truly did not want to deal with Mike just now. After he'd left her yesterday morning, she'd stood motionless in the middle of her living room while the awful ache in her chest caused her throat to burn and her eyes to sting. Had he been any other man, she'd be cutting a berth around him a mile wide. But it wasn't that simple with them. He wasn't willing to give her his heart, but she still wanted him so badly she ached. Another part of her was missing the friend he'd been, and clutching the hope that he wanted their friendship back, too.

That hope, however, had dimmed considerably half an hour ago.

The contact had been so brief it scarcely qualified as an encounter, but his coolness had been unmistakable. Coming out of a patient's room, she'd spotted him on a phone at the nurses' station. He'd looked straight at her as he'd spoken into the mouthpiece. Then, having held her glance long enough for her heart to take a few erratic beats, he'd simply turned away.

The blatant rejection had frozen her in her tracks. Seconds later, she'd returned to the patient's room on the pretext of having forgotten something.

She hadn't seen him since.

"You can leave it and go."

That was exactly what she planned to do. "Here are your gloves."

Mike's head jerked around as she picked up the contaminated setup from the patient's tray table and slid the new one into place. Standing with his back to the door, he hadn't seen who'd come in. He'd just heard the squeak of soft soles on the polished floor.

His expression cooly professional, he took the tan packet she'd set atop the covered tray and tore it open. "I thought you were that other nurse. If you're not tied up right now, I'd appreciate an assist. We're prepped for a central line."

Nothing about his manner indicated that this was Mike talking to Katie. This was a doctor speaking to a nurse. Every bit as professional as he was, Katie put her anxiety on hold and moved to the opposite side of the bed.

As Mike had pointed out, the patient had already been prepped. The emaciated gentleman with the tufts of silver hair surrounding the liver spots on his scalp, lay with his head to the side, his jaw hidden by a sterile blue drape that exposed his neck through a hole, and reached the covered tray table at his waist. The skin visible on his neck was stained orange from the surgical scrub used to clean it and, by now, deadened with an anesthetic.

Mike slipped his hand into the folded cuff of the first sterile glove. Touching only the part that would touch his skin, he pulled it on. "We'll get this done now, Mr. Weineke," he said, lifting his hand so the cuff fell down, covering his wrist. Picking up the other glove with his "clean" hand, he snapped it on and offered a smile that didn't come quite as easy as usual. "I'm sure you'd like to get back to your television show."

Katie glanced toward the silent TV mounted high on the wall. As she opened the blue cloth with a rip of tape and exposed the assortment of instruments and supplies, she couldn't help thinking that the elderly gentleman didn't care whether he got back to the game show or not. He was sick and he clearly felt terrible. From the apprehension in his rheumy eyes, she could tell he was also nervous about what the surgeon was going to do.

Katie offered him a smile of her own as she slipped on her gloves. She would stay "dirty" so she could handle any nonsterile item the doctor might need moved, so she didn't hesitate to rest her hand on the patient's thin, wrinkled arm. The fact that his assigned nurse had just departed under less than ideal circumstances probably hadn't done a whole lot for his comfort level, either.

"I've told Mr. Weineke this won't take long at all." Mike reached toward the tray. "He knows we're putting in this line because all his other intravenous sites are shot."

His deep voice held a wealth of reassurance for the patient, and a verbal nudge for Katie. Some doctors didn't like unnecessary conversation when they worked. Others, like Mike, understood the value of letting certain patients know what was going on.

"That means no more poking in your arms for a vein," she elaborated, promptly picking up the cue to focus on whatever positives she could find for the man. "And no more blood draws. We can get them out of your new line."

"That's what the other nurse said," the man replied, his voice a rusty warble. "She's a sweet girl."

Reminding herself to pass on the comment to Jan, she murmured, "She's very nice."

"She didn't mean to mess up, you know."

"I'm sure she didn't. She's an excellent nurse." She cast a careful glance at Mike. "She's just not having a very good day."

"Neither is Mr. Weineke," Mike defended. "I'm sure he'd rather be just about anywhere else, doing something other than this." The censure in his voice was mirrored in his tight expression as he peeled open a pack he'd taken from the tray. Whether the other woman was having a bad day or not, he clearly didn't want to hear excuses. "Ready?"

The question was for his patient. But the man didn't answer. He just looked apprehensively at Katie, who calmly met the shuttered expression in the doctor's eyes. Knowing she was not the person to go to bat for Jan, she took Mr. Weineke's hand.

"Hold your head still," she gently reminded him, watching Mike feel for the vein. "You're doing fine."

His features fixed in concentration, Mike deftly inserted a needle long enough to skewer a turkey. Had Mr. Weineke seen the size of it, his anxiety level would have shot through the ceiling.

"You're halfway there already." She gave the cool, bony hand a comforting little squeeze, then waited a beat before telling him that all he needed now was a couple of stitches and he was through.

Her quiet commentary visibly eased the man. He closed his eyes, his breath sighing out as if he'd been holding it forever. He didn't even care that the capped catheter had to be sewn in. As far as he was concerned, the worst was behind him.

Katie wished fervently that it were so for her and the doctor wordlessly placing the neat stitches that would keep the catheter in place. But as she clipped the sutures for him, marveling at the deftness with which his long fingers tied off the delicate filaments, she had the awful feeling that, for the two of them, the rough part was only beginning.

"Mrs. MacAllister called me yesterday afternoon," he informed her when they left the patient's room a few minutes later. Glancing down the hall to make sure no one was within earshot, he motioned her to a stop. The distance she'd sensed in him seemed to increase even as he stepped closer. "She invited us to a reception she's giving for her son."

"Us?"

"She specifically asked me to bring you."

"What did you tell her?"

"I haven't talked to her yet. She left the message on my answering machine." A muscle in his jaw twitched, his bridled tension twining around her like smoke. "I wanted you to know about it before I called her back. I thought if Dr. MacAllister happened to mention it to you and you didn't know the invitation had been extended, it might be kind of awkward. Under the circumstances, I don't think we should go. Not together, anyway."

It seemed that Maggie MacAllister was either thinking of them as a couple already or planning to do a little nudging to see that they became one. It was also as plain as the cafeteria's custard that the last thing they needed was someone trying to push them together.

An orderly moving an empty gurney was threading his way between laundry carts. Taking her arm, Mike nudged her back so the young woman in the blue surgical cap and booties could navigate between the wall and the portable monitor someone had left in the hall. His nearness brought the clean scent of his soap. With that same breath came disturbing memories. But his touch was deliberately businesslike, clearly intended only to get her from point *A* to point *B*. The instant they were out of the way, he pulled back and pushed both his hands into the pockets of his lab coat.

"You're right," she told him, feeding off the defensiveness she could feel radiating from him. The last thing they needed was another evening like the last one. "We probably shouldn't."

"I thought you'd feel that way." He gave her a tight nod, his eyes deliberately avoiding hers as the accusation sunk in. "Thanks for the assist in there."

He turned away without another word, leaving Katie to stare numbly at his retreating back. She didn't know if he was angry with her, annoyed or plain old disgusted. He'd never been any of those things with her before—except for the time she'd borrowed his car when he was home from college and she'd dented the fender, but that was light years from the coolness she sensed in him now. He was almost acting as if she were somehow at fault for the way things were falling apart.

"I know you say you and Dr. Brennan are just friends," Alice said when Katie returned to the nurses' station after Mike had gone, "but you two sure looked intense down there."

Thinking that the last thing she needed was Alice's good-natured nosiness, Katie picked up the list of diet changes she'd been entering in the computer earlier and tapped her ID number out on the keyboard. "We'd just finished with a patient," she hedged, dangling the possibility that they'd been talking about the procedure.

Knowing a false lead when she was tossed one, Alice didn't bite.

"You weren't talking about a patient, honey. When you were standing down there," she said, using the papers in her hand to indicate where Mike had stopped her, "you looked edgy as a doe cornered by a buck." She peered over the top of her orange rims. "You went to that heart thing with him Saturday night, didn't you?"

"What's that got to do with anything?"

"Nothing," she said, sounding dismissing despite the shrewd look in her eyes. "He's just been acting kind of strange around you for nearly a month now, and I've never seen him as short with people as he's been this morning. Now, if he was Dr. Aniston, I'd say his mood was downright pleasant. But that man," she continued, apparently meaning Mike, "isn't himself at all."

"You're losing me, Alice."

"I'll catch you up here in a minute," she assured her, adding more paper to her stack as she rattled on. "And when was the last time you brought in a plate of brownies or banana bread? Or that caramel-fudge torte that adds a pound to each thigh with every bite?"

"I am now officially lost."

Alice rolled her eyes. "You always bake when you're happy, girl. You know that. And since you're always on a diet, you always bring in what you bake for the rest of us to stuff ourselves with. Not lately, though," she said, standing up to take her stack of papers to the copier. "I'd say you haven't been happy in about a month. I'd say the same for Dr. Brennan. If there's nothing going on between the two of you, I'll eat these reports."

"If you need salt, there's some in the lounge."

Alice stopped in her tracks. "You're serious? There's nothing?"

Katie kept her attention on the computer screen. As astute as Alice was, she'd never believe her if she could see her eyes.

"Nothing, Alice. Really."

It was the truth. At that moment she couldn't honestly even say they were friends anymore.

Chapter Nine

The night was cold and breathtakingly clear. Mike stood on his deck, his breath trailing off in a fog as he looked at the glittering sky. He should go inside. Check his answering machine. Unpack. But there was nothing inside except space. Nothing living. Nothing breathing. No plants. No pets. At least out here he could hear the rustle of the trees in the wind, the murmur of the creek that ran through the woods, the distant bark of a dog.

Maybe he should buy a fish.

He shook his head grimly at the thought and looked away from the swath of stars to run his hand over his face. The constellations usually seemed to jump out at him, their patterns immediately emerging from the millions of other stars surrounding them. Tonight, though he'd stood staring for the past five minutes, nothing even registered.

He'd been on a natural high all day. His modest presentation at the conference in Seattle had been well received this morning, and the demonstration surgery he'd performed yesterday had gone flawlessly.

It wasn't often that he allowed himself to feel truly pleased with an accomplishment. Making certain he got his next effort right was more important than relishing a victory or massaging his ego over something he'd already done. In his mind, there was always room for improvement, an edge to be pushed, a different approach to be explored. But he hadn't been able to deny the sense of satisfaction he'd felt when he'd left the conference that afternoon. That ebullient feeling had stayed with him on the plane, and accompanied him on the drive to his house. Then he'd walked in his front door, dropped his bag in the empty entry—and felt the pleasure slowly die.

Not wanting to think about why that was, he'd come outside to enjoy the first clear night he'd seen in ages and wound up thinking, anyway.

He'd actually felt better walking into a strange hotel room.

Shaking off the depressing thought, he left the redwood railing and headed for the sliding glass door behind him, ignoring the telescope he could see in the angled window farther down the deck.

He was a logical man. If he'd been on a natural high, then it followed that what he felt now was nothing more than a natural letdown. He'd been surrounded by the energy of his colleagues for three days. On the way back, the plane had been full, the airport busy. He'd had the radio on in the car so he could catch up on the local news, the chatter continuing to connect him with the outside world. His home was his sanctuary. It was supposed to be quiet.

Overlooking the fact that it wasn't supposed to feel like a tomb, he closed the big sliding door and wandered through the vacant, vaulted space to the kitchen. After staring at the meager contents of his refrigerator—none of which held any appeal—he tossed a frozen dinner in the microwave. It was barely six-thirty in the evening. With his current research project completed and his findings delivered, he no longer had results to study or a paper to write. That gave him plenty of time to return calls, unpack and eat while he checked the status of the patients he'd left in his colleagues' capable care.

It took all of ten minutes for him to link to the hospital's computer and get the information he was after, another five to hang his suits and dump everything else in the laundry hamper. Since his friends, family and office knew he'd been out of town, there were no calls to return. After spending ten minutes flipping through TV channels in his study while he refueled with the meal that tasted pretty much like the cardboard container it had come in, he punched off the electronic diversion and tried to decide if he should call his workout buddy and go to the gym or drop in on his parents. But he'd worked out at the hotel gym that morning, and if he'd intended to see his folks, he should have called before he'd subjected himself to the solitary meal. Feeling oddly restless, he wandered back to the kitchen and dumped the disposable plate in the trash.

Swearing he'd heard the plate echo, he headed back to his office to turn on the stereo—only to find himself stopping on the polished parquet tiles as he passed the empty dining room. A brass chandelier hung from the coffered ceiling—the room's total adornment. He didn't even know if the teardrop-shaped bulbs all worked. He'd had no reason to turn it on. Looking to his right, his glance swept the unhampered expanse of neutral carpet to the vaulting stone fireplace.

The muscle in his jaw twitching, he slowly took in the long, empty planter, the empty niches, the stark white walls. Katie said he needed greenery. She'd said he needed textures and natural colors. He should call in a marker on one of the favors she owed him—or maybe *he* owed *her* by now—and ask her if she wanted to go with...

He cut the thought off even before it completely formed. He'd been doing that a lot over the past couple of weeks. He'd be thinking of something he should tell her, only to remember that her interest would be polite at best. Or thinking he should ask her something, then have to remind himself he needed to keep his distance.

He'd had no choice but to step back from her. As much as he could, anyway. Working together presented a challenge at times, but a veneer of professionalism masked the unease between them at the hospital. He simply wasn't around her otherwise. He felt too constrained talking with her, too conscious of how he had to avoid touching her when they spoke. It had always felt so natural to touch before, even though he hadn't realized how often he'd brushed her arm, her shoulder, her cheek—until he'd stopped. Their relationship had changed, become burdened with the differences between them that truly hadn't mattered before. Before they'd simply enjoyed each other's company. Now, it was easier on them both if he just left her alone. She didn't want him, anyway. Not the way he wanted her.

The unwanted thought was blocked as quickly as it formed. Turning his focus back to the room, his gaze settled on the expanse of bare carpet in front of the fireplace. He didn't know squat about decorating, but he knew what he *didn't* like. And he did know where a couch and coffee table should sit.

There was a furniture store on Willamette Boulevard, an upscale-looking place that probably charged an arm, a leg and a lung for a sofa. He didn't know of any place closer. He had no idea exactly what style he was looking for, either. But even as he denied the empty feeling driving him out of his own home, he was going to find it if it took him the rest of the night. Textures and naturals. How hard could that be?

"'Oatmeal, nutmeg or coffee. Cinnamon or cranberry. I'm looking for a couch. Not stocking my kitchen.' I couldn't believe how frustrated he sounded."

Beth Brennan stood with her back to the crackling fire in the Sheppards' spacious living room. Her chin-length salt-and-pepper hair framed her friendly face, her green eyes dancing as she quoted a conversation she'd had with her oldest son a few evenings ago. The son under discussion was running late for Katie's dad's birthday dinner, but he was due to arrive any minute.

It was that knowledge that made Katie's smile feel a bit stiff.

"He said he ordered oatmeal and nutmeg," she continued to Katie and Trina Holgate, Katie's dad's long-suffering office manager. "I'd called to see how his presentation had gone in Seattle and as soon as he'd said 'fine,' he'd launched into this. I didn't have the heart to tell him that it sounded awfully bland. Anyway, I'm glad he's finally getting some furniture in there. Have you seen it yet?"

Masking her own surprise, Katie shook her head, her curls brushing the shoulders of her bronze wool sheath. She hadn't even known that Mike had bought furniture until she'd brought over a plate of hors d'oeuvres a moment ago.

"No, I haven't," she replied, more interested than she wanted to be. "But it sounds just like what he needed in there." Still holding the plate, since she was circulating it among the guests in the colonial-style room, she started to ask how his speech had gone. But the minute she opened her mouth, so did Tracy Ames.

"A few touches of poppy would help." Tracy, the generously proportioned wife of the Sheppards' accountant, set her glass on the mahogany table beside her and eyed the offerings Katie held. "What sort of fabric did he choose?"

Mrs. Brennan's smile deepened with motherly affection. "He said 'bumpy,' but I suspect it's a popcorn weave, like Berber or something. You know men don't care about that sort of thing." Floral-print silk rustled as she raised her arm to sip her wine. "I never thought I'd see the day he'd go off by himself and do something like that. Now, sporting equipment, a sailboat, a different car—those I could see him buying on impulse. But furniture?"

"Mike bought furniture?" Karen Sheppard, looking as delicate as a hothouse flower in a winter white pantsuit, stepped into the group and smiled at Beth. "You didn't tell me that," she good-naturedly accused, placing her perfectly manicured hand on Katie's arm. "I need to steal my daughter, if you two don't mind. I need her in the dining room.

"Mike just got here," she added, the information intended for the man's mother. "Randy took him to the library to get him a drink. We'll give him time to enjoy it, then sit down to dinner."

Mike was here.

The thought settled like a piece of hot lead in Katie's stomach. Uncharitable as the thought was, she'd really hoped he wouldn't be able to make it.

"You must have been rushed getting here," her mom quietly remarked, her glance targeting the unadorned neckline of Katie's simple, calf-length sheath. "I meant to ask when you arrived. Would you like to borrow a scarf or necklace?"

The intimation that she'd been too hurried to remember to accessorize was her mother's way of softening the suggestion that she looked a bit plain. When Katie had been a girl, her mom had fussed over everything from her piano lessons to her posture and, though she'd backed off considerably after Katie had left home, some habits were definitely hard for her to break.

"Do I *need* a scarf or necklace?"

The gentle emphasis had her mom frowning at herself. "No, I don't suppose you do," she admitted, smoothing the fabric on Katie's shoulder. "I was only thinking of what I would need in something so understated. The clutter would detract from your eyes."

Katie's mouth curved. Her mom would still be fussing in her dotage. "What do you need help with?"

"The Tylers had to cancel. We have to rearrange the table."

Heels tapping on polished hardwood, Karen headed into the formal dining room. Thinking she'd much rather have her mother pointing out a potential fashion faux pas than hinting at her lack of a potential mate, something she'd overheard her bemoaning to Beth in the kitchen, Katie dutifully followed. She was there mainly to assist her mom anyway—as her dad had more or less indicated to one of the guests a few minutes ago.

"It must be nice to have your daughter live in the same town," a woman he'd introduced to her as his partner's domestic associate had said.

"We actually don't see much of her," he'd replied with a benign smile. "But it's nice that she could come tonight and help her mother."

Though Katie didn't exactly feel like a servant, after that, she hadn't felt like a member of the party, either. But then, she'd spent a good many years in this house feeling like a third wheel when her dad was around, anyway.

The long mahogany table was set for twenty with pewter chargers and white china on lace placemats. White tapers in pewter candleholders flanked a bouquet of brightly colored trumpet lilies. Her mother loved to cook and to entertain. And she did both exceptionally well.

Katie was still working on the cooking part.

"Help me pull two of these settings. If we take one from each side and spread the rest out to fill in the space, it'll look fine."

Silverware clattered lightly as a setting was removed. The tinkling sound echoed across the table as Katie did the same.

"I'm not sure what to do about the seating arrangements now," her mom continued, taking the crystal Katie held out to set in the mahogany-and-glass china cabinet behind her. "I'd planned to put you at this end with Mike because I thought you young people would like to visit, but now that Ellen won't be here to separate Joe and Andrew, the two of them will be talking with each other all evening and completely ignoring everyone else. Would you mind if I moved you between them?"

"Not at all," she replied, hoping her relief didn't show as she pulled out the extra chair and began to deftly rearrange the settings. Her mom hadn't a clue that she and Mike were barely speaking. Judging from her conversation with Mrs. Brennan, Mike's mom didn't, either.

Katie's goal was to keep it that way.

Or so she was thinking as she turned to put away the extra chairs.

"Oh, Mike," her mother called. "I'm so glad you could make it. Listen, as long as you're handy, would you mind setting these chairs in the library? Let him do it, Katie," she admonished, motioning for her to put down the chair she'd just picked up. "I need you to bring out the salads."

Mike hadn't exactly been handy. He was on the far side of the long entry hall, passing the dining room door on his way from the library to the living room. But he was close enough. And her mom regarded him as family. As family, he could be pulled in for duty she wouldn't have imposed on another guest.

The rest of the small party remained gathered in the living room, an occasional bark of laughter drifting through the doorway. Katie scarcely noticed. Mike was walking toward them.

He stopped in the doorway, seeming to fill the space with his powerful presence. He had a drink in one hand and his other was falling from where he'd been rubbing the back of his neck. The charcoal suit and collarless white shirt he wore gave him a look of casual elegance. But the tense set of his broad shoulders and the fatigue etched in his attractive features made him look like a man only the foolish or the brave would cross.

It was that dangerous aura that made his effort to be accommodating so obvious. The lines bracketing his lips carved more deeply when the corner of his mouth kicked up in a tight smile. "Be glad to," he said, and strode into the room.

Karen didn't notice that he'd yet to make eye contact with her daughter. Offering her thanks, she turned to the door leading to the kitchen, her mind clearly on her next task.

Taking her cue from her mother, Katie attempted to focus on her next task, too. With Mike moving toward her, the effort was wasted. Or maybe it was what he did that made thinking of anything else impossible.

Halfway across the room, his eyes met hers for a scant second. Deliberately pulling his glance, he raised his drink, ice cubes tinkling as he took a long swallow of the amber liquid. It was almost as if he needed fortification just to be with her.

Stung by the thought, it was all she could do to keep from backing away when he stopped to set the chunky glass on the sideboard. Evidence of a recent encounter with a razor marked the underside of his jaw. Considering that he'd called her mom from the hospital only forty-five minutes ago to tell her he was running late, he must have showered and changed at a dead run.

He'd been in surgery since seven that morning. She knew that because he'd been needed for one of his patients, and another doctor had had to take the call. Based on what she'd overheard another nurse say, he'd been in that same surgery when Katie had left at four.

He picked up the nearest chair.

"Where does she want these?"

"In the library. By the bookcase is probably best. Mike?" she called, causing him to hesitate as he turned away. "Did it go all right?"

What she really wanted to ask was if he was okay. She didn't doubt for a moment that it had been one of those days they'd talked about when it would be nice to turn to each other just to be held. But turning to each other was out of the question. She didn't know if her concern would be welcome or even if she should let it show. It hurt too much when he pushed her away.

"The patient was stable when I left."

She lifted her chin in acknowledgment, but before she could tell him she was glad to hear that, he was on his way out of the room. By the time he'd returned for the other chair, she'd been hauled into the kitchen to play servant.

"I've known you for thirty years, Randy, and you've never taken a real vacation." Andrew Brennan's gravelly voice rumbled the length of the dinner table. A big, barrel of a man, with steel gray hair and the same intense blue eyes he'd passed on to his sons, he was blessed with an easy-going nature and a heart the size of his ancestral Ireland. He was usually pretty laid-back, too, for an attorney.

"Those weekends you joined us and your wife and daughter at the beach don't count," he added, holding up his hand as if to stop a protest. "I'm talking about taking some real time off. You're entering your seventh decade here, buddy. It's time to not only smell the roses, but to think about planting the garden. You'll have retirement coming up here in a few years, you know?"

"If you think he's going to slow down just because he turned sixty, you don't know him at all, Andrew." Karen smiled at her old friend, then at the man she'd been married to for thirty-three years. "As for him ever retiring from his practice, I don't dare even suggest it."

"Good," Marty Heber, the other pediatrician in her dad's practice intoned. Beneath dark slashes of auburn eyebrow, kind hazel eyes sparkled behind preppy, wire-rimmed glasses. "I don't want to have to look for another partner."

Karen's smile slipped a bit. "I do worry about him pushing himself so hard, though."

"Nonsense." Dr. Sheppard frowned at his wife, the expression laced with fond amusement as he tucked his hand beneath his tie and absently rubbed his breastbone. "An interesting job keeps a man young. What would I do if I weren't working?"

"Oh," Karen drawled, "you could travel, play golf, take up a hobby, plant that rose garden Andy mentioned."

"Honey, you're the gardener around here. Inside of a month, I'd be bored to death and underfoot so much that you'd be begging me to go back to the clinic."

Katie was scarcely listening to the banter. Since she wasn't contributing to the conversation and everyone had finished eating, she motioned to her mom for her to stay seated and started clearing plates so the guests would have more elbow room. Leaving the table also had the advantage of giving her something to do other than avoid Mike's glance—which she managed to do rather brilliantly, she thought, by coming up behind him to take the plate he'd scarcely touched.

She wished she could go home. As Mike murmured a quiet, "Thanks," when she took his plate and he handed her his mother's plate, too, she suspected he felt much the same way. She'd had to come. It was her father's birthday, after all. But after the day Mike had, his absence would certainly have been forgiven. The fact that he'd made it a point to be there, especially knowing she would be, spoke volumes about his affection for the man.

He didn't look too affectionate now, however. When she moved to the end of the table, his brow was furrowed in a deep frown.

"Are you okay, Dr. Sheppard?" Mike asked, cutting into the conversation when he saw her dad press his fingers against his chest.

"Me? I'm fine," he dismissed, dropping his hand. "I just ate too much. Karen knows I love her Cornish hens." A smile of appreciation for the concern dug lines into his lean, leathery cheeks. "What was that, Beth?" he asked, returning to the discussion. "You've got Andy here talking retirement?"

"I've got him thinking about it," Beth corrected. "It'll be a while, but he made the first move toward it by hiring a new lawyer in his office."

"Had to." Andrew lifted his big shoulders in a shrug and winked at Mike. "I couldn't get either of my sons to follow in my footsteps. I can't understand it, either. Who'd have thought an attorney would lose his children to such shady pursuits as bettering people's lives. A doctor and a social worker. My only hope was the one still in school, and he's leaning toward being a pro athlete."

"Say, Katie." A conspiratorial gleam glinted in Beth's eyes as she crossed her arms on the square of white lace. It was the same gleam she'd glimpsed when Beth and her mother had been in the kitchen speculating about how long the Sheppards would have to wait to be grandparents. "I was telling your mother a while ago about the new man Andy hired. He's single. Nice. And very attractive," she added before Katie could wince. "He's in his early thirties, never married, adores children—"

Mike's eyebrows jammed together. "How do you know that?"

"I've met him."

"I mean about the kids."

"I asked how he felt about them," his mother admitted, looking surprised that he hadn't figured that out.

"Of course you did."

"Anyway, Katie, he really is very nice. Bright, funny. Drives a new BMW," she added, her voice taking on a confidential note. "Are you interested?"

Katie saw the muscle in Mike's jaw jump when he lay his napkin on the table. No one seemed to have noticed that all evening their exchanges with each other had been limited to the polite and the necessary.

Watching him dig the fingers of his right hand into his left shoulder as if the muscles there were knotted tight, she couldn't help remembering that the last time they'd had dinner together, *his* single status had been under the microscope. That had been the evening he made it so abundantly clear that he was perfectly happy with his life as it was.

"I don't know, Mrs. Brennan." She avoided Mike's gaze, not wanting to be concerned about the fatigue etched into the corners of his eyes. If his own mother didn't seem to notice that he looked particularly drained tonight, then she was obviously seeing something that wasn't there. "I'm not much on blind dates."

Looking pathetically grateful for the excuse to escape, she took the plates and headed into the kitchen. Mike watched her go, his glance reluctantly straying over the curve of her hip, the graceful length of leg exposed by the unexpected slit in the side of her slim, calf-length dress. The figure-skimming sheath that covered even her wrists was utterly plain, but its rich bronze color saved it from being uninspired. He liked her simplicity, her lack of artifice.

He supposed he always had.

The thought brought a faint frown, but he didn't let himself dwell on why he'd only now realized that about her. Mrs. Sheppard had just announced that dessert would be served in the living room.

"Do you know if she's dating anyone right now?" his mom quietly asked him, setting her own napkin aside.

Over the refined commotion coming from the other end of the table as chairs were pushed back and people rose, Mike replied with a terse, "No," and pushed back his own chair.

This wasn't his mom's first attempt at matchmaking for Katie. But as she went on to repeat the virtues of Mr. Wonder Lawyer and pointed out that Katie might really like the young man, Mike experienced a personal first of his own. He felt the heat of pure, unadulterated jealousy.

He truly had never experienced the feeling before. But there was no doubt in his mind what it was. He couldn't imagine anything else that would make him hate another man sight unseen, or make a man dedicated to healing hearts want to tear one out.

He'd been watching her all evening, catching whiffs of her soft perfume or powder or whatever it was that smelled like spring and reminded him of seduction. That he'd been so aware of that scent hadn't made any sense at all. It was so subtle a person normally had to be standing right next to her to notice it at all. After their thirty-second encounter when he'd put away the chairs, the closest he'd been to her all evening was when she'd taken his plate.

He took a deep breath, slowly blew it out. It had to be the stress of the day catching up with him. He knew he was tired. He was edgy with fatigue, and his neck and shoulders ached from the hours he'd spent bent over an open chest. It had been one of those surgeries that had yielded one unpleasant surprise after another and just about everything that could go wrong had.

The miracle was that the patient survived. God willing, she would be sitting on the edge of her hospital bed tomorrow feeling as if she'd been blindsided by a Mack truck.

"We could invite Jeff to the club for dinner," his mom suggested, too busy watching Trina surreptitiously unbunch her slip from under her skirt to notice that Mike wasn't sharing her enthusiasm. "You could bring Katie to join us. If she was with the three of us, it wouldn't be a blind date. And if they hit it off, well…" She shrugged, her eyebrows arched in anticipation. "What do you think?"

He thought he needed air.

Pulling himself to his feet, he gripped the back of her chair to pull it out for her. The tightness in his jaw made his words sound the same way.

"I don't think I'll be able to make it."

"We haven't decided on a night," she chided, dismissing the excuse. "We'll work around your schedule. And Katie's…if she wants to go. I'm not trying to push anything on her."

It sure sounded as if she were to him, but Mike bit back his response. Katie had just returned, her soft smile curving her rose-tinted mouth as she graciously told her dad's office manager that she'd be in to join them in a few minutes. Everyone but Dr. and Mrs. Sheppard and his own parents had vacated the room, and they weren't far behind when his mom caught Katie's eye.

"I just had an idea," she began, only for Mike to interrupt.

"Leave me out of it."

"Oh, Michael, don't be a spoilsport. If you *are* interested in meeting Jeff," Beth continued to Katie, though the perplexed look was for her son, "you could join us at the club."

"She wants me to take you to meet the lawyer." Mike's eyes locked on Katie's, his expression a study in stone. "That way it won't be a blind date."

Caught totally off guard by the plan that had been hatched in her absence, Katie could do nothing but blink in incomprehension.

Tension fairly rolled through Mike's body, but his voice dropped as he turned from his mother, leaving only Katie close enough to hear what was meant just for her anyway. "I don't know if *he's* what would interest you or not."

Katie slowly crossed her arms, the motion blatantly protective. There was an attack in those cool, terse words, as well as a heavy hint of something that sounded suspiciously, unbelievably, like hurt.

"Dr. Sheppard," he continued, stepping back to extend his hand to her father. "I'm afraid I won't be able to stay for your cake. But I appreciate being included tonight. Happy birthday."

"That's quite all right, son." Returning the handshake, her dad clapped Mike on the shoulder. "Thanks very much. Oh, and let me know if you decide to do any more clinical research. A friend of mine in Portland is looking into pediatric applications of the drug you were talking about. Maybe you could collaborate.''

Mike thanked him for the information and, looking more agitated by the second, said good-evening to Katie's mom, pecked his mom on the cheek, and gave his dad a pat on the shoulder.

He didn't say a word to Katie. He didn't even glance toward her as his long strides carried him out of the room. But no one had seemed to notice. Their parents were turning to each other in confusion before it occurred to her mother, usually the perfect hostess, that no one was escorting him to the door.

''Did he get a call?'' Karen asked, her glance bouncing between Andrew and Beth. ''I didn't hear a beeper.''

Beth shook her head, her glance searching her husband's. ''I have no idea what that was all about.''

''I think it's about exhaustion.'' The explanation Katie offered was the easiest, the one that would raise no questions she'd have to hedge. ''He was in a marathon surgery today. Nine hours that I know of.'' Concerned despite herself, mystified by his growing displeasure with her, she heard his footfall fading down the entry hall. ''As late as he was leaving the hospital tonight, he'd probably been at the operation longer than that.''

''Well, I've seen him tired before,'' Beth said, lines of bewilderment fanning from her eyes. ''But he's never short-tempered with his family. Did something…go wrong?''

''He said the patient was stable when he left. That's all I know,'' Katie added, because more questions were forming in Beth's eyes.

''Well, it must just be fatigue then. We all have our limits.'' Maternal defense warred with maternal concern. ''Do you think he's all right to drive home, Andy?''

"I'm sure he's fine," his father replied. "The man's had a long day is all. He's entitled to not feel like socializing."

As far as Katie knew, Mike had had only one drink, but he was undoubtedly tired. He was too agitated to fall asleep behind the wheel, though. Still, hearing the door quietly close, the sound somehow deliberately restrained, she was overwhelmed by the feeling that it had all gone far enough. Before she and Mike had overstepped the bounds of their friendship, he never would have acted that way toward her. And she wouldn't have hesitated to make sure he was okay.

She didn't question what she was doing as she murmured, "I'll check anyway," and headed past the library and into the foyer herself. Beyond the dark wood of the door, she heard his car start, the engine revving just a little louder and a little longer than was probably necessary. Not bothering with a coat, she hurried past the parson's bench and the antique mirror gracing the entry, telling herself she'd find the words she needed when she reached him. But he was already leaving the driveway as she hurried onto the porch, and all she could see were his taillights.

The cold suddenly seemed to seep through her dress and into her skin. She became aware of her breath drifting off in rapid puffs of fog, of her heart hammering against her rib cage. She shivered, chafing her arms to warm herself, but the chill came from within as well as without.

There had been a time when she'd thought losing his friendship was the worst thing that could possibly happen. She'd been wrong. The worst thing was not knowing how to get it back.

"Katie? Did you talk to him?"

She turned with a start at the sound of her mother's voice. In the lemony glow of the porch light, she saw concern reflected in eyes very much like her own.

"No, I...no. He was already gone."

"Well, we'll call in a while and make sure he got home all right. Come back inside. You're going to catch your death out here.

"We're going to serve your father's cake now," she continued, sliding her arm around Katie's shoulder, hugging her to warm her up. "You never said what you bought him for his birthday."

"I got him a picture for his office." Mike never had gotten back to her with a suggestion. "It's an old photo that I had blown up and framed."

"What a sweet idea. Of you and him?"

"Of him and Mike. Mike's about fourteen and Dad's teaching him how to use a microscope. It was the only thing I could think of that he'd like."

Chapter Ten

"**W**hat were you thinking? Good grief, Katie. He's a doctor!"

Katie sat on her sofa, knotting her tissue as Lee paced a rut in front of her drapes. Dana, curled up at the opposite end of the couch, snatched the box of tissues from the coffee table and held it out.

"Blow."

"Thanks."

"I've got to admit," Dana muttered, setting the box back after Katie had quite inelegantly done as she'd suggested. "When you screw up something, you do an exceptionally fine job of it."

"Neither one of you is helping."

"But sleeping with Mike?" Lee exclaimed. "Okay," she conceded, holding up her hands when Dana glared at her. "We'll forget that he's on the forbidden list for a minute here. Of *course* nothing is the same between the two of you. It can't possibly be. He's a man. Now that he's had carnal knowledge of you, he's not relating to you with his brain...clinically speaking."

"She's absolutely right, Katie. Once you've slept with a man, the entire dynamic of the relationship changes. It shifts power and vulnerabilities and who knows what else. Just look at how vulnerable you are to everything he's doing now."

"Or not doing," Lee added, ever so helpfully.

Tearing another shred from the tissue, Katie glanced up with red-rimmed eyes. She wasn't crying. She was considering it, though. "Where do you guys get this stuff?"

Dana and Lee gave a simultaneous shrug. "We read a lot," Dana said.

"So what do I do?"

This time it was Dana who held up her hands. "You know how lousy I am with relationships. I haven't a clue."

"Well, I'm hardly an expert," Lee piped in, "but as torn up as you are about this, I think there's only one thing you can do."

"Fine. Just tell me what it is."

"You and Mike have been friends forever. Even longer than the three of us," she said, including Dana with the sweeping gesture of her arm. "If any of us had a problem with each other, the only way to work it out would be to sit down and talk it through."

"But there's a difference here, Lee. Mike isn't only a friend to Katie. She's in love with him."

Katie's glance darted to them both, then promptly fell to her lap. "I never said that."

"You didn't have to."

"You are? Oh, Katie," Lee murmured, her voice falling more in disquiet than disappointment. "Be careful."

The concern in Lee's expression was mirrored in Dana's.

"Don't worry," she assured her friends, feeling a tug of affection for them both. "It's not like he loves me back, so there's no problem. Right?"

Anyone else would have found her conclusion totally confusing. All her friends did was give her a look that said they wouldn't trade places with her for all the sales at Nordstrom's.

"Lee's right, you know." Dana's voice held as much sympathy as conviction. "You have to sit down and talk to him. Just tell him what you told us. Tell him you can't stand what's happened between the two of you and that you need your old friend back. Look at it this way," she suggested, brightening, "at the rate you're going, there's no way it could get worse."

There was no arguing Dana's conclusion. After last night, Katie figured she couldn't possibly mess things up any more than they already were.

But he was in surgery when she got to work the next morning.

And by that afternoon, their little problem was the last thing on her mind.

"I just don't believe this, Katie. He was fine when he left home this morning. And Trina said he seemed perfectly all right to her until he came back from lunch. Then he started having chest pains, and she said he got all gray, and he just…he just…"

"It's okay, Mom." Katie reached for her, unable to bear the fear welling in her mother's eyes. She'd never seen her look so frightened. She'd seen that fear in the eyes of patients' relatives before, but never had she fully appreciated their anxiety until now. Other people had heart attacks. Not her father. The man kept himself in excellent shape. "I'll take you to the waiting room, then find out how long it'll be before he comes up."

"Where have they taken him?"

"To the cath lab. They need to do an angiogram."

"Oh, Katie."

"It's all right, Mom." Where was Mike? Still in surgery? Back at his office? she wondered, not bothering to qualify her need for his presence. "The test doesn't hurt," she hurriedly assured.

"Are you sure?"

"Positive. He stays awake for the procedure," she began, and found herself slipping into the teaching mode she relied on with patients' relatives when they were faced with this very sort of confusion and uncertainty. Explaining the procedure, why it was necessary and how it was done, prevented her from focusing too closely on who the patient was. Detaching was the only way she could help her mom right now. And right now, since she couldn't do anything for her father, taking care of her mother was all she cared about.

Only minutes ago, Alice had pulled Katie from a patient's room to tell her that her dad was on his way to the cath lab from emergency. After a couple of frantic calls, she'd learned that her father had suffered a heart attack, that he was unstable and that Dr. Chapman was prepping for the angiogram. Her mother had been notified by Trina and torn out of the house in the middle of a bridge luncheon. Katie had intercepted her at one of the elevators in the third-floor lobby.

Because the CICU waiting room was small and a couple of other families had pretty much taken it over, they had more privacy in the sitting area of the lobby. So that atrium-like space with its forest green carpet and mint green chairs was where they paced after Katie called Mike's office to see if he was there. She didn't consider why the knot in her stomach tightened when she punched the numbers, or why she'd instinctively needed him the moment she'd heard the news about her dad. She just made the call.

He wasn't in, so she'd tracked him down to the OR and left a message with the secretary to tell him that Dr. Sheppard was in CICU before returning to join her mom at the window overlooking the street. They were still there, Katie's tightly crossed arms mirroring her mother's stance as they watched umbrellas bob along the sidewalk, when Dr. Chapman stepped off the elevator.

"Dr. Chapman," she called, hurrying forward to stop him before he reached the wide, double doors leading to the Cardiac Intensive Care unit. "The angiogram you just did on Randall Sheppard. He's my father," she hurriedly explained. "How is he?"

"Katie. Of course," he said, the relationship immediately registering. "You'd be who I was coming to see. They're bringing him up now."

He nodded to her mom, the silver rims of his glasses glinting when Katie introduced them. His manner straightforward as always, he then returned his attention to the person he knew would understand him best.

He didn't waste time softening the news for Katie. "He has triple vessel disease and needs a CABG."

"A cabbage?" her mom echoed.

"It means coronary artery bypass graft. It's a bypass, Mom. All three arteries are blocked and he needs open-heart."

"Open-heart?"

"Surgery," she translated, wondering at the amount of verbal shorthand the medical staff used over the course of a day.

"The sooner the better," the cardiologist added. "I'll call scheduling and see if we can get him in in the morning."

"Have you told him?"

"Not yet. I want you both present. I'll need you as a buffer," he explained, motioning them toward the doors marked Restricted Entry. "He's not going to like the idea of being out of commission for a while. Once we had the pain under control, he was already trying to talk us into letting him go back to the office so he could finish out the day."

Karen Sheppard's distress visibly increased. "His work is his life, Doctor. He won't listen to me."

"Then, Katie," Dr. Chapman replied flatly, "it's up to you to convince him."

The proclamation had her reaching out to stop her mom from following any farther, which caused the doctor to pause with his hand on the door he'd just pushed partway open. Behind him, the long wide room was divided by curtains, the areas inside those open spaces crammed with so much equipment that it looked like a launch room for NASA.

"I think we should wait for Mike. Dr. Brennan," she expanded, for Dr. Chapman's benefit. What the doctor wanted was impossible. Her father wouldn't listen to her. "He was still in surgery when I called down over an hour ago. Dad will listen to him." She swallowed past the hint of envy she hadn't wanted to admit was there. "He thinks of him as a son."

"I knew your families knew each other, but I didn't realize you were that close. I'd better get someone else to review the films. I was going to recommend him for the surgery, but he won't want to do it."

"But I'm sure he will," her mother interrupted, looking a little frantic. "He's very fond of Randy."

"That's exactly why he won't want to, ma'am. No surgeon wants his or her concentration hampered by a personal involvement. I don't think you'd want that, either.

"Katie," he continued, drawn back to her by her composure. "I'm going to call surgery to schedule your father for the morning. While I'm at it, I'll check on Dr. Brennan." He nodded toward Mrs. Sheppard. "I'll see you both in a few minutes."

With that, he disappeared into the CICU.

Her mom's worried glance darted from the closing door to her daughter. "Can't we go in?"

"Not yet."

"Why not?" she demanded, tears gathering in her eyes. "If he's in there, I want to see him. I want to see my husband."

Of course she did, and seeing her so distraught severely tested Katie's outward calm. Her mom's entire life was devoted to the man lying somewhere on the other side of those doors. And while Katie didn't understand how she could be so devoted to someone who'd missed the birth of his own daughter, who'd routinely missed anniversaries, and who had sent his family off for summer vacations without him, she knew she needed to be strong for her.

"It'll take them a few minutes to get him hooked up to everything. And we need to wait until Dr. Chapman finds out about scheduling and Mike gets here. Dad will have questions and it's best to have as many answers as possible before confronting him with all this."

"But, if I could just—"

"He's in good hands in there," she told her, wanting to relieve as many fears for her as she could. "You'll want those answers, too. Come sit down until Dr. Chapman gets back."

Her mom didn't budge.

The entire time the doctor had been speaking to them, Katie had been aware of the furrows pinching her mother's brow. That consternation was undoubtedly due to what she was hearing, the enormity of the news, the foreign-sounding lingo. But there was censure in that pinched look now, and no small amount of disbelief.

"You sound just like the people downstairs who wouldn't let me see him when I got here. He's your *father,* Katie. How can you stand there and calmly talk about waiting for answers when you haven't even seen for yourself if he's still breathing. Aren't you even a little upset?"

"Mom," she said, forcing patience past the sudden burning in her throat. "I sound like them because I am one of them. And I am upset. It's just not going to do either one of us any good if we both fall apart."

"She's right, Mrs. Sheppard." Mike settled his hand on the older woman's shoulder, his incisive glance sweeping the distress in both women's faces. He was still in scrubs and sounded just a little out of breath, as if he'd taken every flight of stairs on the run. "Why don't we do what Katie suggested. Let's sit down over here so we can talk."

Mike had heard their conversation as he'd crossed the lobby from the stairwell door. He'd also seen the tortured accusation in Mrs. Sheppard's face and caught the stiffening of Katie's shoulders as she'd braced against the attack. Katie was well aware of how the stress of such a situation could cause even the closest of relatives to lash out. But this wasn't someone else's distraught relative, and he knew her armor wasn't anywhere near as thick as she pretended it was.

"I saw your dad's films," he told her, a chink pitting his own armor at the confused hurt she tried bravely to mask. "I called to check his status and see what had been done as soon as I got your message when I came out of surgery. Who's Chapman calling in?"

Having seen the seriousness of the problem himself, Mike's priority was getting the best surgeon available for his friend. Right behind that came concern for Katie. He didn't question it. Nor did he wonder at the protectiveness that had made him step between mother and daughter a moment ago. While he listened to Mrs. Sheppard tell him how glad she was that he was there and Katie asked if he would talk to her father about how imperative it was that the surgery not be delayed, he considered only that she hadn't hesitated long to call him.

After the way he'd acted toward her at her parents' home a couple of nights ago, he considered it a miracle that she was still speaking to him.

Dr. Chapman returned a minute later. After a quick consultation between the two doctors, they were all moving through the surreal atmosphere of the critical care unit. The place seemed bathed in twilight, the voices here sounding softer somehow. Computer screens and monitors cast glows of gray and green. Machines blipped and beeped. Screens danced with oscillating and spiking lines. There were only three patients in the unit, each in curtained spaces, but all had what looked like miles of tubing coming and going from various parts of their bodies, and every vital sign was emblazoned on the appropriate digital readout or monitor for anyone passing to read.

Mike's expert glance slid over the displays on the array of instruments surrounding Dr. Sheppard. His bed had been elevated at the head so he could breathe more easily and the neckline of his white hospital gown was pulled down on one side, exposing swirls of gray hair and the cardiac leads attached by adhesive circles to his chest. Despite the look of war in his eyes, Dr. Sheppard's skin was the color of ash.

Mrs. Sheppard was already at her husband's side, worry etched in her face as she clutched his hand.

"There's no reason for all this fuss," he insisted, his voice gruff with irritation. "I told them there was no reason to scare you, Karen. And there's certainly no reason to pull you away from your work," he admonished Mike. "I feel fine."

"That's because you're loaded to the gills with drugs to stablize your heart and cut the pain," Mike muttered.

Preferring to ignore what he regarded as a minor detail, Dr. Sheppard's glance sharpened on his daughter.

Katie hung back, looking as if she weren't sure she should be there at all. She'd been all right before she saw her dad. Now, Mike watched her glance move from the IVs, to the oxygen cannula under her father's nose, to the monitor above his head. He knew she understood the lines and waves and readings on the instruments, but it didn't appear that anything registered. She wasn't a nurse at that moment. She was a daughter looking at her father, and finding him far more vulnerable than she'd ever believed him to be.

"Katie?" Dr. Sheppard took in the ID tag and her scrubs. "You don't work here, do you?"

From the way he lifted his hand toward the room, it was apparent that he meant the CICU, not the hospital itself. Katie obviously realized that as she quietly told him that she worked across the hall, and approached the silver side rail near the foot of the bed.

"Well, they shouldn't have bothered you, either," he insisted. "Except I'm sure your mother needed you. Trina probably scared her half to death. Now," he said, dismissing her and everything else that didn't immediately concern him. "Who do I talk to about getting out of here?"

"That would be me," Dr. Chapman announced. The doctor nodded to Mike, the glances passing between them making it clear each understood what had to be done. "But it's in your best interest to stay put for a while."

In his briskly efficient manner, he explained why that was by slapping chest films onto the light box on the wall to show Dr. Sheppard exactly which arteries were blocked where. There was no worse patient than a doctor, even one whose specialty had little to do with his own problem. As a pediatrician, her dad knew enough about what was going on to question everything. Which he did. Up to and including the need for the surgery being recommended.

That was when Mike stepped in.

As the cardiologist had suspected he might, her dad balked big-time at the idea of immediate surgery. But when he was told he'd be laid up for about three months after the operation, he nearly went ballistic—which had three of the four people around the bed casting quick, edgy glances toward the cardiac monitor. He rattled off every excuse in the book, ticking them off on his fingers as he recounted each one. He had patients scheduled for the next two months. His partner had the same backlog and he couldn't put the burden of his patients on him and expect him to cope with all the emergencies that arose during the course of a day with a practice devoted to children, many of whom were dealing with serious illnesses. Some of his patients wouldn't see anyone but him, anyway. Children and their parents were counting on him. As an afterthought, he remembered that he had a conference to attend and a meeting of the medical review board he chaired.

When he finished, no one said a word. But just as he seemed to think he'd driven home his point, Mike slowly shook his head.

"No disrespect, sir," he began, in a no-nonsense tone. "But there's something you need to understand. No one's going to be counting on you for anything if you don't have this surgery. You don't have the luxury of waiting until you have time to fit this into your schedule.

"You told me something I've never forgotten," he continued, crossing his arms in a stance that made him look as inflexible as a granite pillar. "When I was fourteen years old, you told me that the only way a man ever accomplished anything was to keep his priorities straight and his sights on his goals. I've kept that advice in mind every day since then, and I can honestly say I wouldn't be where I am without it.

"Now, I don't know if you've accomplished everything you've set out to do," he continued, conscious of Katie's eyes on him, "but the fact that you've driven yourself the way you have for the past thirty or forty years could well be responsible for why you're where you are right now."

The strong angle of Mike's jaw tightened with that conclusion, his words jerking hard at something inside himself as he swept a dispassionate glance over the lean frame in the bed.

"You're only sixty years old," he finally said, wanting to drive home the point of how young that actually could be. "With your energy and determination, you have *decades* left to contribute. But your heart is a ticking time bomb. If you don't want to do this for yourself, then do it for your family and all those other people who count on you. Take your own advice and get your priorities straight. You won't be around much longer if you don't."

There wasn't a soul in that crowded little space who would accuse Mike of mincing his words. But then, her father wouldn't have listened to anyone who'd soft-pedaled his prognosis. Hearing it laid out so bluntly hadn't been easy for her mom, though. She had visibly paled at the stern warning.

Praying her mom wouldn't do what some spouses did and faint, Katie was about to move to her side when she saw her dad reach out to touch her mother's cheek. An instant later, her parents' eyes were locked on each other, blocking out everyone else. Including her.

Knowing she wasn't needed, she stepped back, her arms tightly crossed.

"Dr. and Mrs. Sheppard," Dr. Chapman said to the silent, stunned couple. "I'm sure you'll want a few minutes alone to discuss this."

"Mom, I'll be…"

Katie started to say she'd be right outside, but her mother was already nodding, seeming to know she'd be where she could find her. Her father, looking as if someone had just kicked a ladder from under him, said nothing.

She felt the brush of Mike's hand against the small of her back as she turned away. For one brief moment, she teased herself with the idea that he meant the gesture as one of support. But his oddly pensive expression became shuttered, and when his hand fell, she realized he only wanted her to move so her parents could have some privacy. Her father was already nodding to her mother, agreeing to the surgery. Now, there would be releases to sign, tests to run, things to be explained to both of her parents about the procedure and what they could expect afterward. But the CICU staff would take care of all that. And Mike and Dr. Chapman would take care of getting the best surgeon available. She could hear their hushed conversation behind her even as she turned for the door.

"Don't worry about him," Rick, one of the CICU nurses, said to her as he headed toward her dad's cubicle. "We'll take care of him for you."

Lu, a tiny Asian nurse with a billion kilowatt smile, echoed the sentiment on her way past with a tray of medications for another patient.

Murmuring a quiet, "Thanks," feeling a little numb, Katie kept going. There was nothing for her to do but wait. As critical as the patients were in this area and as busy as the staff was, she didn't need to be hanging around and getting in the way.

That was exactly how she felt, too—as if she was in the way. She'd grown up with that feeling.

Jamming down the unwanted thought, she hurried toward the doors.

Mike was right behind her.

"We've got more tests to run," he said, hitting the button that swung the doors inward, "but your dad seems to be in good shape except for his heart. You know how well bypasses work. There's no reason to think he won't be just fine."

The assurance was appreciated, especially considering the expertise of the man delivering it. Mike was speaking as a surgeon, as a man well versed in the very surgery her father needed to save his life. On a certain level, to him, it was strictly a matter of plumbing and parts, and if he saw no particular cause for alarm, then she shouldn't, either.

Intellectually she knew that. She knew, too, that she would accomplish nothing by thinking of all that she'd personally seen go wrong with such patients. But she wasn't feeling terribly intellectual at the moment. What she felt was…lost.

"It's my mom I'm worried about. He's her whole life."

The strain she tried to mask in her voice was visible in her eyes when she stopped by a tall, potted ficus in the lobby. Looking around the comfortable area, she felt as if she'd never seen the place before. She was never in this area except to pass through it on her way to somewhere else. Now, having been relegated to it twice, she understood how exposed people forced to wait here felt to everyone who walked by.

She felt exposed to Mike, too. She hated the way he was watching her, his intense blue eyes seeing too much, offering so little.

Turning to the wide window, she avoided him and the curious glances of a couple talking quietly near one of the sofas. It was nearly dusk now, and it had stopped raining, but the cars moving along the street below scarcely registered.

"Thank you for talking to him," she quietly said, crossing her arms over the nerves jumping in her stomach. "I knew he'd listen to you."

Mike stood behind her, his hands on his hips, his faint reflection towering over hers in the window glass. He hadn't seen her since he'd left her parents' home two days ago, and he'd tried very hard to put his behavior that evening out of his mind. His conscience hadn't allowed it, though. He couldn't escape what he felt for this woman. And he couldn't deny his purely selfish reaction when he'd received her message a while ago. He could think of a couple of reasons why she would have called him about her father. But underscoring his immediate concern for the seriousness of her dad's condition had been the hope that she'd wanted him there for her.

Apparently that hadn't been the case at all. If her body language was any indication, she didn't want him anywhere near her.

Her head was bent, her face hidden from him, but she held her back straight, as if she refused to lean on anyone. Despite the rigidity of her shoulders, something about the position struck him as oddly vulnerable.

She'd said she was concerned about her mom. He didn't doubt that for an instant. Karen Sheppard had never struck him as a particularly strong woman. But it was the worry Katie wouldn't express about her father that bothered him. For years, he'd watched her take care of everyone but herself, putting other's concerns, other's needs, before her own. Just as she was doing at that moment with her mom. But watching her now, seeing her hold herself in, he had the uneasy feeling she might well be using her concern for others to deny her own needs; to deny what she felt the strongest, the deepest.

As a man whose profession demanded a certain detachment, suspecting he'd mastered the art a little too well himself, he recognized exactly what she was doing. He'd bet every skill he possessed that she was using her concern for her mother, real as it was, as an excuse to hide from the fear she felt for her father. He just wondered what else she was denying.

"Are you still on duty?"

She shook her head, her soft curls gleaming in the overhead lights. Against the backdrop of dreary gray, the strands of amber and dark wheat glinted like summer sun.

"I reported off to a couple of the other nurses after Mom got here and they divided my patients between them. I'd already finished my discharges and worked up the new admit—"

"I'm not asking if you covered your work," he muttered. "I'm certain you made sure everyone was taken care of. All I'm asking is if you have to go back."

He hadn't intended to sound exasperated with her, but her professionalism was an unwanted barrier at the moment. The fact that he hid behind the same wall himself was something he didn't care to consider. The past forty-eight hours—the past several minutes, for that matter—had given him more than enough to think about.

"I just wanted to know where you'd be," he clarified, trying to ignore the undercurrents shifting between them. "I have to check my patients...unless you need me for something else right now."

He would stay if she needed him. Seeming to understand that, she turned slowly and looked up. "Please. Go do what you have to do," she said, sounding as if she'd imposed enough. "Your talking with Dad was a huge help. He'd probably have talked Mom into letting him wait."

She deliberately avoided mentioning that she'd have had little influence on her father herself. Mike didn't have to ask why that was. He knew she felt her father wouldn't care about her opinion. But she cared about her father whether she wanted to admit it or not.

"I think there are other things he might need to hear, too." He chose his words carefully, cautiously, well aware that he was entering forbidden territory. "Maybe there are some things you'd like to say to him yourself."

He'd caught her with her defenses down, her vulnerabilities exposed. The disquiet that sliced through her eyes was immediately veiled by the sweep of her lashes as she turned. But he wouldn't let her block him the way she did every time he tried to talk to her about her father.

"He's eighteen hours from major surgery, Katie. What if something happens and you don't get a chance to talk to him?"

"Nothing's going to happen." Her voice was as low as his, but her suddenly shaky tone was far more insistent. "You said yourself there's no reason—"

"There isn't any particular reason, but you know as well as I do there are no guarantees. Yes, he should come through just fine. People in Las Vegas would kill for the odds he has of sailing through this." His voice lowered as a visitor and a pink-jacketed hospital volunteer passed by. "No surgeon is God," he continued, his tone hardening to a near whisper. "And you know as well as I do that there are things even the surgeon can't control. If something should happen and he doesn't make it, then you'll have to live the rest of your life wishing you'd dropped the wall between you two."

"And if I do that, and tell him I love him," she countered, "and he just looks at me like he can't figure out why I'm bothering him with such a thing, then I get to live the rest of my life knowing for sure that he didn't want me."

His uncomprehending glance froze on her face.

"Didn't want you? What are you talking about?"

Hurt melded with defiance. Holding herself so tightly that her knuckles went white, Katie turned her head away. Mike had shifted his body to block her from the other people moving behind them, and the window and a potted tree provided barriers of their own. But she suddenly felt more trapped than protected.

"I know what you're trying to do, Mike. I've done it myself when I've worked with families in this position. You try to make everyone set aside their differences and focus on healing. Well, I don't expect you to understand how I feel about him. You know you've always seen him differently than I have."

"Then make me understand," he insisted, truly at a loss. "Tell me why it is that a man I've always admired is practically estranged from his own daughter."

"Because he chose everyone else but me," she snapped back, her throat tightening as a lifetime of hurt surged forth like uncorked champagne. "He was always there for everyone else, Mike. Including you. Remember how you used to come over on Sunday afternoons when you were in high school and the two of you would talk in his library? Sunday was usually his only day off, and Mom never wanted me to disturb him. But you could talk to him any time he was home."

"Katie," he cut in, looking torn between defending himself or his mentor. "He was probably just advising me about colleges or something."

"Stop taking his side!" The words were a fierce whisper. "You always do that. You wanted to know why I feel the way I do, but I can't tell you if you won't listen. What you and he were talking about isn't the point. The incident itself isn't even important." It was just one of dozens over the years. Insignificant alone, it was the constancy that had mattered. "The point is that you could be in there and I couldn't. He cared about you. Not me. You were my friend, but you were my competition, too. There were times when I didn't know if I loved you, or hated you."

The vehement admission had her quickly looking away, protecting herself from his reaction to thoughts she hadn't intended to voice. They were talking about her father, not how she felt about Mike. And the last thing she wanted to deal with just then was how complicated her feelings were for him. "Even if you hadn't been there," she said more deliberately, hurrying past what had only been part of the bigger picture, "he'd still have had something else to do. Work always came first. Other people always came first.

"I know that most of those other people were sick kids," she admitted, remembering her ambivalence over that unfortunate fact. "Mom had always made a point of making sure I understood that. But she had time with him, and when they were together, it was like I wasn't even there." Unprepared for the instant replay of the emotions triggered by the possibility of her father's death, she pulled a breath, forcibly calming herself. "On some level I know I understood that what my father was doing was good, but all I remember is how I felt. And I felt like an ingrate for wanting him to be with me when some sick child needed him."

The knowledge had also made her feel unimportant, self-ish, petty and guilty, feelings most children weren't equipped to handle. But she saw no point in mentioning that. Especially since that was how she was feeling at the moment. She was thirty years old, but in the past few minutes, the years had been stripped away, leaving her feeling more like ten.

Hating how easily the feelings had surfaced, upset with Mike for uprooting them and herself for allowing them, she tightened her arms around her middle.

"I don't expect you to change the way you feel about

him,'' she said, wishing she had Mike's indomitable control. She could read nothing in the blue eyes silently studying her face; nothing to indicate that a word she said even mattered. "I'm not even *trying* to change your mind. I know a lot of people think the world of him, and I'd never dream of mentioning this to anyone else. He's helped a lot of people and he deserves the respect he's earned. But you asked how he and I could have so little to do with each other,'' she reminded him. "Well, that's why. He wasn't interested in me, so somewhere along the line I decided not to be interested in him.''

She averted her eyes, turning to the window. "I'll go in there. I'll tell him I'll be thinking of him. But please stop trying to push a relationship that isn't there.''

Mike said nothing. He just stood still and unnervingly silent. Knowing how analytical he could be, she was sure he was weighing every word she'd said. Considering the way he'd never failed to defend her father, she was also certain he was preparing some sort of rebuttal.

Or so she was thinking when he reached over and tipped her face to his.

Something strangely like apology shifted through his eyes in the moments before she saw his mouth harden.

His pager was beeping.

Without looking from her, he dropped his hand to reach for the small, black instrument clipped to the waist of his scrub pants, and turned it off. A second later, his sense of duty getting the better of him, he glanced at the number on the digital display to see where he was to call.

"That's the unit,'' he murmured, speaking of the area behind them.

"You'd better see what they want.''

His mouth thinned again, his thoughts clearly torn. He didn't move, though. And when he spoke, his deep voice held caution. "Are you going to be all right out here?''

She swallowed as she nodded, her glance falling to the corded mucles of his forearms. Of all the places in the world she could be right now, she found it rather ironic that the only place she wanted to be was less than three feet away.

She was thinking that it might as well have been a mile, when she saw that gap close. Mike reached out, his hand hovering like a blessing near her shoulder. Breaching his hesitation, he slipped his fingers along her cheek and tucked a stray curl behind her ear. The gesture was as familiar as the pattern of her own breathing, and for reasons that went far beyond unexpectedness, it caught her breath in her throat.

"I'll come back when I'm through...if you want. To check on your folks."

She had no idea what thoughts churned in his mind. At the moment, she didn't care. She didn't even care that he'd qualified his concern. All that mattered was that he seemed willing to sidestep the emotional baggage stacked between them for a while if she needed him. Having needed him for as long as she could remember, all she could do was whisper, "Please."

Chapter Eleven

"I promise, Mom. They'll call if there are any changes. He's off the respirator, they've already had him sitting on the edge of his bed, and they're talking about transferring him to the telemetry unit in the morning. You were just with him a while ago. You saw yourself how much better he looks tonight than he did this afternoon."

Katie shifted on the waiting room's well-worn sofa and ran a worried glance over her mother's face. Her mom sat next to her, her back straight and her hands knotted in her lap. She looked to Katie as if she'd aged ten years in the last thirty hours. The lines around her eyes she'd faithfully fought with creams and masks had etched themselves as deeply as the twin furrows between the wings of her eyebrows, and her skin was as pale as milk. Beth Brennan, who flanked her mom on the other side, looked equally concerned about her.

"You haven't eaten and you haven't slept since yesterday,'' Katie continued, sounding more like a parent talking to a child than the other way around. ''You won't do him any good at all if you wind up in the hospital yourself. If you don't want to go home alone, I'll stay with you.''

Threading her fingers through her hair, her mother released a long, steady sigh. ''You don't need to stay with me, honey. I'll be fine by myself.'' She reached over long enough to pat her daughter on the knee. ''I just hate to leave him.''

''She knows that, Karen. But your daughter is right.'' Mrs. Brennan slid her arm around her friend's shoulder. ''You're not doing Randy or yourself any good right now. He's resting, and you should be, too. Let me take you home.''

Clearly outnumbered, and desperately in need of sleep, her mom finally capitulated. ''I'd really rather not drive. Can you bring me back for my car in the morning?''

''Of course.''

''Then you'll stay for a while, Katie? Make sure he doesn't wake up needing something?''

''I'll check on him. I promise.''

''Karen,'' Beth admonished, tugging her to her feet. ''Let's go. If he needs anything, he has a nurse right there.''

With a grateful smile for Mrs. Brennan, Katie rose to give her mom a hug. Her own eyes felt gritty from lack of sleep and her stomach burned from too much coffee and too little to eat herself. It was nine o'clock at night and, except for the snatches of sleep she'd managed on the waiting room sofa last night, she'd been up since five-thirty yesterday morning. The quick shower she'd taken when she'd run home to feed Spike that afternoon had revived her, but those effects had worn off long ago.

Her vision was blurred with fatigue when she noticed Mike standing near the door of the CICU waiting room.

He was in street clothes, a brown suede jacket over a cabled sweater and slacks. The last time she'd seen him, he'd been in a lab coat. Or maybe, she thought, wearily rubbing her forehead, he'd been in scrubs. He'd come and gone several times over the course of the day, relating the progress of the surgery, checking on her dad afterward, staying for a minute, or ten, depending on how much time he had before he was needed for his own patients. He'd been there for her parents and, though neither she nor Mike had said a word that didn't relate to the present circumstances, he'd been there for her, too.

She had no idea how long he'd been standing there now. She didn't even hear what he said to their mothers as he glanced toward her, then returned his attention to them as he walked them out.

She wished he had stayed. He possessed a quiet strength that she needed desperately. She always had, she supposed. But what she needed, what she wanted and what she could get, bore little relation to each other. Even though he'd been there for her, there had been no mistaking the cautious distance he'd kept.

Their truce was tenuous, at best.

Bending to pick up her purse, she became aware of a hollow ache deep inside. She'd never thought of herself as being alone before. She had her family, her friends, her volunteer work, her job and her cat. But as she slipped the strap over the shoulder of her beige jacket, she couldn't deny the dull ache filling her chest.

She missed her friend.

Telling herself not to think about it right now, she headed off to check on her dad.

Visiting times for CICU were severely restricted. No visitors were allowed in at all after eight in the evening, but since she was on staff, the warden of a nurse who intercepted her at the door let her in. Though only for a minute.

The unit was dim, and the voice of her father's nurse was hushed. After he assured her that her father was resting comfortably, and asking her to not wake him, he left her standing at the side rail.

Her dad was asleep, his head turned toward her, his usually neat silver hair falling over his forehead. The equipment surrounding his bed and the tubes and lines running every which way were so familiar to her she scarcely noticed them. The man in the bed didn't seem familiar at all. The ordeal of open-heart surgery had taken its toll, and left him weak and dependent. The circumstance was only temporary. Yet, each time Katie had seen him like this today she couldn't help thinking how very...human...he was.

In her mind, her father had always been an icon of sorts, a walking reputation who cast a shadow a mile long.

"Katie?" Her name was a painful rasp, his throat still raw from where the tubes had been. "Is that you?"

"Yeah, Dad." She moved closer, curling one hand over the rail. "I didn't mean to disturb you. I just told Mom I'd check on you before I go."

"Are you taking care of her?"

She nodded, adding a quiet, "Yes. We just got her to go home and get some rest."

"Good. I worry about her." He lifted his hand and gave hers a weak pat before it fell back to his side. His eyelids drooped, then closed. "She's not like you."

Katie hesitated, old inadequacies waiting to be felt. "I don't know what you mean."

"You're independent. Always have been," he added, the rasp in his voice making the words barely audible. "You don't need anyone."

There was no particular criticism in the observation. No

compliment, either. The drugs in his body could easily be responsible for the lack of inflection in his voice. The man was so heavily sedated that he was already drifting off again. But he'd sounded as if he were merely stating some simple and obvious fact that those who knew her had accepted long ago.

✗ She blinked at the still figure on the bed, disbelief vying with incomprehension. He hardly knew her. Yet he believed she didn't need anyone? She'd once needed *him*. And at that very moment she needed her old friend back so badly she ached. But thinking about Mike just then made the ache deepen all the more. And trying to figure out her father was something she'd given up on long ago.

Suddenly feeling precariously close to tears, she told herself not to think at all and turned away.

Mike was walking toward her.

In the dim light, his features looked hammered from granite, all sharp angles and planes. A man his size shouldn't be able to move as quietly as he did, but he didn't seem to make a sound as he motioned to the nurse that he wasn't there to check a patient and headed straight for Katie.

His glance swept her face, quick, assessing. Visibly displeased with what she was doing, he looked at the man in the bed and back again.

"How is he?"

She echoed his near whisper. "He just went back to sleep."

"You need to go."

"I didn't mean to wake him—"

"I mean you, Katie. You need to get some rest."

She didn't seem to expect his concern. Her eyes already bore a suspicious brightness. They had from the instant he'd seen her turn from her father's bed. Now they simply looked haunted.

"Come on," he murmured, feeling the desolation in her expression slice right through him.

Something had just happened with her father. He was sure of it. But knowing he was the last person on earth she'd want to talk with about him, he said nothing else. Unable to help her, not liking the feeling at all, he just watched her tuck her arms around herself and followed her out of the eerily quiet unit.

"Did our moms leave?" she asked when they stepped into the deserted lobby.

"I saw them to the car myself. This way," he said, taking her by the elbow to steer her toward the elevator. "I'm taking you home."

A moment ago she looked incredibly vulnerable. Now, shaking her head as she pushed her fingers through her hair, she simply looked confused.

"I have my car," she said, looking as if she'd just figured out why she couldn't go with him.

"Mom can pick you up when she brings your mom back in the morning. I'd swing by and get you myself, but I have to be here at seven and I don't think you want to be up that early." He glanced toward her, frowning as he punched the Down button. "You're so tired, you're practically walking into walls."

"Am not."

"Are too," he muttered back, watching her deliberately modify her path to avoid the side of the elevator when the doors opened. He might be the last person she wanted to talk to about her dad, but he could certainly make sure she got home in one piece. "Don't be so stubborn. I told your mother I'd see that you got home safely and that's what I'm going to do."

"You could follow me."

He glanced to where she rested her head against the side of the elevator wall. Her eyes were closed.

"Yeah. Into a ditch."

Out of sheer determination, she straightened her shoulders, blinking like a young owl. That determination drained right out of her a second later. "You win."

"Wise woman."

Mike had left his car near the hospital's front doors when he'd returned from the office that evening. As soon as they were inside, he asked Katie if she wanted to get something to eat on the way to her place, but she didn't seem to care about food. She said all she really wanted was sleep, then proceeded to prove his point about how tired she was by turning sideways to lean her head against the seat back.

She was out in two blocks.

Keeping one hand on the wheel, he reached over and nudged the hair from near her mouth. It was just an excuse to touch her, something he'd wanted to do since the moment he'd seen her turn from her father's bed. He'd had no idea how completely shut out she'd felt when she'd been growing up. He'd been aware of her basic feelings about her dad never being around, but she had never elaborated much beyond that. Probably, he thought, his conscience kicking him in the teeth, because he'd always defended the man the minute they'd started talking about him. As she'd rather eloquently implied yesterday, it was a little hard to talk to someone who wouldn't listen.

It was difficult, too, to reconcile his image of Dr. Sheppard with hers. A man who loved children as much as her father did could never deliberately hurt one. Yet, he'd sacrificed his daughter for his career. Mike was sure that, in his own way, Katie's father loved her. But the dynamics of any family were often a mystery to an outsider, and some damage, whether inflicted by intention or neglect, could never be undone.

He just hadn't realized how much his relationship with her dad had affected her.

I didn't know if I loved you, or hated you.

She'd spoken in past tense, the words so matter-of-fact it had taken a moment for their impact to hit. They'd been friends as far back as he could remember, yet he'd had no idea she'd cared about him enough to love or hate. As he pulled up in front of her house and studied the shadowed contours of her lovely face, he couldn't help but wonder which, and how much, of those feelings lingered now.

"Katie? Honey, give me your keys."

At the low rumble of his voice, she lifted her head. Pulling a deep breath, she pushed her hair back from her face and, in a stupor, reached for her purse. After fumbling for her keys, she handed them over and reached for the door handle herself.

The cold, damp air roused her even more. Pulling her jacket snugly over her blouse and jeans, she forced herself to her feet and had closed her own door by the time he made it around the front of his car.

"You don't have to see me inside," she insisted over a yawn.

"Then why did you give me your keys?" he asked, ever so logically, and steered her up the walk.

Her only response was a faint frown before he slid the key into the lock. Then, doing a commendably quick shuffle when he pushed open the door, she snatched up Spike before the cat could dart through the opening and scooted inside. An instant later, he heard a soft, "Damn."

Stepping in behind her to shut out the night air, he saw that she'd left the lamp on by the sofa. Its soft pool of light illuminated the inviting and comfortable space, reaching into the shadows of the kitchen and hall. Katie seemed concerned only with the carpet in front of the bookcase.

Spike had been at it again. This time, the plant had not survived.

She still held the now-purring feline in her arms. He was curled up tight under her chin, rubbing his head against her jaw as if he'd never been so glad to see anyone in all of his nine lives. Either that, or he was begging for mercy.

Too weary to be upset, she simply dropped to her knees, let the cat go and started picking up bits of wilted leaf.

Curving his hands under her elbows, Mike promptly drew her back to her feet. With one finger, he caught her purse by the strap and dropped it on the chair behind her.

"Go to bed."

"I can't. I have to clean this up."

"I'll do it."

She looked too beat to argue, but, being Katie, she did anyway.

"You don't need to clean this up. It's my mess." Tears of fatigue gathered in the corners of her eyes. "Darn cat."

To Mike, the feeble epithet and the tears she stubbornly dashed away were a fair indication of how exhausted she was. The woman was a rock. Every time he'd seen her since yesterday afternoon, she'd either been reassuring her mom, patiently trying to get the woman to rest or to eat, or standing by her father's bed having, once again, buried her conflicted feelings for the man and moved on. But she was precariously close to crumbling now. Over nothing more than a small pile of dirt and a shredded plant.

She looked desperately in need of holding.

"I said I'd do it," he repeated, wondering what she would do if he pulled her into his arms.

The temptation was strong. Or maybe it was the need. But with his hands on her shoulders, he deliberately turned her toward her bedroom.

"You're through for the day," he quietly informed her,

torturing himself with the thought of taking her into her room and putting her to bed himself. "You've taken care of everyone else. Just take care of yourself now."

The thought that *he* wanted to take care of her hovered in a corner of his mind. But he was too busy wrestling the urge to pull her back against him to consider just how deep that need went. He wanted to feel her sweet little body against his; to push aside her untamable hair and taste the back of her neck and the soft skin behind her ear. He wanted to hear her sigh with pleasure at his touch and melt against him the way she had before.

That was what he wanted. What he did, however, was steel himself against the tight sensation low in his gut and give her a little nudge. An instant later, she'd slipped from beneath his hands. But instead of heading down the hall, she turned to face him.

Something about her expression reminded him of a small dejected child.

"Are we ever going to be all right?"

The quiet plea in her question nearly undid him.

He didn't think. He simply lifted his hands, slipping them into the hair on either side of her head to draw her forward. Pressing his lips to her forehead, he gathered her in his arms, and felt his heart tighten almost painfully when she sagged against his chest. She leaned into him as closely as she could, her small hands clasping the back of his jacket as if she needed to be held even more badly than he'd thought.

"Don't worry about it tonight," he told her, though he couldn't help wondering the same thing himself. "As much as you've had to deal with today and as tired as you are, talking would probably do us more harm than good right now."

Drawing her closer, he pressed her head to his shoulder. The protectiveness of the gesture had Katie squeezing her eyes closed, two unwanted tears finally leaking out to trail down her cheek. He was right. She felt entirely too needy right now. And his wants and her needs were poles apart. All she cared about, anyway, was that he was holding her. They should be able to turn to each other after a bad day. He'd told her so himself. But that had been back when they were still friends.

She had no idea what they were now.

"Thank you for being here," she whispered, willing to take whatever she could get at the moment.

He brushed the top of her head with his lips, trailing his fingers through her hair. With his thumb, he tipped her head back. A tear clung to a spiky point of her lashes. The tracks of others glistened on her cheek. Her doe eyes were luminous, her skin pale and she looked fragile enough to break. The fact that she was totally vulnerable to him just then should have made him think twice about kissing her. All it did was make him want her more.

"Don't mention it," he murmured, and caught the tear before he touched his mouth to hers.

There was no explosion of the senses. Not like the first time he'd kissed her. What she felt in his kiss was tenderness, a deliberate gentleness that was far more devastating than passion could ever be. In those still, scattered moments as he gathered her closer, sensations registered and built slowly. She felt the heat of his breath warming her skin, and the nighttime roughness of his cheek brushing hers when he angled her head to kiss her more deeply. She tasted the salt of her tear and the heady flavor of him on her tongue.

Unclenching her fists from the back of his jacket, she dared to let her hands slide up to his shoulders. His body felt as solid as steel, but it was the quiet, constant strength inside him she craved.

Her dad was wrong. She did need. She needed desperately. She just didn't know how to hold on to what she had.

The panicky thought had no sooner formed than Mike lifted his head. His eyes glittering hard on her face, he eased back and pulled her hands from his shoulders.

"You need sleep," he finally said, his voice tight with the restraint he exerted over himself. "I'm going to take care of that plant and let myself out. Is there anything you need before I go?"

Five minutes ago, all she'd wanted was for someone to point her in the direction of her bed. Now, with her mind still feeling like mush, her heart and body were calling the shots.

"Just you," she whispered. "But I don't know what to do about it."

He'd let go of her to tuck back her hair. Now, he stood motionless, his hand curved at her cheek as he cautiously scanned her face. The naked need in her eyes tore through him, taunting restraint, demanding response.

He drew her closer. "That makes two of us," he murmured, and closed his mouth over hers again.

He held her with only the touch of his mouth and his hands on her face, but the explosion she'd missed before hit now. His heat burst through her, pooling low in her stomach, melting her bones. She slipped her arms back around his neck, holding on because she'd fall if she didn't. But that support was threatened when he lifted his head moments later.

His breathing ragged, he slipped his hands down her sides and pulled her against him. She felt him, hard and straining against her stomach.

"I've spent weeks wanting you, Katie. I can't think about you without remembering how you taste, how you feel." The tension in his body turned his features stark and haunting. "We either stop and I'll hold you, if it's just a pair of arms that you need. Or we keep this up and I take you to bed.''

It was a choice she didn't want. "Don't stop."

She thought she saw his jaw harden in the moments before he crushed her to him. She wasn't really sure. She wasn't certain of anything except the feel of his body, the demand of his mouth and the sensation of floating when he lifted her in his arms and carried her to her room.

He wanted her. She wouldn't let herself think of how long that would last, how long it would be before their differences would drive them apart. When he stood her by her bed to pull back the covers and he began to undress her, she played only that one thought over in her head.

He wanted her.

The phrase shimmered in her mind as he murmured in her ear, soft, seductive words of how, this time, they would take it slow. Standing in front of her, his taut features carved in shades of shadow, he worked his way down the front of her blouse, releasing buttons and tugging the hem from her jeans. His head dipped as the fastenings gave way, his lips tracing a path of fire from the pulse hammering at the base of her throat to the soft skin of her stomach. By the time he'd slipped her blouse over her shoulders and skimmed it down her arms, she was already weak with wanting. Then, she felt the clasp on her bra give, and his lips moved to her breasts.

Tiny shards of heat splintered in her veins as his hot tongue teased her nipple. He cupped her gently with his palm, his thumb replacing his mouth when he ministered to the other peaked bud. The room seemed to tilt. Gripping his shoulders, her eyes closed, her head lolling back as he opened the zipper of her jeans and his mouth continued its torturous play. She responded to him as if they'd been lovers forever and her need to touch him, to make him feel what she was feeling, was like a living thing inside her.

But every time she reached to pull him closer, he caught her hands and guided them away.

"You can have your turn later," he told her, his voice a rough rasp. "It's mine right now."

She knew exactly what he was doing. He was taking over so she wouldn't have to do anything at all. In the process, he was sensitizing every nerve she possessed. She felt the backs of her legs bump the mattress. A moment later, he'd slipped her jeans over her hips and he was guiding her to sit on the edge of the bed. He pulled off her shoes, her socks and stripped away denim and her pink underpants, the scrap of satin and lace somehow looking both dainty and erotic in his masculine hands.

"Head hurt?" he asked when he saw her touch her hand to her forehead.

It had a while ago. It didn't now. She told him that, but the care he took with her when he eased her back and brushed away her hair to kiss the spot she'd touched, nearly stole her breath. He robbed the oxygen from her lungs again a few heartbeats later. She'd started to cover her nakedness when his hand caught her wrist. His hungry gaze raked her body, his eyes devouring her in the moments before he pinned her arm by her head and he picked up the trail of kisses where he'd left off before.

She was taut as a bow, her body vibrating beneath his touch. Mike took his time, savoring the little sounds she made, soothing her with his hands, wringing another moan from her with his tongue. He wanted to chase every thought from her mind, except thoughts of him. He wanted to be all that mattered to her right now. All that she needed. And he wanted to know every inch of her long, lovely body.

He shaped the feminine flare of her hip with his hand, drawing it down her thigh to brush the exquisitely soft skin inside. Her legs were incredibly supple, the muscles smooth and strong. The thought of how they would feel wrapped around him jolted heat deep in his gut, and he was already so hot he burned. She was so beautifully responsive, so artless in her need. He didn't think he'd ever get enough of her. The taste, the feel, the scent of her was fused in his brain. She was like some strange drug in his blood. One taste and he'd been addicted.

Or maybe, he thought, groaning at the feel of her small, soft hands sliding under his sweater when he found his way back to her throat, she'd been in his system long before he'd ever kissed her.

The mattress dipped as he rose over her and stripped off his sweater. She moved with him, their hands colliding at his zipper.

"My turn." Her voice was a breathless whisper.

"Next time." He growled the words against her mouth, catching her hand before she could close around him. "I won't last thirty seconds if you touch me."

He doubted he'd last that long as it was. He'd tested his control about as far as it would go, and he was already perilously close to the edge. His shoes hit the floor, slacks and briefs landing beside them. The corded muscles of his chest and thighs pulsed with the tension coursing through his body when he slipped between the sheets and pulled the covers over them both.

He slid over her, drawing her legs around him, seeking her mouth. Her arms welcomed him, urging him closer, her tongue tangling with his. In one smooth thrust he was inside her. Hot, tight, she surrounded him, making him feel as if his brain had momentarily ceased to function and all that existed were sensations. It should have been enough. But it wasn't. He wanted more from her. Needed more. Raised on his elbows, his hands cradling her face, he knew she might well possess something he might not survive without.

"Look at me, Katie."

Her lashes lifted as he withdrew, her head tipping back as he slowly thrust forward again. The feel of her nearly shattered his senses. But in that moment, he knew that what he needed was right there in her eyes, and in the soft sound of his name when she breathed it out.

She was his.

His heart seemed to catch at the thought, but the demands of his body were overtaking his mind and soon he wasn't thinking at all.

What he'd felt with her before was a hot blast of white heat. What he felt now was more like life being poured into his soul.

Katie slept.

Mike didn't know how long he lay holding her. She'd been out in seconds, it seemed, sated, exhausted.

She lay with her head on his shoulder, one hand between his chest and her cheek. In the pale gray light filtering in from the living room, he picked up one of the long curls near her bare shoulder and absently wound it around his finger. He liked the soft way it coiled and clung, then sprang back as if it had a mind of its own. He liked the way she fit in his arms, too—the way she fit in his life. Except, she really wasn't in it anymore—the evening notwithstanding. Tonight had been a hiatus, a few moments away from the confusion of feelings that had pulled them apart. Once her father was out of the woods, they'd be right back where they were before.

Almost.

He'd discovered a few things about himself lately that had ripped gaping holes in his assertion about being happy as he was. One of the more jarring had been last night when he'd talked with her father. Standing beside that bed, he'd felt as if he'd walked around a corner and run right into a mirror. He hadn't liked what he'd seen at all. In some ways, the man in that bed could be him in another twenty-five years. Only, at the rate he was going, if he drove himself to a heart attack, he wouldn't have a partner as devoted to him as Mrs. Sheppard to see him through. He would have spent so much time on work and research over the years that he'd have blown off or destroyed the most important relationships a man could ever have. The way Dr. Sheppard's devotion to his work had damaged his relationship with Katie.

She nestled closer, her soft sigh feathering the hair on his chest. Feeling his heart hitch at the way she sought him in her sleep, he pressed a kiss to her forehead. Seeing himself twenty-five years down the road was disconcerting enough. But that mirror had flashed a bright beam of reality on his present, too.

Since the morning he'd first left her bed, it seemed that every time he'd turned around, he'd found another piece of himself missing. Now, he suspected that all those pieces were right there in the woman he held in his arms, and he wasn't entirely sure how to keep her.

Even now, he wanted her again. He craved her like a thirsting man craves water. But there was far more to consider than physical need. He'd thought he could keep it neat: they were good friends, the chemistry was incredible, they could have sex.

Looking back, he had no idea how he'd thought he could separate one from the other. With Katie it was all or nothing. And even though she'd just proved that she cared for him in ways she wanted to deny, she still had her needs, which did not happen to include a relationship with a doctor.

Chapter Twelve

She couldn't believe they'd done it again.

Katie stared at the coffee in her cup, oblivious to the voices drifting around her in the hospital cafeteria. She'd awakened that morning to find Spike's handiwork with the plant cleaned up and a note from Mike on her kitchen table. In the barely legible scrawl he'd mastered in medical school, he'd said he hadn't wanted to wake her and that he would see her at the hospital. They needed to talk.

The knot in her stomach felt strangely like the one that had been there the first time he'd left her bed. Only bigger. She needed him as a friend. Not a lover. If she didn't set a few ground rules for both of them—starting with "hands off"—they were never going to get their relationship straightened out.

"The doctors say your dad is doing fine, honey. They wouldn't have transferred him out of intensive care if he wasn't. If you're going to look so worried, I'm going to start worrying again, too."

Katie looked up from her coffee and blinked at the woman across from her. Her mom looked more like herself today, more rested, more together. She'd taken her usual care with her wardrobe, her silk blouse matching her mauve wool jacket and slacks. Her gold earrings even had mauve-colored stones in them. Katie matched only because she was in her blue uniform scrubs. She was working half a shift today.

"I'm sorry. Did you say something?"

"I want to know what you're so concerned about."

Apologizing again, she forced a smile. "I'm just pre-occupied, I guess."

"Well, you've been that way ever since Beth and I picked you up this morning. Did Mike keep you up after he took you home?"

No, Mom, she thought, *I pretty much hauled him right off to bed.* "I got plenty of sleep," she replied, evading. "I didn't get up until eight."

That she'd lain for an hour with her head buried under her pillow wishing she'd only dreamed what had happened was something she didn't need to mention. She didn't want to talk about this morning or last night at all. If her mom suspected that she and Mike were anything more than what they'd always had been, she would be picking out silver patterns with Beth Brennan by noon.

Katie, on the other hand, was desperate for an argument that would convince her former friend that their relationship had to be platonic. Considering that Dana was right, that she was hopelessly in love with Mike, she had no idea at the moment what that argument was going to be.

Assuring herself that she'd come up with something by the time she saw him, she motioned to the bowl of fruit her mom hadn't touched.

"You should eat. That's why we came down here." Her expression filled with sympathy as she picked up her cup.

"Dad really is going to be okay, Mom. I won't be assigned to him, but I'll be on the floor, so I'll know if there are any problems. Okay?"

"It does make me feel better to know you'll be there. I think it makes him feel better, too." Picking up her fork, she toyed with a seed in a piece of watermelon. "He said you came in to see him after I left last night."

"I told you I'd check. As medicated as he was, I'm surprised he remembered."

"He did. He told me he wanted to make sure you were taking care of me. I've been taking care of myself for years," she said, her soft smile full of affection, "and he knows it. It's just his way of saying he cares."

That wasn't the impression she'd gotten from her father, Katie thought, slowly sipping the industrial-strength brew. Considering that he regarded his daughter as being far more independent than his wife, it sounded more as if he thought her in need of protection.

Katie rarely spoke to her mother about her dad. And never had she asked about their marriage. But something that eluded her completely held that relationship together. And because the most important relationship of her life was falling apart, she couldn't help but wonder what that something was.

"May I ask you something personal, Mom?"

At the unexpected question, her mother glanced up from the seed she was burying under a slice of cantaloupe.

"Of course you can."

An image of her mom sitting alone in the front row of a grade school play flashed in Katie's mind. "Do you ever regret marrying a man who is so rarely there?"

"Regret?" The fork clattered lightly as it was set on the table, a thoughtful expression stealing over maturely attractive features. "There have certainly been times when I've wished he was around more. But regret?" She shook her head, looking every bit as certain as she sounded. "Never."

"But what about everything you had to do alone? For as long as I can remember, you've had the responsibility of the house and the yard and the cars. And, for all practical purposes, you raised me alone. You must have felt like a single parent."

"He wasn't always physically present," she agreed, the light of curiosity entering her eyes at the consternation in her daughter's expression. "And he certainly missed a few anniversaries and birthdays over the years, but it wasn't as if he forgot them. And we always talked.

"I had to make decisions without him sometimes," she conceded, looking as if she were remembering back to when Katie had been a child, "but he always supported me on them. Just like I always supported him when he'd get a call at two in the morning and he'd have to leave for the hospital. He had his job and I had mine. Mine was to see that his home ran smoothly, to raise you and make everything as perfect as I could. I'm sure I spoiled him," she admitted with a sheepishness that wasn't familiar to Katie at all, "but I wanted to."

"It just seems to me that you gave more than you got."

"Because other people were always needing him?" she asked, as if that were simply the lot of a doctor's wife.

"Yes," Katie replied flatly.

Karen placed her hand over her daughter's, her eyes searching and serious.

"It was his generosity and caring about other people that attracted me to him in the first place, Katie. I knew when I married him that I'd have to share him. But I needed him. I always will. How can I complain about the very thing that makes him the man he is?"

Katie had no answer for that. But in those moments, she began to understand more about the woman sitting across from her than she ever had. Karen Sheppard didn't need to be taken care of. She just needed the man she loved. In her own way, she was actually the most formidable sort of woman—the kind who looks fragile as glass, but has a backbone of solid steel.

As she looked from the wrinkles on her mom's manicured hand to her neatly styled blond twist, she also began to understand why her mother was always finding some little fault with her. If she wanted everything perfect for the husband she adored, then it followed that she would try to be the perfect wife—and raise the perfect daughter.

Feeling about as flawed as they came, Katie turned her hand over and gave her mother's a squeeze. "I don't know if I could ever be as generous as you are."

"Oh, sweetie, you're far more generous than I am. I'm just flexible is all. And I know I made a lot of mistakes. But you're right. I did raise you pretty much alone. Which means I get to take most of the credit for you," she said, catching Katie off guard with the unexpected touch of pride. "I just wish sometimes that I hadn't raised you to be so independent."

Katie instantly went on alert. Her mother had that look in her eyes, the same one she got whenever she started talking about how precious Katie would look with shorter hair, or how nice it would be to have a grandchild.

"It's good for a woman to be self-sufficient," her mom said, actually looking more like a confidante than a critic, "but I never wanted you to be so independent that you didn't need someone of your own." Her head lifted, a quick smile flashing on her Marvelous Mauve lips. "There's Mike."

There seemed to be an echo of her father's words in her mother's quiet statement. But it wasn't the realization that both of her parents seemed to think her resistant to a relationship that had her pulling her hand away. "He's coming over?"

"I don't know. He's talking to someone by the cashier." Her smile disappeared. "What's the matter? Is your stomach bothering you?"

She hadn't realized she'd crossed her arms so tightly until she saw her mother frowning at the wrinkles she was pressing into her scrub top. Telling herself she was going to wind up with an ulcer if she didn't get this mess with Mike straightened out, she deliberately loosened her hold.

"I'm fine, Mom. We should probably go, though. They'll have finished pulling Dad's lines by now," she added, referring to the internal monitors and tubes his nurse had gone in to remove.

Surprisingly, her mother made no effort to get up. She simply sat, her head tipped as she watched Katie avoid her eyes.

"You know," she observed, her tone a little too casual, "Beth said the other night that she thought Mike was awfully reluctant to have her introduce you to the new man in Andy's office.

"She thought there might be something starting between you two," she continued, finally reaching for her purse. "But I told her it was just wishful thinking on her part. You two have always been so much like brother and sister," she went on in that same offhand way, "that I couldn't see it at all." She glanced up, smiling beyond Katie's shoulder, before looking back to her daughter. "You have always thought of him as a big brother, haven't you?"

There was a wealth of speculation in that innocent-sounding question. But Katie didn't have a chance to answer before the light in her mother's eyes brightened.

"Hello, Michael. How are you this morning?"

"I'm doing fine," he replied, the warm brandy burn of

his voice flowing over Katie's rapidly knotting nerves. "Am I interrupting?"

Diplomatically curbing her speculation, her mother assured him that he wasn't and asked him to join them. Katie glanced up as the offer was extended, doing a little curbing of her own. He was wearing the same charcoal suit he'd worn at her father's party. That dark color and the sapphire of his shirt turned his eyes the shade of blue flame. Feeling her pulse scramble as that flame touched her, she took a deep, calming breath and watched him look back at her mom.

"They said upstairs that I'd find you down here," he said, dropping his overcoat on the chair back. Over the scrape of chair legs on tile, he added, "I was just with your husband. He looks good, Mrs. Sheppard. Tired and uncomfortable, but that's to be expected." Sitting down beside her, he offered an easy smile. "He wanted to know where you were, though."

"May I see him now?"

"I don't know why not."

The prospect of seeing her husband suddenly took on the urgency that had been lacking when Katie had mentioned going upstairs herself only moments ago. With her purse already in hand, she rose as Mike did to help her with her chair.

"Thank you," she said, smiling at his chivalry. "Oh, and thank you for taking Katie home last night. You've been wonderful to us." Her wedding ring flashed as she caught his arm and gave it a squeeze. "I'll see you upstairs later, Katie."

"I can come with you."

"No need." She sliced a meaningful glance toward the man still towering beside her. "Take your time," she encouraged, and, looking entirely too happy for a woman whose husband was barely out of critical care, she strolled away.

"Why do I have the feeling you just got rid of her on purpose," Katie murmured when Mike sat down in the chair her mom had just vacated.

"Because you're a relatively astute woman. On occasion." Letting the qualifier pass, he eyed the fruit plate. "Which one of you isn't eating?"

"Mom."

"Did you get my note?"

Her glance flicked to his, her heart stalling at the directness of his gaze. No one would ever accuse him of beating around the bush.

"Yes. And you're right," she told him, thinking of what the note had said. "We do need to talk." She reached for her coffee, and promptly pulled her hand back so he wouldn't see it shaking. "There was something I wanted to tell you before all this started with Dad, but I obviously didn't get a chance. I really would like to talk to you before anything else happens."

"Are you expecting a disaster?" he asked, looking as if he were trying to prompt a smile.

"Just trying to prevent one."

He didn't look as if he cared for the sound of that. He also looked as if he, too, had something rather specific on his mind.

"I don't want to discuss this here," he muttered. Nodding to one of the OR nurses as she passed, he ignored the envious glare the woman gave Katie and glanced at the burgundy raincoat hanging on the chair beside her. "How long before you have to be upstairs?"

"Cindy has to leave at noon, so I'm finishing out her shift for her. I have another hour."

"That's about what I have before my next appointment.

Would you rather drive somewhere or go for a walk?''

Feeling a definite need to pace, she opted for the walk.

The park across the street from the hospital took up two city blocks and was lined from one side to the other with hedges and pines. In March, the winter-dead lawns and concrete benches were pretty much the domain of the squirrels who ran, chattering, from one barren oak tree to the next. Few people wandered its walkways, unless it was to cut from one street to the next. Especially when the weather was bad.

The leaden clouds overhead were actually separated by streaks of blue sky when they crossed the wet street near the emergency entrance. As anxious as Katie felt, the sun could have suddenly come out, or it could have started pouring rain and she might not have noticed. All she could think about with Mike walking beside her was the look of quiet determination carved in his face.

"Thanks for cleaning up the plant," she said, unwilling to let silence magnify her disquiet. "You really didn't have to do that."

"I just got the big pieces. I didn't want to wake you with the vacuum."

"Still, I appreciate it," she told him, entering a section of barren rose garden. She took a deep breath, part of her wanting only to get this over with, another part wishing it weren't necessary. "You're a good friend."

The cool breeze tugged at her hair, tossing loose curls against her cheek. "That's what I've wanted to talk to you about." She twisted her head so the wind could remove the bothersome strand. "About being friends."

"Is that how you think of me?" he asked, his voice deceptively mild. "As a good friend?"

"My best." Her footfall matched his, the slow cadence mocking the erratic beat of her heart. "I've known you all my life, Mike. I can't imagine you not always being there." The wind flipped her hair into her face again. Agitated, needing desperately for him to know how important he was to her, she swiped at it and started to look toward him. "That's why all this has been so awful."

Her hand was falling from her cheek when Mike caught her by the wrist. Stopping her in her tracks, he turned her to face him.

Sometime in the past few moments determination had become defense. His glance slid the length of her body, the visual caress so deliberate that when he lifted his eyes to hers again, she felt as if he'd just stripped her bare. "All of it?"

"Except that part," she admitted, her voice singed to nearly a whisper. Pulling her hand away, she willed herself to ignore the heat he ignited all too easily. "But I'm going to overlook that."

"How?"

"I don't know yet. I haven't figured that out. But I'm not going to bed with you again. That's the part that's complicating everything."

She didn't trust the stillness that stole over him, or the way his eyes narrowed on her face. She didn't know what he was looking for, either, but she knew he wasn't at all pleased with what he found.

"Just what is it that you want from me, Katie? The signals I'm getting from you are totally screwed up."

"Don't be angry—"

"I'm not angry," he insisted, eyes flashing. "I'm confused. Last night you wanted me as much as I wanted you. It was the same way the first time. And now you're pushing me away again."

"Forget last night," she begged, well aware of how mixed her signals had been. "And I'm not pushing you away. All I want is for us to be the way we were before. I want us to be comfortable with each other. I want us to be able to call each other and ask for help or to talk or to have dinner or watch a movie or...or...borrow something.'' Her voice caught on a plea. ''I want my old friend back.''

The pleading in her eyes confounded Mike even more than what he was hearing. He didn't care what she said— she *was* pushing him away. Yet, he could swear she didn't look as if that was what she wanted to do at all.

''Let me make sure I have this right.'' He stepped back, shoving his hand through his hair in disbelief. Having come from her bed less than twelve hours ago, her responses to him fresh in his mind, he'd had an entirely different agenda than the one she was proposing. ''You want to be friends. You want to go back to the way things were between us a couple of months ago. And you want to forget last night. Right?''

Though clearly wary of his terse summation, she nodded.

''Well, you know what, honey? That's not going to happen.''

''Mike—''

''It can't possibly be the way it was,'' he insisted, frustration with her logic goading him on. ''I don't understand how you can even think it could be. It would be like trying to turn a flower back into a bud. Or making a tree viable after it had been burned to ash. Some changes are just plain irreversible, and this happens to be one of them.''

''We could try.''

''Why do we even have to?'' he insisted, amazed by how naive she was being. ''I know you've said you'd never marry a doctor because you don't want a man who won't be there for you and your children, but you won't even give me a chance to prove what kind of a husband and father I'd be. And you know what?'' he demanded, ignoring the way he'd just barreled over what he'd intended to talk to her about, "I think that's just an excuse anyway. You've said for years that you want marriage and a family, but you've made it next to impossible to meet *any* man who could qualify as a husband. You're either at the hospital around the very sort of man you say you don't want, or you're working at the free clinic with pregnant women and their kids. Don't you see anything wrong with that picture?"

Katie opened her mouth, but all she could do was stare at him before she closed it again. Totally stunned by what she was hearing, incredibly confused herself, she had no idea where to begin.

Mike didn't give her a chance anyway.

"What is it you're really afraid of?" he demanded, his voice lowering to a near whisper. His eyes searched hers, their intensity burning clear to her soul. "Is it just me, Katie? Or is it every man?"

The moon was playing hide-and-seek with the clouds.

Mike stood in the dark in his living room, watching the disk of pale light slowly disappear and listening to the recording on Katie's answering machine. He'd called every fifteen minutes for the past two hours and still there was no answer.

He pushed the Off button on the portable phone and set it on the edge of the flagstone hearth. Since she hadn't picked up on either of the two messages he'd left, he could safely assume she either wasn't home, or she simply didn't want to talk to him.

Considering the way he'd left her standing alone in the park, he was pretty convinced it was the latter.

"Jerk," he muttered, using one of the less inventive names he'd called himself that evening.

Instead of coming down on her, he should have talked with her about why she felt as she did, not gotten in her face and demanded an explanation. It was obvious she had hang-ups he didn't understand. But he was a reasonable man. He was a patient man. He'd even been known to be sympathetic on occasion. Yet he'd reacted to her request with nothing but anger.

What he'd actually felt was fear, because he was deathly afraid of losing her, but the knee-jerk emotion was so much easier for a man to deal with. The reaction wasn't like him at all, either. He could usually keep his emotions in check. He demanded it of himself, in fact. But she pushed buttons he didn't know he had and he couldn't hold much of anything back where she was concerned. He couldn't distance himself. He'd tried, and it simply hadn't been possible. With her, he had no choice but to feel.

She kept him human.

He wanted her.

And he needed her as more than just a friend.

He turned to the window, resting his hand on the cool metal cylinder of the telescope and thought about losing his thoughts by searching for stars. The clouds continued to part, leaving huge sections of clear, velvet black sky. But escape wasn't possible just now. He couldn't conveniently block the thoughts clamoring in his brain any more than he could block the love in his heart.

And he did love her. He'd been falling in love with her for the past year. He didn't know the exact moment he'd realized it. It could have been when they were working together on a patient. Or when she'd been nagging him about getting furniture. But he suspected it had been the moment he'd realized she could be pregnant. He'd never been able to shake the feelings he'd experienced that night. Beneath the initial apprehension, there had existed a profound sense of rightness about creating a child with her. He'd never felt that with any woman before. Not even his ex-wife. If he'd let himself think about it, he might even

have acknowledged the same sense of disappointment
however ill-timed the event, that Katie had said she'd felt
when she'd learned she wasn't going to have a baby.

A baby.

The thought had him dragging his hand down his face
and looking back at the telephone. A moment later, the
chime of the doorbell drifted through the house.

It was nearly ten o'clock, rather late for his brother to
be dropping by. Moving through the dark of the still-empty
room, he flipped on the light in the foyer and opened the
door.

Katie stood with her arms wrapped around her raincoat,
her unruly hair pulled up in a listing ponytail and uncertainty clouding her lovely pale features.

"I was driving around and noticed your porch light."

"Come on in."

"You sure?"

Katie watched Mike step back, his expression guarded
as he motioned her in. Tightening her hold on herself, she
stepped across the threshold and heard the door close behind her with a quiet click.

"I've been trying to call you."

"I haven't been home. I mean I went home to change
clothes after work and to feed Spike," she added, inanely.
"But I….left."

She'd been driving around for the past couple of hours,
too agitated for the confines of her house and too upset to
talk to anyone else. She had no idea how she'd made it
through the afternoon; how she'd handled work and her
mom's heavy-handed hints about how perfect she and
Mike were for each other. But she had made it. Just as
she'd made it through countless other days when life threw
her a curve.

Running a glance over Mike's dark slacks and the
rolled-up sleeves of his sapphire dress shirt, she swallowed

hard and let herself meet his eyes. There was an unchar-
acteristic uneasiness in those seductive blue depths. Judging from the hesitation she could see there, too, he appeared no more certain of what to expect at the moment
than she did.

"Do you want to take off your coat?"

For a moment, the only sound in the quiet house was
the rustle of fabric as she slipped out of her coat and
handed it to him. Crossing her arms over her long navy
sweater, she watched him turn away to toss the garment
over the empty planter. As he did, her glance slid past him
to the living room.

Had it not been for the light in the foyer the space would
have been completely dark, but it was still easy enough to
see that nothing was there.

"Where's your furniture?"

"It hasn't been delivered yet." His rich sable hair
looked as if it had been combed with his fingers. Beneath
the locks falling over his forehead, his brow pleated in a
frown. "How did you know about it?"

"Your mom told me. The night of Dad's party," she
added, when the frown didn't go away. "She said you
ordered nutmeg and oatmeal."

She'd said he needed natural colors, and that was what
he'd got. But he was clearly no more interested in discussing furniture than she was. He didn't even respond.
He just stood an arm's length away, looking as if he didn't
know if he should touch her to invite her farther in, or if
he should just let her come in on her own.

His office was the only room with anywhere to sit. But
he made no move toward it. Thinking he was waiting for
her to go first, she started past him, but two steps were all
it took for her to see that it was as black as pitch in that
direction. There were no lights on behind them in the

kitchen, either. There wasn't a light on anywhere except for where they stood.

"Were you in here in the dark?"

He was as unreadable to her as Sanskrit when he nodded toward the tall windows in the corner of the living room. "I was over there," he said. "Looking out the window."

If that was where he'd been, then that was where she wanted to go now. She wasn't sure why. Maybe it was because she really didn't want the glare of lights herself. Having spent a considerable portion of the day and the evening pulling herself apart and examining all the pieces, she wasn't up to much more close scrutiny.

With a knot of anxiety coiled in her stomach and her heart beating in her throat, she silently crossed the expanse of plush carpet to where two walls of window intersected. Normally, she would have been able to see the deck from there, but he'd even turned off the security lights.

Because the angle of the windows didn't directly reflect the diluted light from the foyer, the pale winter moon and a scattering of stars were visible beyond the tree tops. Katie scarcely noticed them, though. Mike had stopped a step behind her.

"It isn't all men," she said, because that was the only answer she'd been totally sure of when he'd turned and walked away. "It's just you."

She heard his slow intake of breath, but she didn't wait for any sort of response. There were also a couple of other things she'd known—along with a couple she'd just discovered—that she needed to tell him before she lost her nerve.

"It's really always been you," she admitted, hugging herself as she slowly turned to face the broad expanse of his chest. "You're the reason my dad thinks I don't need anyone. And you're the reason my mom thinks I'm too independent to let myself commit to a relationship. I've just never wanted anyone the way I've wanted you."

He lifted his hand toward her. "Katie—"

"Please." She stepped back before he could touch her, her glance barely skimming his chin. "I need to just say this. Okay?

"You asked what I was afraid of," she reminded him, hurrying on. "I think there's only one thing that truly frightens me, and that's being abandoned by people I love. But, with you, it's always been more frightening, because I don't just love you, I'm in love with you. I have been since I was nine years old. But you never saw me as anything but a friend, so keeping you as my friend was the only way I had of never losing you.

"That's why I didn't want us to get involved." She spoke quickly, quietly, wanting her admission to sound more like simple fact than anything that required a response on his part. "Affairs end, and you want your life the way it is. You don't want a wife and children. At least, that's what you said," she added, afraid to believe what he'd alluded to in the park, "and I didn't want to be an ex-girlfriend because then I wouldn't have you at all.

"That's why you've been getting so many mixed signals," she concluded, feeling more vulnerable than she ever had in her life. "And that's why I didn't want us to get involved any more than we already are. I don't know if that makes any sense to you or not, but I don't know how to explain it any other way."

She blinked at the front of his shirt, listening to the sound of her pulse pounding in her ears and wishing he'd say something now, but half-afraid of what she might hear. He didn't say a word. He just lifted his hands, curving them at the sides of her neck, and tipped her chin up with his thumb.

In the dim light, the beautiful angles and planes of his

face looked sculpted from stone. His glance swept over her, his eyes searching hers.

"Since you were nine?"

All she could do was lift one shoulder in a faint shrug, "Maybe I was nine and a half."

Mike wasn't sure what he was feeling at the moment. Disbelief, amazement, wonder—they were all in there somewhere, along with a heavy dose of hesitation. What she'd feared most was being emotionally abandoned, and she'd spent most of her life denying herself what she wanted because of it. He knew where the fear had come from. It had begun with not having the father she'd needed. But what bothered Mike more was that he'd contributed to her fears himself. The thought that she'd always been afraid of losing him made his heart hurt.

He tucked a curl behind her ear, his touch as cautious as his expression.

"I had no idea," he said, threading his fingers into her hair. The gathered piece of fabric holding it atop her head fell to the floor, leaving her curls to tangle in his hands. "But then, it's taken me a while to figure out that I'm in love with you, too." He brushed his thumb over her mouth, his pulse feeling a little erratic. "I really did think I was happy with my life the way it was, but that was only because you were already a part of it. It wasn't until things started falling apart that I realized nothing was the same without you."

Her fingers curled over his wrist, her heart so full she could barely speak. "So what do we do now?"

He answered her by drawing her closer and slanting his mouth over hers. A heartbeat later, he'd gathered her in his arms and she was sinking against him, absorbing the hunger, need and longing in his kiss. He wasn't going to let her go. He left no doubt of that in her mind in the long moments before he pulled back and pressed her head to his chest.

"What we do is work this out," he murmured.

"How?" she asked, echoing the demand he'd often made himself.

"Well," he began cautiously, "I was thinking about that baby."

Her head came up. "What baby?"

"The one we didn't have. I'm not your father, Katie," he said, not giving her a chance to resurrect her old arguments. "My children will not grow up to be strangers. I'm sure I'll make plenty of mistakes, but something else I've learned from your dad is that I'm not raising my children the way your parents raised you. I might not be there for every soccer game or ballet recital, but I'll put in my share of time in the stands or wherever it is they need me. I'm scaling back on the research, and what projects I do take on we can do together. We'll just bring the playpen into the office."

He pulled her closer, his glance darting to his right. "We can even teach him how to use a telescope."

Katie's eyes narrowed on the light in his eyes as she tipped her head. The idea of Mike going over statistics with their toddler in his lap was a sight she couldn't wait to see. But the thought of him showing their child the stars the way he'd once shown them to her nearly lodged her heart in her throat.

"The playpen would work," she agreed mildly, pretty certain her heart was in her eyes, too, as she skimmed her hands over his strong shoulders. "But there's just one little detail I'm curious about."

"What's that?"

"Did you by any chance propose to me yesterday?"

He grinned, the expression feeling rare, but amazingly good. "I was going to. Yes," he amended, her smile warming him clear to his soul. This woman was as vital to him as the oxygen he breathed; as necessary to his existence as the blood pumping through his heart. From the moment he'd first kissed her, he simply hadn't been the same. "I suppose I did."

Looping her arms around his neck, she grinned back. "Then I suppose I'd better say yes," she murmured, pulling his head toward hers.

With her mouth a breath away from his kiss, she whispered, "I can't imagine anything better than being married to my best friend."

* * * * *

Turn the page for a sneak preview of

PRINCE CHARMING, M.D.
by
Susan Mallery

the next book in
PRESCRIPTION: MARRIAGE
an innovative new medical miniseries
Special Edition
November 1998

Nurse Dana Rowan is suddenly experiencing
strange symptoms: sweaty palms,
rapid pulse, visions of doctors...and love.
Could marriage be the cure?

Prince Charming, M.D.

"Good thing he's a gifted surgeon. He'll be able to repair all the hearts he breaks."

Dana Rowan took a sip of her coffee and resisted the urge to roll her eyes. She'd made a special effort to get to the meeting early enough so she could have her pick of seats. She'd deliberately chosen one in the back…as far from the podium as possible. She wanted to avoid gossip, her nurses who had—collectively and overnight—seemed to have lost their minds and most especially the "gifted surgeon" in question. So far she hadn't seen any sign of Dr. Trevor MacAllister, so she'd accomplished a third of her goals. Guess that would have to be enough for now.

The two women sitting in front of her continued to talk about "young" Dr. MacAllister, differentiating him from "old" Dr. MacAllister who was Trevor's father and the chief of staff at Honeygrove Memorial Hospital.

"Have you seen him?" Sally asked, then continued

without waiting for an answer. "He's gorgeous. Serious studmuffin material." She leaned back in her chair and sighed loudly.

"I know," her friend Melba said. "Don't forget I grew up here. I was a few years younger than him, but I remember Trevor back when he was in high school, and let me tell you, he was just as good-looking then." She strained her neck as she peered toward the open door. "I'll bet time has only improved him."

Dana wished there was somewhere else she could move to. She didn't think she would be able to stand listening to this kind of talk through the entire staff meeting. Unfortunately, judging from the buzz flying around the room, she would have to leave the hospital or possibly even Honeygrove itself to escape the excitement generated by Trevor MacAllister's return.

"He's just a man," she muttered under her breath. "He puts his pants on one leg at a time, just like other mortals. No doubt he has other human frailties like an occasional bad temper and morning breath."

But they were not listening to her and even if they were, they wouldn't care. She wasn't saying what they wanted to hear. In the world of hospital gossip and lore, Trevor was a god-like creature. A hometown boy returned to the fold after making his name out in the world.

Dana took another sip of coffee and tried to disconnect from everyone around her. Regardless of what she personally thought of the man, he was now a surgeon at the hospital. Her job was to schedule surgical nurses and keep the OR, pardon the pun, operating efficiently. That meant working with the "young" Dr. MacAllister. Fine, she would put her personal opinions aside and be as professional as the job required. She would survive the daily contact and do her best to ignore the inevitable stories that would circulate. After all, they meant nothing to her. Like

Melba, she'd grown up in Honeygrove and had personal experience with Trevor's considerable charm. She'd fallen hard and she'd been burned big-time. If she allowed herself to examine her heart closely, she might even still see a few of the scars. But that was in the past. As far as she was concerned, Trevor was just another surgeon. As such, he held no interest for her.

Sally tucked a loose strand of dark hair behind her ear and leaned close to her friend. "He's divorced," she whispered although not softly enough to keep her words from drifting back to Dana. "It's been two years and he hasn't gotten serious about anyone since. Think he's trying to get over a broken heart?"

"Are you crazy?" Melba asked. She made a dismissive gesture with her hand. "A man that good-looking? You don't actually think his wife left *him*, do you? I'm sure he's been real busy these past couple of years. From what I've heard, he's already been out with a couple of nurses here and he hasn't officially started work yet. I'm not saying you couldn't have fun with him, but don't make it more than it is or you'll end up with a broken heart."

Amen, Dana thought to herself and hoped Sally would listen to her friend. The brunette nurse was pretty enough to tempt Trevor, but he'd never been much on commitment.

Sally grinned at Melba. "You're warning me off so you'll have a clear shot at him yourself."

Melba smiled in return. "I wouldn't mind having a little fun with the good doctor, but I'm not going to make it more than that. He might have grown up but I don't think he's changed all that much."

Suddenly there was a slight commotion by the door. Sally spun back to face front, then drew in an audible gasp. "It's him! Oh, look, Melba, he's stunning. I want him desperately."

Then you'll probably get him, at least for the night, Dana thought, then glanced toward the door.

He, of course, looked incredible. She was too far away to be able to distinguish the color of his eyes, but she knew them to be an impossible shade of hazel-green. Tall, tanned, with the perfect masculine features of a movie heartthrob. But Trevor was more than model perfect—he was also a tremendously gifted and compassionate surgeon. His colleagues respected him, his patients worshiped him, women desired him. A true paragon, Dana thought grimly.

There were a couple dozen people milling around and talking, now that the initial hush had faded. Dana had felt confident that she would neither be noticed nor acknowledged. So when Trevor looked in her direction, she didn't bother to look away.

"He's looking at me!" Sally exclaimed.

"Don't be ridiculous," her friend told her.

Dana barely heard them. Despite the physical distance between them, despite the number of years since she'd last seen him, despite the stern lectures she'd given herself to avoid making a fool of herself over this man ever again, once he caught her attention, she *couldn't* look away.

Trevor seemed to single her out in the crowd. All his attention, all his considerable energy flowed toward her, around her. She wasn't breathing, she realized with dismay and forced herself to inhale and exhale slowly. Noises in the room faded to faint buzzing, while the corners blurred into nothing. A wanting as powerful as a force-three hurricane built up inside of her.

If she'd been standing, she would have collapsed into the nearest seat. As it was, all she could do was lean weakly against the chair back and wait for her strength to return.

What had just happened? She shook her head. Scratch

that. She didn't want to know the answer. She absolutely, positively refused to be attracted to Trevor MacAllister. No way, no how, not again. She'd sung that song and danced that dance.

And just because she had to work with him didn't mean she would fall prey to his wily charms...again!

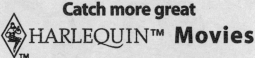

FOLLOW THAT BABY...

the fabulous cross-line series featuring the infamously wealthy Wentworth family...continues with:

THE DADDY AND THE BABY DOCTOR
by **Kristin Morgan**
(Romance, 11/98)

The search for the mysterious Sabrina Jensen pits a seasoned soldier—and single dad—against a tempting baby doctor who knows Sabrina's best-kept secret....

Available at your favorite retail outlet, only from

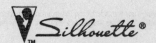

Look us up on-line at: http://www.romance.net   SSEFTB2

> We, the undersigned, having barely survived four years of nursing school, do hereby vow to meet at Granetti's at least once a week, not to do anything drastic to our hair without consulting each other first and never, _ever_—no matter how rich, how cute, how funny, how smart, or how good in bed—marry a doctor.
>
> Dana Rowan, R.N.
> Lee Murphy, R.N.
> Katie Sheppard, R.N.

Christine Flynn
Susan Mallery
Christine Rimmer

prescribe a massive dose of heart-stopping romance in their scintillating new series, **PRESCRIPTION: MARRIAGE**. Three nurses are determined _not_ to wed doctors— only to discover the men of their dreams come with a medical degree!

Look for this unforgettable series in fall 1998:

October 1998: **FROM HOUSE CALLS TO HUSBAND** by Christine Flynn

November 1998: **PRINCE CHARMING, M.D.** by Susan Mallery

December 1998: **DR. DEVASTATING** by Christine Rimmer

Only from

Silhouette®SPECIAL EDITION®

Available at your favorite retail outlet.

Looking For More Romance?

Visit Romance.net

Look us up on-line at: http://www.romance.net

Check in daily for these and other exciting features:

Hot off the press — View all current titles, and purchase them on-line.

What do the stars have in store for you?

Horoscope

Hot deals — Exclusive offers available only at Romance.net

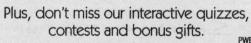

Plus, don't miss our interactive quizzes, contests and bonus gifts.

PWEB

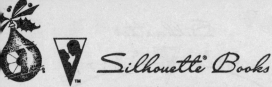

Silhouette®

SPECIAL EDITION®

COMING NEXT MONTH

#1207 A FAMILY KIND OF GAL—Lisa Jackson
That Special Woman!
Forever Family
All Tiffany Santini wanted was a life of harmony away from her domineering in-laws. But a long-ago attraction was reignited when her sinfully sexy brother in-law, J.D., decided this single mom needn't raise her kids all alone. Could he tempt Tiffany to surrender all her love—to him?

#1208 THE COWGIRL & THE UNEXPECTED WEDDING—Sherryl Woods
And Baby Makes Three: The Next Generation
Once, headstrong Lizzy Adams had captured Hank Robbins's heart, but he'd reluctantly let her go. Now they were together again, and their pent-up passion couldn't be denied. What would it take for a fit-to-be-tied cowboy to convince a mule-headed mother-to-be to march down the aisle?

#1209 PRINCE CHARMING, M.D.—Susan Mallery
Prescription: Marriage
Just about every nurse at Honeygrove Memorial Hospital was swooning shamelessly over debonair doc Trevor MacAllister. All except disillusioned Dana Rowan, who vowed to never, ever wed a doctor—much less be lured by Trevor's Prince Charming act again. But *some* fairy tales are destined to come true....

#1210 UNTIL YOU—Janis Reams Hudson
Timid Anna Collins knew what to expect from her quiet, predictable life. Until she discovered a sexy stranger sleeping on her sofa. Suddenly her uninvited houseguest made it his mission to teach her about all of life's pleasures. Would he stick around for the part about when a man loves a woman?

#1211 A MOTHER FOR JEFFREY—Trisha Alexander
Leslie Marlowe was doing a good job of convincing herself that she wasn't meant to be anyone's wife—or mother. But then young Jeffrey Canfield came into her life, followed by his strong, sensitive father, Brian. Now the only thing Leslie had to convince herself of was that she wasn't dreaming!

#1212 THE RANCHER AND THE REDHEAD—Allison Leigh
Men of the Double-C Ranch
Matthew Clay was set in his ways—and proud of it, too. So when virginal city gal Jaimie Greene turned his well-ordered ranch into Calamity Central, the sassy redhead had him seething with anger and consumed with desire. Dare he open his home—and his heart—to the very *last* woman he should love?